Seti's Secret

Text copyright 2014 Fiona Deal
All Rights Reserved

This is a work of fiction.
Names, characters, places and incidents
either are the product of the author's imagination
or are used fictitiously.

Chapter 1

Summertime 2013

Of all the people I might have expected to find standing on the gangplank of our dahabeeyah at daybreak, my ex-boyfriend was not one of them. But there he was, in the flesh, arms folded, feet planted apart, and with a deep scowl on his face.

'Dan!'

His expression may have had something to do with the fact that I myself was not actually inside the *Queen Ahmes*, but approaching it from the riverbank. Judging by the look of him, he'd been there for some considerable time waiting for me – us, I should say, for I wasn't alone – to return. He must have heard us pull up in Ahmed's car, now parked under the knot of palm trees behind us.

'At last!' he barked, confirming my assessment of his long wait.

I quickened my pace as I negotiated the steep stone steps leading down to the crumbling causeway where our dahabeeyah is moored. This wasn't a good move. The steps are treacherous at the best of times; and with Dan now striding angrily towards me, this didn't seem likely to be one of them. I lost my balance and let out a yelp. Thankfully, Adam was right behind me and shot out a steadying hand.

I recovered my voice along with my footing. 'Dan! What on Earth…?'

'I've been waiting here for *hours!*' he growled. I use the terms *barked* and *growled* advisedly. Dan's ability when annoyed to sound a little less than human is second to none. 'Where the hell have you been for half the night?' Then he ran an appraising glance over the small party of whom I was just one. His raking gaze took in the dusty, dishevelled and sweat-stained appearance not just of me, but also of Adam, Ahmed, Ted and Walid, clustering protectively around me as we made it without further mishap to the foot of the stone steps. I daresay the vexation in Dan's expression was as clear to them as it was to me as the sky lightened with the breaking dawn.

My ex-boyfriend's sweeping glance didn't miss the linen wrappings clutched protectively against the professor's narrow chest. 'No, don't tell me,' he swept on. 'It's stark staringly obvious where you lot have been; as if I hadn't already guessed it!' His tone became downright accusatory. 'You've been inside that bloody tomb again!' He glared at each of us in turn. '*Haven't you?*'

There was no point in attempting to deny it of course. I'm sure our guilty expressions were a dead giveaway, if further proof were necessary.

The strange part, if that's what it could be called, was that for the first time in all our experiences with it, we'd locked up and left the tomb without any trouble. Nobody had come to confront, incarcerate or attempt to kill us. It had been an odd feeling to pick up the Aten disc from the floor inside the Hathor Chapel in Hatshepsut's Temple and watch the stone panel grind back into place wondering how long it might be before we next opened it, and in what circumstances that might be.

We'd piled back into Ahmed's police car, thinking only to come back to the *Queen Ahmes* for some much needed sleep, before gathering again to exclaim over the night's discoveries, and wonder what to do about them.

But we'd reckoned without the sudden, unexpected and, I have to say, unlooked-for appearance of the ex-boyfriend I'd thought was happily – or resignedly at least – up to his neck in wedding preparations back home in England. I had no idea what he was doing here. But I felt sure I was about to find out.

'Dan!' Adam exclaimed in rather more welcoming tones than mine. 'What a surprise! You should've let us know you were coming! Please, come on in.' He ushered us along the causeway and onto the gangplank as he spoke. Pulling a key from his pocket, he set about unlocking the door that opened into the little wood panelled reception area on board our dahabeeyah.

Dan allowed himself to be swept along by Adam's bonhomie. But I wasn't fooled. This was no social visit. I could only imagine the difficulty he'd had getting here.

'I thought international tourist flights into Luxor had been suspended since the Foreign Office imposed a ban on all but essential travel to Egypt,' I blurted my thoughts aloud.

Dan looked daggers at me. 'Damn right, and a devil's own job I've had to get here, I don't mind telling you! I had to take a scheduled flight from Heathrow into Cairo, since the commercial charter flights from Gatwick into Luxor were cancelled. On arrival I suffered an impertinent interrogation at the immigration desk from some jobs-worth official who spoke the worst English of any Egyptian I've ever encountered!' He broke off briefly at this point and cast a quick and, I have to say, rather disparaging glance at Ahmed. 'Well,' he amended. 'Maybe with one or two exceptions... Anyway, after much to-ing and fro-ing I managed to get the halfwit to understand that I needed to travel because I had family out here. Once he finally condescended to let me on my way, I hailed a taxi to the station only to find I'd just missed the sleeper train down here to Luxor. So I had to wait for the ordinary passenger one, and then travel third class in a packed carriage without air conditioning. I've been travelling for *hours*. And then to turn up here late last night only to find you weren't here ...' He left this hanging. There was no need for him to spell it out. Dan was quite clearly not a happy man.

But none of this was what made me stare at him in consternation. '*What* family?' I challenged. I knew for a cast iron fact that there was not one solitary person on Egyptian soil to whom Dan could claim to be related.

He let out a puff of impatience and glared at me. '*You*, Meredith!'

This was another bad sign. When Dan calls me by my full name, rather than the abbreviated version or a nickname, it's a clear-cut indication of bad temper.

'But I'm not... I mean, we're not...' I trailed off in confusion.

'We were together for ten years,' he announced as if I needed reminding. 'I think that entitles me to sta – er – state some connection.' I had no doubt he'd been about to say '*stake a claim*' but with a quick glance at Adam he performed a neat verbal swerve at the last moment. 'Besides which, your mother...'

My mother?!' I cut across him. 'What does my mother have to do with this?'

But I wasn't the only one who'd spotted his quick rethink mid-sentence. Despite Dan's split second glance at Adam, and his lightning recovery, there was someone else who had cause to question the claim or *connection* Dan seemed to be staking to me.

Ted coughed, interrupting my demand to know where my mother fitted in. He was far too polite to cut across me in the same way I'd done to Dan. 'Eh hum,' the professor started. 'Is my daughter here in Egypt, Dan? Is Jessica with you?'

Dan cast a somewhat uneasy glance at his future father-in-law. It's fair to say their relationship hadn't got off to the best of starts last year. But since Dan – for all his bluster – was so far superior to Jessica's first husband (about whom the less said the better), Ted had decided to overlook his character flaws and welcome him to the family. I thought this was to Ted's great credit. Dan can take some getting used to. As he'd just pointed out, I'd had a full decade to come to terms with his quick temper and tendency to lecture. And, if my current raised blood pressure was anything to judge by, I still wasn't sure I'd completely cracked it.

'Er, no,' Dan shook his head. 'Jessica stayed at home. I considered it was potentially too dangerous for her to come. All the News reports have been describing Egypt as a war-zone since President Morsi was toppled.'

'These News reports are grossly exaggerated.' Ahmed cut in, using pure and faultless English, and flashing his beautiful new white teeth. He'd been practising his 'th's' since his teeth were fixed, with some success. I was quite sure his flawless pronunciation was intended to put Dan firmly back in his place.

Dan ignored him. 'When I turned up to find you weren't here, it did occur to me you might have been sensible and gone away for a while. But then I saw you'd left one of the

8

windows on the latch, so I knew you couldn't be far away. You'd never lock up and leave for any length of time without making sure the dahabeeyah was secure. Besides...' he treated me to another accusatory glare, '...when did you ever do the sensible thing, Meredith?'

Ted subsided now he knew his daughter was safely at home, and that his prospective son-in-law had shown a modicum of care for her wellbeing. I was grateful for Ted's forbearance since I didn't appreciate Dan's hectoring tone and had every intention of telling him so.

I opened my mouth to retaliate but Adam forestalled me. 'Why don't we make some coffee and toast and head up onto the sundeck, so we can all say hello properly?'

Lovely Adam. Always the voice of reason. I bit back my angry retort, contenting myself with a fulminating glare at my former boyfriend. Then I allowed Adam to take my hand and lead me down the narrow corridor towards the back of the boat, where the kitchen is situated.

'What the hell is he doing here?' I muttered once we were alone, putting thick slices of bread in the toaster while Adam busied himself with the coffee machine.

'I imagine your mother sent him,' Adam said equably. 'You can't blame them for being worried about you, Merry. It's because they care.'

'Yes, well, his timing stinks,' I complained, getting butter out of the fridge and banging down jars of marmalade, honey and jam on a tray. I didn't want to be reminded that people I loved were concerned about me. I wanted to get on with the excitement of the discovery we'd made overnight.

I felt sure Adam equally could do without the interruption and the distraction of my ex turning up unannounced like this. But Adam and Dan had formed an unlikely friendship of sorts – thanks, I think, to Adam's never-to-be-forgotten rescue of Dan from a dice with death on a cliff-top not so long ago. And Adam suffers less with impatience than I do. Whatever, he didn't comment further while we finished preparing the breakfast things.

As we reached the top of the spiral staircase that leads up onto the sundeck, it was to find Dan frowning as he contemplated the charred furniture and stripped back floorboards. 'What in God's name happened up here?' He turned towards us, sounding shocked.

'The small matter of a fire,' Adam said grimly, setting down the tray with the coffee things on it.

Dan gazed about him, his frown deepening. 'That much I can see for myself! But how...? Surely you're not stupid enough to allow people to smoke up here?' He must have caught something in the brief look Adam and I exchanged. He sat down with a thump, swinging his gaze between us. 'It wasn't an accident, was it? Someone set the *Queen Ahmes* alight on purpose. Oh God, it's worse than I thought. Who have you made an enemy of this time?' This was said with a kind of weary resignation, as if it were almost boringly predictable that we'd be up to our necks in some sort of trouble.

I shifted uncomfortably under his critical gaze. 'Before we start on all that, I want you to answer my questions,' I demanded. 'What are you doing here in Egypt? And where does my mother fit in?' I was quite keen to deflect Dan's interrogation. I decided I'd much prefer to give an accounting of our recent activities once I had some reinforcements to back me up. And since Walid, Ted and Ahmed were taking their time about joining us up on deck (discretion being perhaps the better part of valour), I felt it was in my best interests to stall for time. Besides, I'd asked my questions first.

'We want you home, Pinkie.'

I stared at him in dismay, shocked into overlooking his casual use of my nickname.

'That goes for you too of course, Adam,' Dan added quickly, clearing his throat. 'Look, we all know how much this business venture means to you both. But you knew from the start what a huge risk you were taking given Egypt's dodgy political situation and its impact on tourism.'

'Hang on –' I started to interrupt.

But Dan was not to be diverted now he'd started. 'The fact is, none of us could have foreseen this second revolution coming so quickly on the heels of the first one. And now the

News reports are of running battles in the streets and rivers of blood. Put simply guys, it's just not safe for you to be here anymore. It's time to call it a day and come home.'

'But –' I tried again, shooting Adam a look of appeal.

Dan steam-rollered verbally over the top of me, yet again. 'Your parents are worried sick, Merry. The very fact that your mother picked up the phone to *me* of all people should show you just how frantic she and your dad are. She said she's left you voicemail messages, but you haven't returned her calls. You sent just one short text message last week to let her know you were ok. Nothing beyond that. Can't you understand how concerned they are?'

I bit my lip, feeling like a balloon that had been burst. All my indignation deflated in a heartbeat. I hated to admit it but Dan was right. I'd been so caught up in everything else going on, I really hadn't given my family back in England more than a passing thought. But, even so, going home? No. Going home was the very last thing I wanted to do.

'I'm sorry.' I looked directly into Dan's eyes, wanting him to see I meant it. 'I've been horribly thoughtless. Of course I should have phoned Mum back. It's just –'

I broke off at the sound of a heavy footfall on the wooden planks behind me. Ahmed was the first one brave enough to join us up on deck. Walid followed. And, bringing up the rear, Ted came up the spiral staircase just a few paces behind them. I had the strongest impression they'd arrived together to have strength in numbers.

Adam poured the coffee while our friends pulled up a selection of chairs and recliners that had fared best in the fire and were still sturdy enough to sit on.

'I can't even think about coming home right now,' I started. 'It's not just that we need to give Khaled time to finish his repairs of the *Queen Ahmes*. You see...' I broke off, not really sure how to begin to tell Dan everything that had been happening.

'You've made another blasted discovery!' Dan finished for me. 'Credit me with a bit of intelligence, Meredith! I do have eyes in my head. I saw those wrappings the professor was carrying when you got back. You've been back inside the tomb, and you've found something else to rock the world, as if the damned tomb itself wasn't enough! And you no doubt have a whole host of criminals chasing after you, baying for your blood like a pack of hungry wolves. Am I getting close?'

The professor cleared his throat. 'Closer than you may think, my boy.' He leaned forward and stirred milk into his coffee. 'Except they're not criminals. And they're not chasing after us. At least, not anymore. One of them, the one who attempted to blackmail poor Walid here, was killed in the rioting in Cairo. The other, who so cavalierly set light to this dahabeeyah, is missing, presumed drowned.'

'*Blackmail*?!' Dan spluttered, looking as if he might be about to succumb to a bad case of apoplexy. He made a visible effort to get a grip on himself, and glared round at us. 'I think you'd better explain, and quickly.'

'Both individuals worked for the Ministry for the Preservation of Ancient Monuments here in Luxor,' Walid rushed into speech. 'They found out about the tomb because a copy of that letter we all signed turned up in Mustafa Mushhawrar's bank box when his possessions were cleared after his death. It was my fault, of course, for insisting on the stupid letters in the first place. It left us all dangerously exposed. I'm truly sorry for my error of judgement. But we must now hope the danger is past, since the blackmailer is assuredly dead. Our friend Ahmed had the unhappy task of delivering his body to the hospital morgue.'

Dan assimilated this in silence, no doubt recognising the implications in the blackmail scenario for he and Jessica without needing to have them spelled out. I'd thought he might rant and rave a bit more but he didn't. 'So, the tomb is now an open secret,' he concluded instead, in a flat tone of voice.

'Not quite,' Adam put in. 'We have no reason to believe that anyone outside of these two young men knows about the tomb.'

Dan looked far from convinced. 'But surely the blackmailer must have made copies of Mustafa's letter. He'd have wanted an insurance policy to back him up for sure. How do you know he didn't lodge a photocopy of it with everybody he knew?'

'We don't.' Walid said baldly. 'We just have to hope it is not so. As it is, the one copy of the letter we know he had in his possession has disappeared. It was not found among his paltry belongings after his death.' He'd obviously decided it was best to come clean and have the whole sorry state of affairs out on the table.

Dan frowned. 'And the man you presume to have drowned?'

'Gamal Abdel-Maqsoud.' Adam supplied. 'He jumped into the Nile in Cairo after setting light to the *Queen Ahmes*. He didn't resurface. We waited and scanned the riverbanks on both sides. There was no sign of him. We presume he may not have been able to swim and might have been caught up in reeds under water. He certainly knew of the tomb and its location. But we don't believe he had a copy of the letter.'

Dan didn't look any happier. 'So, you have no idea where the letter is now. Anyone could have got their hands on it.'

'That's about the size of it,' I agreed flatly.

'Well, it's an unholy bloody mess, that's all I can say.' Dan made this pronouncement as if delivering a verdict.

'It's potentially a ticking time bomb,' Adam agreed. 'That's why we knew we had not a minute to waste in getting back inside the tomb to see if we could find the evidence to debunk Nabil Zaal's latest theory.'

'Nabil Zaal?' Dan queried, looking momentarily confused by the change in subject before his expression cleared. 'Ah yes, I recollect him now. He's the author you hooked up with earlier in the year. You sent us that long newsy email about him, Meredith; remember? He claims some of the key figures of the Old Testament were in actual fact Egyptian pharaohs, isn't that the one?'[1]

I nodded, recalling the glee with which I'd written to tell Dan and Jessica the story of how we'd come to be acquainted with the writer, and as a by-the-by, the claim to fame our dahabeeyah could boast, having once played host to Egypt's last reigning monarch, King Farouk.

'Well, we all know the Old Testament is a tissue of lies from start to finish,' Dan declared bluntly and, quite possibly, blasphemously. 'So, what preposterous theory is he peddling to the gullible this time?'

It was Ahmed, however unlikely that may sound, who paused in the action of liberally buttering a slice of toast to respond. Perhaps he saw an opportunity to practise his newly perfected English and prove Dan wrong in his earlier insulting denigration of his command of our language. He sat up straighter in his chair, thrust out his feet and looked Dan full in the face. 'He claims that the father of the Jewish faith, and the

---

[1] Farouk's Fancies – Book 4 of Meredith Pink's Adventures in Egypt

forefather of both Christianity and Islam, the man we know from religious teachings as Moses, was, in actual fact, the pharaoh Akhenaten. He believes Akhenaten was the one who led the Israelites out of Egypt towards the Promised Land in the Exodus.'

I nearly jumped up and applauded. Every 't-h' was enunciated to perfection. Allowing for the Arabic accent it was impossible for him to disguise, Ahmed had delivered this speech, no matter how pompously, as if English was a language he'd been speaking all his life. It was only a matter of a couple of weeks since our friend, Selim, had fixed his dental implants in place. But aside from the startling physical improvement, something in his new dentistry seemed also to have untangled Ahmed's tongue from his teeth.

Sadly, Dan seemed to notice neither Ahmed's transformed appearance nor his flawless pronunciation. 'Akhenaten? He was the one who uprooted everyone from Thebes to Amarna when he decided he'd had enough of Egyptian tradition and wanted to go his own way, right? And now your writer-chum would have us believe he uprooted everyone all over again, well, some of them at any rate, and led them off into the sunset of the Sinai? Sounds like a damn fool theory to me! Besides, I thought Akhenaten was one of the fossilized occupants of that gold-stuffed tomb you found. How's it possible for a man to be leading his previously enslaved people through the waters of the Red Sea and trooping up Mount Sinai to collect the Ten Commandments, or whatever the hell it was he's supposed to have done, while simultaneously lying safely mummified inside a secret tomb only a stone's throw from here?'

I heard a choking sound to my left and realised Adam was swallowing down hard on a bubble of amusement. 'See, Merry, some of your knowledge rubbed off on him after all,' he murmured quietly out of the corner of his mouth. Then he nodded his head at Dan to show his agreement and addressed him in his more everyday tones. 'You're quite right, of course. But I'll admit some of Nabil's arguments were quite compelling. He got us doubting ourselves. We took it into our heads to check, just to be sure.'

'So, you broke back into the tomb and, what? Lifted the lid on the sarcophagus?'

'Yes,' Ted confirmed. 'That's exactly what we did.' Somehow, it sounded better coming from him. As an Egyptologist of the most unimpeachable scholarly credentials, his involvement lent a tenuous kind of credibility to our activities. Under his watchful eye, we could convince ourselves our actions were less about adventure hunting, and more about the search for historical truth.

Walid too, with his senior ranking position at the Egyptian Museum in Cairo, and his contacts in the Ministry of Antiquities, added the weight of authenticity to our trespass into this throwback to antiquity. It was Walid who spoke up now. 'And, thankfully, we were able to satisfy ourselves that Akhenaten, or, more accurately, his mummy, is indeed one of the occupants of the tomb. I am perfectly convinced the other is Nefertiti. Nabil Zaal's hypothesis has indeed proved to be wide of the mark on this occasion. Sadly for him.'

Dan stared round at us. 'Why am I sensing a "*but*"?'

We exchanged glances. Telling Dan everything we had so far was perfectly reasonable. Dan knew all about the tomb. He'd been inside it. More than that, he was one of the small band of what we might call co-conspirators who'd signed their names to the letter Walid had insisted upon. The letter that had subsequently proved so troublesome and ill judged. There had been a time, very recently, when I'd been worried Dan himself might fall prey to our blackmailer's malicious threats. I'd even toyed briefly with the idea of warning him. I'll admit it was *very* briefly. I'd been put off by the prospect of Dan hotfooting it out here to Egypt to throw his weight around. But now he was here anyway. The spanner was well and truly in the works. Even so, I wasn't sure it was necessarily sensible to share the rest of the story with him. Dan could be hot tempered, unpredictable and occasionally irrational. There was no telling how he might react. Besides, we'd barely had a chance to draw breath ourselves. It was still only a scanty few hours since we'd made our latest discovery. Dan's precipitate arrival had denied us the opportunity to talk it through and decide what to do next.

'There's more you're not telling me,' Dan pressed, watching our faces. 'Isn't there?'

I felt rather than observed the long breath, almost a sigh, the professor let out and knew he'd made the decision to come clean. As Dan's future father-in-law, perhaps he felt he had no choice but to trust him. And since Ted was something of an elder statesman amongst us, I knew we'd all defer to his judgement and take our lead from him. So I decided to sit back with my coffee and my toast and hear the story told, rather than attempt to be the one to tell it myself. The warmth of early morning was stealing across the deck as the sun lifted higher in the sky. The pinkish light of dawn was giving way to the golden tones of daytime. I watched an egret flapping its wings against the stretching sky, pale blue and endless above the dahabeeyah. The Nile lapped gently against the hull below us at the waterline and I could hear the slinky feral cats mewling on the causeway. Settling comfortably against my sadly scorched cushion, I looked across at the professor, interested to hear how he would put it all into words.

Ted placed his coffee cup on the table, adjusted his glasses and looked through them at Dan. 'Yes,' he admitted. 'There's more.'

Dan crunched on a square of toast and waited politely for him to continue. If he was impatient he managed not to show it as Ted allowed a long pause to draw out before he went on.

'As Adam rightly said, the proof of Akhenaten lying mummified inside his sarcophagus enabled us to debunk Nabil's assertion that the heretic pharaoh was also Moses. But, hidden inside the sarcophagus, we found evidence to suggest another candidate for the role.'

'You're saying Akhenaten wasn't Moses, but you think you know who was?'

'Quite so, my boy. Quite so. Although I'm still not sure I can believe the evidence of my own eyes.'

Stillness seemed to settle over our small party as we waited for the professor to continue. I'm not sure any of us could quite believe it either. Yet we'd all been there and witnessed the discovery.

'What we found suggests in the strongest possible terms that the man who led the Israelites out of Egypt in what the Bible calls the Exodus was the high priest who served at the temple of the Aten in ancient Akhet-Aten. His name was Meryre.'

'And what exactly did you find?' Dan asked, narrowing his gaze on his future father-in-law's face.

Ted cleared his throat. 'We found a set of clay tablets wrapped in linen secreted inside Akhenaten's outer coffin. The first of them reads as a kind of promise made by Meryre to the dead Pharaoh.'

'Oh God,' Dan groaned, rolling his eyes upwards. 'It sounds just like the dratted papyrus all over again!'

I stared at him. I simply couldn't understand why he wasn't transfixed with wonder. But then, the Egyptology bug had never bitten Dan in the way it had the rest of us. He stared back, and I could see his inability to grasp our excitement was every bit as strong as my own failure to comprehend how it could leave him so cold. The trouble was, to Dan's way of thinking, since the life had gone out of these ancient relics several millennia ago, he just couldn't see the relevance of them to the modern world. And he'd made his opinion on the Old Testament of the Bible abundantly clear already.

Ted managed not to react to the rudeness his daughter's fiancé exhibited with this less than enthusiastic response. Instead he chose to carry on as if Dan hadn't spoken at all. 'On the tablet Meryre promises to lead Akhenaten's people out of Egypt, to keep his teachings alive, and to keep the treasures of the temple safe.'

I'd noticed Ahmed had been fidgeting and twitching in his chair as the conversation progressed. As he's such a big man, his fidgeting and twitching were hard to ignore. I'd swear I could feel the tremor he was sending through the charred floorboards underneath our feet. Since it was impossible to take no notice of him, I sent him a questioning glance.

His dark eyes snapped and flashed back at me. 'I wondered how long it would take for someone to get around to mentioning the treasure,' he announced. And then, forgetting his newly perfected English in his excited agitation, he added, 'Tell to him about de treasure map, professor.'

Chapter 2

We all stared at the clay tablets lined up neatly on the bar in the lounge. We'd come inside, since outside the heat was rising along with the sun. Egypt in July suffers ferocious temperatures, even in early morning.

There were twelve tablets in all, not counting the slightly larger one on which the high priest Meryre had transcribed his pledge to Akhenaten. Each was the approximate size of a reporter's notebook. The professor had collected them from his cabin and very carefully removed them, one by one, from their protective linen wrappings, setting them out side-by-side so we could study them.

'This is a treasure map?' Dan asked in disbelief.

Ted ceased leaning forward over the tablets. He lifted his head to look at his future son-in-law. His pale blue eyes seemed lit from within behind his glasses, and his skin was flushed. 'Certainly the next best thing to one,' he said in a strangely hushed tone of voice. 'If my reckoning is correct, what we have here is a prototype of the Copper Scroll.'

'The Copper Scroll?' Dan asked inevitably.

'The most mysterious, and unique, of the Dead Sea Scrolls,' I volunteered.

Dan looked at me and raised one eyebrow. He didn't need to comment. That winged brow was silently eloquent, and quite effective in dampening my excitement.

Luckily, Adam was impervious to Dan's unspoken scepticism, and shared my enthusiasm in equal measure. 'From everything the professor has told us so far, the Copper Scroll stands apart from the rest of the Dead Sea Scrolls which, as you know, comprise the oldest known collection of Biblical texts ever discovered. Unlike the traditional Dead Sea Scrolls, which were written on parchment, papyrus and leather, the so-called Copper Scroll was engraved peculiarly on copper pieces. It doesn't fit into the category of being a religious or literary document like the others. Instead, it appears to be a list of buried treasure.'

Dan cast a doubtful glance at the clay tablets lined up on the bar. 'They don't look much like copper to me,' he said flatly.

Ted frowned at him, looking as if his patience was wearing thin. 'No, of course not! What I consider we have here, as I believe I said, is an early *prototype* of the Copper Scroll. The Copper Scroll itself is on display at the Jordan Museum in Amman.'

'The professor has been studying the Dead Sea Scrolls, and the Copper Scroll in particular.' I said a bit defensively. As usual, Dan's whole demeanour was making my hackles rise.

'Quite so, my dear,' Ted smiled at me, and then explained for Dan's benefit. 'My interest was sparked earlier in the year when we came into possession of a document we thought might have been stolen from among the original collection of Dead Sea Scrolls.'

'It turned out to be a fake, if I remember rightly,' Dan said in studiedly neutral tones. 'Yes, Merry told us about it in her email.'

'Indeed it did,' Ted acknowledged. 'But, as I said, it got me interested. So I started reading up on the subject. I stumbled across some recent research apparently linking one of the scrolls, the mysterious Copper Scroll, to the pharaoh Akhenaten. The suggestion seems to be that the followers of the pharaoh's new religion left Egypt after his death, but not before they'd hidden or buried quantities of his temple treasures. The Copper Scroll appears to be a kind of record, a map if you like, of where they stashed these precious objects; perhaps so they could come back later and recover them.'

'Which, if true, is no doubt precisely what they did.' Dan declared. 'Honestly! You lot are carrying on as if none of this treasure has ever been discovered!'

Ted pushed his glasses up his nose and levelled his gaze on his future son-in-law's disbelieving face. 'It is, of course, entirely possible that any buried treasure itemised in the Copper Scroll was dug up centuries ago. Or perhaps those who apparently kept such a meticulous record of its whereabouts did indeed return to reclaim it. But a couple of points lead me to believe this may not be the case.'

Seeing us all attentive – even Dan, who was staring back at the professor with the light of challenge in his eyes – Ted cleared his throat and started to elucidate.

'First, I think it unlikely those who so painstakingly transcribed the Copper Scroll at around the time of Christ would have done so if the treasures whose hiding places they were recording had already been recovered.'

'So, you're saying the Copper Scroll itself was created at the same time the Dead Sea Scrolls were being written?' Adam interrupted. 'You don't think it was an earlier piece, handed down through generations and simply stored alongside the scrolls in those caves in Qumran?'

Ted looked back at him. 'Everyone seems to agree it is contemporaneous with the other Dead Sea Scrolls. But many specialists believe the Copper Scroll was copied, possibly from a much earlier document.'

I felt my gaze pulled back to the clay tablets lined up on the bar. They were unquestionably an earlier document. 'What makes them think that?' I asked.

'The scroll was engraved in an unusual form of ancient Hebrew – a square-form script. It contains many previously unknown word forms and apparently numerous mistakes. So it seems quite plausible that the people who copied it onto copper did not in every instance understand the language they were transcribing. The theory seems to be that the Qumranites obtained the text from a much earlier source community and were dealing with a language, or an archaic form of a language, that was not altogether familiar to them.'

'Which would make sense if the original text was written in ancient Egyptian,' Adam said.

'Hieratic,' Walid murmured, his gaze resting on the clay tablets. 'The abridged form of hieroglyphics used by priests.'

'Exactly so,' the professor concurred.

Ahmed was shifting his feet impatiently. I could sense he was desperate to bring us back to the point. 'Professor, you said there were two reasons why you believe the treasure was not found. You have given us only one.'

Ted's lips twitched as he contemplated our police pal. 'You're right to remind me,' he smiled. 'The other, of course, is that the collection of Dead Sea Scrolls lay undisturbed in the caves in Qumran on the shores of the Dead Sea for two thousand years, presumably since their writers stored them there.'

'And if the creators of the Copper Scroll engraved it in the belief the treasures they were recording still lay undisturbed...' Adam finished for him, '...then there's no reason to suppose anyone should have attempted to dig them up all the time the Copper Scroll lay undiscovered among the Dead Sea Scrolls.'

'Precisely my point, my boy.' Ted nodded. 'The Copper Scroll was found in March 1952 by a team of Bedouin led by an archaeologist from the École Biblique in Jerusalem.'

Dan looked around at our faces as if we'd all taken leave of our senses. 'It may have escaped your attention, but 1952 was over sixty years ago!' he said abruptly. 'I'd say more than half a century was plenty of time for the initiated to indulge in a spot of illicit treasure-hunting.'

'That's just it!' Ted responded excitedly, ignoring Dan's rudeness. 'Those you call *the initiated* – the scholars and philologists who've translated and studied the Copper Scroll – seem to have been searching in the wrong place!'

We all stared at him.

The professor pushed his glasses back into place on the bridge of his nose and peered through them at each of us in turn. 'It has taken a generation to achieve a viable translation of the Copper Scroll. Even now, there is scholarly disagreement about how its contents should be interpreted. That it lists the hiding places of quantities of treasure is not in dispute. But no one can seem to agree where these burial sites are. Those who originally analysed the Scroll identified four likely locations for the lost treasures of the Qumranites.' He proceeded to tick them off on his fingers. 'One, The Dead Sea region. Two, Jericho. Three, Jerusalem. And four, Mount Gerizim, which is situated in historical Canaan. The

Biblical land of Canaan, of course, later became known as Judaea, Palestine, and finally, the modern State of Israel.'

'Hmm,' Adam remarked thoughtfully. 'Considering how unsettled things have been in the Middle East in recent decades, I'm not sure any of those is a promising location for a treasure hunt.'

'Indeed,' Ted concurred. 'Many of the locations mentioned appear to refer to Jerusalem, or its close vicinity, namely the Temple Mount area where the first and second Temples of Jerusalem were situated before they were destroyed by the Babylonians and Romans respectively. Both temples were known to be places where considerable wealth was accumulated through donations of sacrificial gifts and tithes.'

'Well I'd certainly think twice about excavating the Temple Mount area for buried treasure,' Adam said. 'I'd be too afraid of attracting a hail of machine-gun fire and stirring up all sorts of religious trouble.'

'Yes, and sadly the political sensitivies mean that official permission is nigh on impossible to obtain,' Ted agreed.

I couldn't contain myself any longer. 'But you don't think any of these is the correct location for the secret hiding places?'

Ted took a little while about answering. Finally, after ordering his thoughts, he met my gaze and said, 'I'll admit my own view, based on what I've read, is rather different from that of most other scholars. It seems indisputable that the Copper Scroll describes a Temple – it certainly refers to Temple-associated objects – but the most recent research suggests the contents describe *another* Temple altogether.'

It was slowly dawning on me what he was leading up to. And I could see enlightenment creeping across Adam's expression when I glanced at him.

But Walid was the first to put the pieces together and make them fit. He spoke into the expectant hush that had fallen over us. 'The Temple of the Aten in Akhet-Aten,' he whispered.

Ted smiled beatifically and gazed at the clay tablets. 'And I think we have now stumbled across the proof that the Qumranites were guardians, not just of treasure, but also of a religion that belonged to a much earlier time and a very distant place.'

'Amarna,' Ahmed pronounced sonorously, proving he was not a police officer for nothing. 'Professor, you believe the treasure, it is buried in Amarna.'

I felt my gaze drawn back to the clay tablets, and I wasn't alone. When I glanced up it was to find everyone was staring at them.

'There's one thing I don't understand,' I frowned. 'Ted, you said researchers had only recently made a link between the Copper Scroll and the Pharaoh Akhenaten. What is it?

Afterall, *we're* the ones who've found these clay tablets inside Akhenaten's sarcophagus. No one else knows they exist. So how could the latest researchers possibly have dated the contents of the Copper Scroll back to the Amarna period of ancient Egypt without these?'

Ted's pale blue eyes gleamed at me through his wire-rimmed glasses. 'What put scholars onto the connection to Akhenaten is the insertion in the Copper Scroll of a series of Greek characters into the columns of text. These would seem to have very little to do with the content of the scroll itself. The Greek letters are interspersed, apparently randomly, at the end of sections of the text. Until now, no one has ever claimed to understand them. Some suggested they appeared to be a cryptic code. But nobody was able to propose how to crack it. Until...' He reached behind the bar for the small notebook and pencil I keep there.

We all watched as with slow and careful precision, Ted drew a string of characters on the paper.

'Now,' he turned the notebook around, so we could see it. 'What do you make of this?'

I stared at the letters the professor had meticulously transcribed.

'I studied them so closely, I learned them by heart,' he explained. 'Now, what I have done is positioned the letters sequentially, having pulled them out from the end-sections within the Scroll.'

Reading across from left to right, the characters were as follows:

♯ K ε N ♯ χ A Γ ♯ H N ♯ Θ ε ♯ Δ I ♯ T P ♯ Σ K

'It's all Greek to me,' Dan murmured, no doubt trying to be funny.

'I never learned Greek,' I admitted. 'It may as well be written in Martian for all the sense it makes to me.'

But I could feel Adam had gone very still alongside me. 'The first letters spell AKENHATEN!' he exclaimed. 'Oh my God, it's the pharaoh's name!'

'Well, at least a very close approximation of it,' Ted smiled. 'I guess some misspelling is forgivable after a gap of some twelve hundred years between the holy city of Akhet-Aten during the Amarna period, and the community at Qumran at about the time of Christ.'

'But what about the last few characters?' Dan asked dubiously. 'Presumably, they *don't* refer to the pharaoh?'

Ted was unfazed by this challenge. 'The reason Akhenaten's name appears in the earliest sections of the Copper Scroll is, I believe, because the earlier columns relate to locations in Egypt – specifically Amarna, as this fine fellow Ahmed has already pointed out. As the Scroll is essentially a list, I think the later sections describe the hiding places of the precious objects Akhenaten's followers were able to smuggle out of the country when they left, perhaps during the Exodus. I suspect, as other scholars have noted, the later locations are most likely to be in Canaan, that is to say, modern-day Israel. When we study these clay tablets I'm sure we'll find these later sites are not included.'

'Because these were transcribed before they started on their journey out of Egypt,' I breathed in wonder. 'Before the Exodus.'

'That's my take on it,' Ted nodded. 'Of course, the link to Akhenaten was all theory and supposition, an intriguing hypothesis,' he added. 'But now ...' He trailed off, his eyes drawn back to the clay tablets as if magnetised.

'Now we have the proof,' Adam finished for him.

'Now we have our own copy of the treasure map,' Ahmed amended. 'And we should go in search of the treasure!' He stared around at us with the supreme self-confidence of one to whom this conclusion and course of action were as clear as the nose on his face.

It took long seconds for it to start to dawn on him that something so obvious to him wasn't quite as straightforward to the rest of us.

I blame his tomb-robbing ancestry. Put simply, treasure hunting is in Ahmed's blood. His smart black-and-white uniform, courtesy of the local tourist and antiquities police department, might serve as a useful disguise; but I'd swear its only skin deep. He could shed it as easily as he could remove his shirt and tie.

'Not so fast...' Ted chided calmly. 'We need to take stock.'

'We can't go surreptitiously digging all over Amarna.' Adam cautioned. 'We don't have a proper excavation permit, beyond the temporary one the Ministry granted to Walid and Nabil Zaal last month. And, just imagine if we should find something ...! What the Hell would we do then?'

Dan was nodding his head vigorously. 'It strikes me you lot are up to your necks in enough trouble, without courting more! You can't possibly set about making more fantastical discoveries, when you've still got a bloody great unannounced tomb you're keeping secret from the world! If you want my advice, you need to hand these tablets over to the proper authorities. And you need to hand them over fast!'

I was tempted to tell my ex-boyfriend he sounded like a broken record. He'd been banging on about handing things over to the authorities right from day one, when I'd accidentally discovered some cryptic hieroglyphics hidden inside a picture frame in the Howard Carter Museum. I'll say that for Dan; he's remarkably consistent. Pig-headed might be another way of putting it.

Restraining the impulse as best I could, I instead pointed out quietly, 'I'm not sure we need your advice, thank you Dan. We're lucky enough to have one of the foremost authorities in Egyptology right here in the room with us.' I turned towards Walid Massri with some deference as I spoke.

'Walid holds the most senior ranking position at the Egyptian Antiquities Museum in Cairo, as you know. He counts as "the proper authorities".'

I'm not sure how Walid felt about me dropping responsibility in his lap like an unexploded bomb because Dan started on me before I could see his reaction.

'Walid's proved himself no better than the rest of you!' Dan rapped out. Then, perhaps hearing his voice rising to the point of a shout, he took a hold of himself, levelled his tone and addressed himself somewhat more respectfully to the museum curator. 'Forgive me, Walid; you're a fine chap and all that, and I know you've helped hook this pair... ' – He jerked a thumb at Adam and me – '...out of more scrapes than they've had hot dinners, but, let's face it, if you'd only decided to come clean about the tomb from the start, then perhaps I wouldn't need to be pointing out to you the trouble you'll be courting if you don't leave well alone now.'

'Don't blame Walid!' I immediately leapt to his defence. 'You know his reasons for keeping quiet about the tomb as well as I do. You were there when he explained them. And, let's face it; he's been proved right! Egypt is a nation in turmoil. That's the whole reason you're here! Who knows what might have happened to the tomb if we'd owned up to discovering it? There have been enough political power struggles and violence on the streets as it is, without throwing the tomb into the mix.'

I stopped abruptly as Walid reached out and gently but firmly gripped my arm. 'Enough, Merry,' he said. 'I have heard enough. And perhaps Dan is right in what he says.'

His voice held an air of authority I'd heard there before, as if it had a thread of steel running through it. When Walid speaks in that tone, people listen. We were all listening now.

'I fear I have made a mistake, my friends, in withholding that magnificent tomb from the world.'

We all gaped at him. 'But...' I started to interrupt.

He silenced me with a gesture, holding up one hand in an unmistakeable plea for quiet while he collected his thoughts. When he spoke again it was more slowly, but still with that same mettle. 'I now wonder if perhaps a discovery like this is exactly what Egypt might need to set her on her feet again, to unify opposing factions, and to invite the world's tourists back once more.'

Funnily enough, I'd thought he might be wavering when we were inside the tomb last night. Maybe the discovery of the clay tablets and all the discussion about the Copper Scroll had helped him to make up his mind. At least, I hoped it was that, and not Dan and his imperious way of riding roughshod over everybody's feelings.

'But how on earth...?' Adam started. 'I mean, it's been more than a year...! How will you... I mean how will we...?'

'It is quite simple,' Walid said calmly. 'We will have to stage the discovery of the tomb.'

37

Chapter 3

'Do you think if we told Dan we're married, it might stop him ordering me about?' I asked Adam later that day.

We were in our stainless steel kitchen situated in the hull towards the back of the dahabeeyah, preparing the evening meal. Dan had spent the afternoon sleeping off his travel-fatigue in the cabin we'd allocated him. To be fair, we'd all succumbed to the need for a mid-day nap after being up all night. But the excitement of our discovery had roused all of us except Dan after only the briefest of forty winks. Ted and Walid were now in the lounge-bar sharing a huge pot of coffee, both studying the clay tablets with expressions of absorbed pleasure on their faces. Khaled had turned up to put in a few hours of repair work up on deck, but had now gone home again for his tea.

Adam gave me a soft but rather quizzical smile. 'If I thought it would help, I'd tell him in a heartbeat. But, considering the mood he's in, I have a feeling it might just make things worse!'

'You mean, he might start bossing you around too?'

Adam grinned. 'Something like that! You see, Merry, I'm just a great big coward at heart, and your ex-boyfriend scares the living daylights out of me!'

Since I knew this wasn't true, I grinned back, feeling my mood lighten.

The trouble was, Adam and I weren't actually married. We might – and did – consider ourselves to be happily joined in wedlock, but there was nothing official about it. We'd said our vows to each other in the pitch dark while locked inside Akhenaten's tomb, not knowing if we'd ever see the light of day again. There'd been no witnesses, no register to sign, and no marriage certificate. Nothing at all, in fact, to prove it had happened beyond our own memories, and the sense of renewed commitment we felt towards each other.

'Maybe you're right,' I acknowledged with a shrug. 'But it would give me immense satisfaction to wipe that insufferable look off his face, as if he's doing me some enormous favour being here! I'm sure he'll start on at me again about going home as soon as we sit down for dinner.'

I didn't like the fact my ex-boyfriend could turn up all gung-ho, thinking he could bully me into submission – even if my mother, technically speaking, was the one who'd put him up to it.

Adam looked at me with a sad-edged seriousness. 'Maybe we should consider it.'

'Consider what?'

'Going home.'

I stared at him in disbelief.

'We're going to have to face up to it sometime, Merry,' he said. 'If business was bad in the post-Mubarak period, I should think it will be non-existent now Morsi's been ousted and the army is running the show.'

'I told Dan I wasn't coming home,' I said flatly.

'And he said he wasn't leaving without you,' Adam reminded me. 'That's a stalemate that can't last forever.'

'But he has no right to tell me what to do! This is my home now. Here! In Luxor! With you!'

Adam took me lightly by the shoulders and turned me towards him so I had no choice but to look into his eyes. It was to find them shadowed with concern. 'You heard what he said about the way this latest Revolution has been reported in the Western press. The British Foreign Office has slapped a ban on tourist travel to Egypt, and Americans have been ordered home. We don't stand a hope.' He squeezed my shoulders to emphasise his point. 'Maybe our best bet is to go home and sit things out for a year or two. We can start earning again while we wait for things to settle down and the tourist trade to pick up, so at least we won't be living on our savings for a bit.'

'I won't go home until Khaled's finished the repairs on the *Queen Ahmes*,' I said obstinately. 'It's not fair to leave him in the lurch. He needs the work. And that's going to take a good few days more solid effort. Besides, I want to be here while Walid decides how we're going to go about staging the discovery of the tomb. If you think I'm missing out on that, you've got another think coming. I was there from the start, and I'm not opting out now!'

Adam looked at me unhappily and dropped his hands from my shoulders. 'Ok, Merry, have it your own way. I'll admit, I want to stay as much as you do. Things have just started to get exciting again. But I don't think we'll be able to put it off indefinitely.'

* * *

It was only five of us for dinner, since Ahmed had been on duty at the local police station today, and had no doubt gone home now to catch up on some much-needed sleep.

'I don't think he was much looking forward to his shift today,' Adam remarked as we were setting the table.

'Ah yes, today was when the delegation was due to arrive on secondment from the Ministry of State for Antiquities in Cairo,' I remembered with a smile. 'You're right; Ahmed seemed very disgruntled at being the one selected to take them under his wing. Almost as if he suspects the Ministry of putting spies in the camp.'

'Considering all the reports of illicit digging at Egypt's archaeological sites since law and order broke down, I should think that's exactly what the Ministry has in mind,' Adam said with an ironic lift of one eyebrow. 'They don't think the local police force is on top of it. And the Military quite clearly has enough on its plate already.' Then he grinned at me. 'But I'm not so sure that's what's got poor old Ahmed so riled. I think it's more that he resents his selection as babysitter. What's added insult to injury, so far as I can make out, is that it's not actually a delegation the Ministry is sending.'

'Oh?'

'At least it *is*,' he amended. 'But not in the sense of it being a *group* of people.'

'It's only one person?'

'So it seems,' he nodded. 'But in the worst possible sense.'

'I don't follow...?'

'The person the Ministry has seconded to oversee the police security of the sites in and around Luxor isn't just any old official they've sent to breathe down poor Ahmed's neck. It's a *female* official...!'

'They're sending a *woman*?'

'Apparently so,' Adam nodded.

'Ah,' I said. '*I see*.'

The door opening interrupted our conversation. Adam looked up with a smile as Ted and Walid came into the room. They'd both returned to their cabins to spruce up a bit before dinner.

Dan has never mastered the art of dressing for dinner. He arrived a couple of minutes later looking as crumpled as

43

ever. Thankfully, he seemed well rested. He accepted the beer Adam offered him with a smile of thanks. Trying not to look too astonished at this unexpected show of good humour and nice manners, I suggested we might want to eat up on deck. It was a balmy evening, the stars were bright, and I still relished the novelty of eating our evening meals outside. The weather back in England was rarely settled enough to permit this little luxury on more than a handful of occasions each summer. And since it seemed my days here in Egypt might be numbered, I was more determined than ever to make the most of them.

'But we've just set the table in here,' Adam protested lightly.

'It doesn't matter. It's easy enough to move everything upstairs.'

Walid and Ted proved themselves willing helpers. Even Dan mucked in. He collected everyone's pre-dinner drinks onto a tray and carried them up the spiral staircase. Adam set about lighting the hurricane lamps, and soon everything was sorted. Khaled was doing a fine job of the repairs. In no time at all I was quite sure he'd have the *Queen Ahmes* looking as good as new. 'See?' I smiled. 'In the candlelight you'd never know we'd had a fire up here.'

'Speaking of which…' Dan started.

I immediately regretted my decision to relocate from the lounge-bar.

'Yes, we can claim on insurance,' Adam cut in smoothly.

I'm sure that wasn't the question Dan had been about to ask but, for once, he allowed himself to be diverted. I breathed a sigh of relief. I didn't want to be quizzed about our run-ins with Gamal Abdel-Maqsoud. I was perfectly content just to be thankful they were now over, since he'd had the common decency and good sense to drown himself in the Nile.

We sipped our drinks, listening to the chorus of frogs along the riverbank, while the waves gently lapped against the starboard side of the dahabeeyah. We still had a little time to relax and enjoy the warmth of an Egyptian dusk before dinner was ready.

'I was successful in getting hold of Nabil Zaal on the telephone earlier,' Ted informed us conversationally.

We all sent him looks of interested enquiry.

'It took me a while to calm him down at first. He was extremely agitated.'

'Oh?' Adam prompted.

'It seems his computer crashed as a result of some kind of virus. There were signs it had been uploaded deliberately.'

'Someone tried to sabotage his computer?' I exclaimed.

'So it would seem. You see, it had his draft manuscript stored on it.'

'The book he was writing claiming Moses was Akhenaten?'

'Yes. And, of course, the virus corrupted the file. He lost the lot.'

'Oh my goodness! Poor Nabil. No wonder he was upset! Was it those same anti-Jewish protesters who were dogging his footsteps while he was here in Egypt last month?'

'Well, it's impossible to prove, of course. But it seems likely.'

Walid looked concerned. 'Considering they let off that smoke bomb during Nabil's lecture at the Museum, and then tampered with the brakes on our jeep, I wouldn't put anything past them,' he said. 'They've proved themselves remarkably tenacious.'

Dan had been following this exchange, his head moving side-to-side so he could focus on whoever was speaking. Now he interrupted. It was immediately obvious his earlier good humour had evaporated. 'Am I right to deduce from all this that you've had yet *another* bunch of thugs on your trail?'

'They're not so much after us,' Adam corrected. 'It's Nabil they've been trying to silence.'

'We just happened to be there both times,' I added.

My comment was probably unhelpful. Dan didn't look in the least bit reassured. 'Then I'd say you should choose your friends more carefully! By the sound of it, you could have been killed!'

'It wasn't as bad as that!' I protested, remembering the way Adam had steered the jeep into a sand bank in a semi-controlled crash. 'I think they were just trying to put the frighteners on us... I mean, on Nabil.'

'And why should they want to do that?' Dan asked, eyes narrowed. He looked as if it would take a great deal to convince him this wasn't yet another good reason to haul me onto the next flight home, by the hair if necessary.

Ted sighed. I wondered if he was starting to find Dan every bit as trying as I did. Fortunately for me, my relationship with Dan was over, at least in the official sense. Ted's was just beginning. I wasn't sure it boded well for the future. 'It's a little bit hard to explain,' he started.

'Try me,' Dan invited.

Haha, I thought, *you asked for it.* And I waited with malicious anticipation to see how much he would enjoy what followed.

Ted pushed his glasses back up onto the bridge of his nose as they'd slipped forward again. 'Well, it stems from Nabil's construction of Tutankhamun's family tree. Remember, Tutankhamun is big business for Egypt. Outside of the pyramids, he's one of the most significant draws for visitors to the country – at least, he was, before all the political upheaval of the last few years. Anyway, put it this way: Egypt has a huge vested interest in keeping Tutankhamun as a pure-blooded Egyptian pharaoh.'

'You mean; he wasn't one?'

I'll say that for Dan: he's quick on the uptake.

Ted smiled at him. I'd swear I caught a malevolent glint in his eyes that mirrored mine. 'Possibly not! You see, if Nabil is correct then Tutankhamun was the great-grandson of Biblical Joseph.'

Dan stared back at him without comment.

'It means Tutankhamun was possibly descended from the Biblical Patriarchs, including Abraham and Jacob,' I explained. 'In short, he was of mixed race. He had the blood of the Hebrews running in his veins.'

'Thank you, Merry,' Dan said short-temperedly. 'I was working that out quite nicely for myself.'

I resisted the urge to poke out my tongue at him. I like to think I'm more grown up than to stoop to such a childish response. But it took some effort, I'll admit.

Ted spoke into the momentary pause, managing to take the heat out of the atmosphere. 'Of course, it rests on Joseph being identified as the Vizier Yuya, who served at the courts of both Thutmosis IV and Amenhotep III,' he said. 'But I think Nabil's scarab has proved the case on that one to the satisfaction of most scholars.'

Dan lifted his bottle of beer to his lips and downed what was left in one big gulp. 'So, why should this make Nabil Zaal

– and all of you by association – the target of a set of small-scale terrorists intent on doing you harm?'

'The link is through Akhenaten,' Walid said, bravely stepping into the conversation. 'He was part of the same family tree as Tutankhamun, and, assuming Nabil is right, would have been Biblical Joseph's grandson.'

'Now, this is where the religious part kicks in,' Adam said, picking up the threads Ted and Walid had left hanging. 'As you know, Akhenaten founded a new religion – worship of the Aten as the sole god – and swept aside thousands of years of polytheistic belief in Egypt. Ancient Egyptians previously, and subsequently as it turned out, worshipped a whole Pantheon of gods and goddesses. Some claim Akhenaten was the first monotheist in history. But our friend Nabil Zaal took things a step further. He claimed the origins of Akhenaten's worship of the Aten were in his Hebrew ancestry. And then, by identifying Akhenaten as Moses, credited with founding the Jewish faith…'

'…He was, in effect, saying the pharaohs of the Amarna period were Jewish,' Dan finished for him. 'Or, at least, an earlier version of it.'

'Precisely,' Ted approved his logic.

Adam finished his own beer, and put the bottle down on the floor beside him. 'And considering the bad blood between Egypt and Israel, you can see how certain factions might take it into their heads to protest.'

'But Moses wasn't Akhenaten,' Dan stated. 'You said those clay tablets you found in his coffin show it was someone else. Won't that take the heat off Nabil?'

Ted shifted back in his chair and took a sip of his martini. Ted was not a beer drinker, and preferred an aperitif he could linger over. 'Not necessarily; because, you see, the tablets seem to suggest the man who led Akhenaten's followers out of Egypt in what we suppose was the Exodus was the High Priest at the temple of the Aten. So, if *he* was Moses, and if *he* founded the Jewish faith, then the links back to the Hebrews through Akhenaten's beliefs would still hold true.'

'But it wouldn't be a blood link,' Dan said. 'This High Priest – what was his name…?'

'Meryre,' I supplied.

'This High Priest, Meryre, might have been a follower of Akhenaten's religion, which, in turn, might have had its origins in the Hebrew belief in one god through the likes of Joseph, Jacob and Abraham, etcetera. But he wasn't one of them. Meryre – or Moses, if that's who you think he was – wasn't part of the family tree of the Hebrew Patriarchs which Nabil says can lay claim to Akhenaten and Tutankhamun.'

'I'm not sure it matters to those who want to ensure Israel can't lay claim to two of Egypt's most famous pharaohs,' Ted said. 'Besides, we've got nothing to show that Meryre led the Exodus, beyond the very suggestive inscription on a clay tablet. It's hardly rock solid proof.'

'That won't matter to Nabil,' Adam said wryly. 'He's made an art form of using the most flimsy evidence to write his books.'

Which brought us back neatly, albeit via a circuitous route, to Ted's purpose in telling us he'd been successful in getting hold of the author on the telephone today.

I drained my glass of white wine and addressed myself to the professor. 'So, how did he react when you told him he had to give up on the idea of Akhenaten being Moses?'

Ted smiled. 'At first, he just seemed mostly relieved that he wouldn't have to re-create his entire draft manuscript from scratch...'

'Has the man never heard of backing things up to an external hard drive?' Dan muttered.

'...But then, naturally, he wanted to know how I could be so sure.'

I bit my lip. 'That poses a bit of a problem; considering he doesn't know about the tomb.'

'You mean to tell me, in all your dealings with him, you've managed not to mention the tomb?' Dan said sarcastically. 'You *do* surprise me!'

Ted chose not to rise to this blatant provocation. 'I equivocated, of course,' he admitted. 'I just said something had turned up that was very similar in content to the transcribed box we found in Panehesy's house in Amarna, but it seemed to point to the High Priest Meryre as being the "my Lord" in question, rather than the pharaoh Akhenaten.'

'You didn't tell him where this "something" came from?'

'I avoided a direct answer,' Ted said with a shrewd look on his face. 'I imagine he thinks another discovery has been made by Barry's team.'

Barry was the field director of the Amarna Project; the multi-national team authorised to excavate ancient Akhet-Aten.

'Oh my god; you'll have him plaguing Barry with calls demanding to know what they've found!'

'I believe I persuaded him to wait until we're more certain,' Ted said with a confidence I hoped wasn't misplaced.

As he spoke, the telephone rang below deck. Adam jumped up. 'I'll get it. I'll top up our drinks at the same time.'

I watched him stride across the deck and disappear out of sight down the spiral staircase.

'I should check on the dinner,' I murmured, and started to get up.

The sight of Adam coming back up the spiral staircase a moment later arrested my movement. He looked worried.

'Ted, it's for you,' he said. 'It's Barry.'

Ted got up and hurried below deck to take the call. Adam and I followed him, Adam to refresh our drinks, and me to check the seasoning on the coq au vin I had in the slow cooker. I could hear the low murmur of the professor's telephone conversation, which was taking place in the lounge-bar. But it was impossible to discern what was being said. I could only hope Barry wasn't too angry if Nabil had indeed contacted him demanding to know all about the latest discovery the professor had been so mysterious about.

As it was impossible to make out the tone, tenor or any of the content of the call, I headed back up on deck. To my surprise, it was to find that, even without Ted present, the bent of the conversation was still Egyptological in nature. I was far less surprised to hear that Dan was still in the mood to be truculent.

'So, are we really supposed to believe that the followers of Akhenaten's new religion were so dedicated to keeping his beliefs alive after his death that they were able to pass them down across some twelve hundred years, and god knows how many miles, until this weird religious sect who lived by the Dead Sea around the time of Jesus hit upon the idea of putting everything down in writing in the Dead Sea Scrolls?'

I accepted my refilled glass of wine as Walid responded to Dan's outright scepticism. 'I see no reason to doubt that Akhenaten's priests could preserve his monotheism across the centuries and the miles. Unless an ideology is completely wiped out, it seems to me that repression only strengthens it. If people have achieved some great insight, and others attempt to suppress it or persecute its advocates, often it goes underground. That may very well be what happened. And so for Akhenaten's beliefs to endure over such a long period would be perfectly possible.'

I wasn't sure I'd completely followed this. Walid's way of speaking could sometimes be a little too scholarly for me. But Adam was nodding, his eyes bright in the leaping lamplight from the hurricane lamps. 'That's exactly what happened following the Amarna period. The city of Akhet-Aten was destroyed. Akhenaten was labelled a heretic and a criminal by later pharaohs. They attempted to stamp out all memory of him and his so-called religion. So his followers would have been very determined indeed to pass on his beliefs to future generations.'

I sat down and leaned forward to join in. 'And, if one of those followers was none other than Moses, in the guise of the High Priest of the Aten, then we can start to see the origins of today's great religions in Akhenaten's break with the traditional Egyptian beliefs.' I said.

Dan was frowning. It seemed fast to be becoming his favourite facial expression. 'But I thought the popular man's choice for the pharaoh of the Exodus was that Ramses fellow. You know, the one with the monumental ego, who littered the length and breadth of Egypt with huge bloody great statues of himself.

'Ramses II,' Adam supplied. 'Also known as Ramses the Great.'

'He's the one,' Dan nodded. 'Wasn't he played by Yul Brynner in that old Hollywood film?'

'The Ten Commandments,' I confirmed. 'Yes, that's right.'

'But I thought Ramses came later,' Dan frowned again, perhaps not realising he was once more giving away the fact that he'd absorbed a lot more about ancient Egypt than he'd want to admit. 'After the timeframe you're talking about.'

Adam nodded. 'Yes, Ramses II came to the throne as the third pharaoh of the 19th Dynasty, something like fifty or so years after the Amarna period.'

'So, won't it put the cat among the pigeons for these clay tablets you've found to date the Exodus earlier than everyone imagined, and in the reign of a completely different pharaoh? Who are you proposing now? Tutankhamun? He came shortly after Akhenaten, didn't he?'

'Well, yes, although Smenkhkare was Akhenaten's immediate successor,' Walid said slowly, looking thoughtful. 'But I'm not sure Meryre led the Exodus straight away. If the Old Testament is to be believed, there are some years in the wilderness to account for first.'

Dan rolled his eyes.

'Lots of different theories have been put forward for the date of the Exodus,' Adam said.

'Including those that claim it never took place at all,' I added.

Dan's eyebrows inched so high they were in danger of merging with his hairline. 'Wasn't the Exodus preceded by Moses supposedly bringing down ten plagues on Egypt?' he enquired in deceptively mild tones. Then added the killer blow. 'If anyone needs convincing that the Old Testament is a load of old baloney, surely they're it! Such pleasant stuff as rivers turning to blood, and infestations of frogs, lice and locusts, among other things; isn't that right?'

Adam sipped his beer thoughtfully. 'You know, there's been lots of research done to suggest the ten plagues of Egypt may have been natural phenomena. If I remember rightly, there was a big hoo-ha in the Press back in the late nineties when some environmental catastrophe in America meant the waters of a major river in North Carolina turned red. The people working near the river found they were covered in sores.'

'Yes! I remember this!' I interrupted him. 'It was because millions of gallons of pig farm waste found its way into the river, causing some kind of genetic mutation in a marine micro-organism – I forget what it was called. But it basically poisoned the water. I remember thinking how gross it was!'

'Pfisteria,' Adam said. 'It turned the river red and more than a billion fish died. I remember reading in the papers that some scientist said something similar could have happened in ancient Egypt, causing the first six plagues. Pfisteria, or something like it, poisoned the water, causing the fish to die and the river to turn red. This would have driven the frogs onto the land. On land the frogs would die, causing an explosion of flies and lice. The flies could then have transmitted viral diseases to livestock, killing them. And, as we've already heard from the American experience, it caused sores – or boils – on the people.'

I couldn't help but be impressed. But, glancing at Dan, it was to see him still looking unconvinced. 'And the other plagues?' he pressed. 'Ok, I'm willing to overlook the death of firstborn children. But darkness? Hailstorms?'

I also couldn't help but be impressed by the knowledge of the ten plagues of Egypt exhibited by both of the men who'd shared my life, past and present. I had vague recollections from my religious education lessons at school, nothing more.

Adam took a quick swig of his beer. 'A volcanic eruption,' he said smoothly.

'Give me a break!' Dan retorted. 'Even *I* know there's no active volcano in Egypt!'

'True,' Adam said calmly. 'But five hundred miles or so north of the Nile Delta is the Greek Island of Santorini.'

Walid stepped back into the conversation. Adam had evidently touched on a subject he'd studied. 'In the 16th century BCE, Santorini was blown apart by a gigantic volcanic eruption.'

'It would have been thousands of times more powerful than a nuclear explosion,' Adam added.

'Yes,' Walid nodded. 'It was one of the biggest eruptions of the last ten thousand years. The ash cloud from the blast would have covered an immense distance.'

'As far as Egypt?' Dan said doubtfully.

'Well, put it this way, samples of Santorini ash have been collected from the seabed in the Nile Delta.' Walid stated.

Even Dan couldn't argue with that.

'The point is,' Adam said, 'the ash cloud overhead would have cut out the sun, plunging the region into darkness. This would have been accompanied by the kind of unusual weather seen after volcanic eruptions – lightening and probably hail.'

Dan was silent.

'But, Walid, you said Santorini erupted in the 16th century BCE?' I questioned. 'So who's reign would that date it to?'

'The best guess seems to be Thutmosis III.'

I frowned, 'So if neither Ramses II nor Thutmosis III is correct as the pharaoh of the Exodus – since Meryre seems to be our prime candidate as Moses, and he sits somewhere between the two – how do we explain the plagues?' I had a nasty feeling I was at risk of siding with Dan as I voiced this.

Thankfully, Adam had his brain in gear and wasted no time in putting forward his thoughts. 'I think if we're right in saying the Old Testament was more a literary work than a strictly factual one...'

'A fabrication from start to finish is more like it,' Dan qualified.

Adam carried on as if he hadn't spoken. '... Then I think we could hypothesise that its writers were drawing on the best bits of what had happened over the last few hundred years and working them into their Biblical stories to add drama to the tale they were telling.'

This sounded so perfectly reasonable, I found myself letting out a sigh.

'And remember,' Walid added. 'If Nabil is correct, then the writers of the Old Testament or, let's say the Dead Sea Scrolls to be more specific, may have wanted very much to shroud their stories in a bit of mystery – throw people off the scent of whom they were actually writing about. Remember, the Bible never names a pharaoh. I suspect if the roots of Judaism, Christianity and Islam are to be found in Atenism, there may have been pressing reasons to want to throw up a bit of a smoke screen. Afterall, Egypt reverted to its pantheon of animal-headed gods and goddesses, seen by many to be the worst sort of paganism.'

I'm not sure where the conversation might have gone from there. We were destined never to find out. For, at that moment, the sound of a footfall on the spiral staircase alerted us that Ted was re-joining us, having completed his telephone call.

'So?' Adam asked nervously as the professor eased himself back into his seat.

'So; I didn't get the grilling or the ticking off I was expecting,' Ted said. He had an air of barely suppressed excitement about him that immediately transmitted itself onto the rest of us.

'So, what did he want?'

'Do you remember those jars we found in Panehesy's cellar in Amarna?'

We all stared at him agog; even Dan, who had no idea what he was talking about. I'd swear there was something electrifying about the airwaves around the professor's chair. The darkness seemed to be humming.

'The wine jars?' I queried. 'Yes, there were loads of them!'

Ted picked up his Martini. I could see his hand was trembling as it held the glass. 'Yes; except, as it turns out, they've never contained wine!"

'Oh?'

'No! They're packed full of parchment documents!'

Adam, Walid and I stared at him in wonder.

'Barry's offered me the opportunity to be the one set about translating them!' Ted rushed on; sounding elated. 'He said that privilege should go to me as I was on the scene when they were discovered!'

'*Ohmygod*, Ted! That's *wonderful*!'

'I argued that I'm retired and, by rights, the distinction should go to one of his team of new-generation philologists. But he was kind enough to say he wanted the best in the business!'

'And that's you,' I said admiringly. 'Wow, Ted, what a feather in your cap!'

'It is an honour indeed,' he smiled. 'So, tomorrow, I will catch the early train bound for Amarna. Barry has offered me accommodation in the dig-house. But, Merry and Adam, if you should choose to join me in a little while, once Khaled has completed his repairs on the *Queen Ahmes*, of course; I would be more than delighted to return to the creature comforts I have grown accustomed to on your fine dahabeeyah. I will pay for my board and lodging, naturally.'

'But...' Dan started to protest.

I silenced him with a peremptory gesture.

Adam reached for my hand and squeezed it. I knew we shared a single thought. We had a bona fide reason to go to Amarna again... And we had a prototype of the Copper Scroll in our possession. Who could say what adventure might await us in Akhenaten's ancient city?

Chapter 4

Suffice it to say, the coq au vin suffered.

Dan spent the rest of the evening doing an admirable impression of the Big Bad Wolf.

'You can huff and puff all you like,' I advised him tartly. 'I am not coming home just yet.'

'But your family…'

'Look! I'll phone my mum, ok? I'll explain it's not as straightforward as simply jumping onboard the next flight home. I'm not here on some extended holiday, you know. I'll tell her we had an accident up on deck and need time to get the repairs done before we can mothball the *Queen Ahmes*. And then, well, we'll see where we go from there.'

'But it's not safe! What if something should happen to you…?'

I let out an exclamation of annoyance. 'Dan, I am a grown woman. I think I should be allowed to run my own life! Besides, this is Luxor, not Tahrir Square! Sure, by the sounds of it, things got a bit sticky around here over the weekend that Morsi was ousted. But that was nearly a fortnight ago. Things are settling down now. I appreciate the Foreign Office's concern for tourists. But Adam and I are not holidaymakers, as I seem to keep having to remind everyone. Yes, I understand it's unlikely we'll be able to get our business off the ground this year. That in itself may force us home. But that decision does not have to be made right this very moment!'

'But...' Dan started to argue.

Adam had heard enough. 'Merry's right,' he said forcibly, taking my hand. 'The decision is ours, hers and mine, about if and when we come home. Your concern means a lot to us, Dan. And, naturally, we don't want to worry Merry's family. You have my word that she'll keep in closer touch. She can phone you all daily if that will do the trick. And as to her safety, well, nobody cares about that more than I do. I will protect her; with my life if necessary.'

Its not often Adam speaks with this hard note in his voice. But when he does it demands respect and compliance. That, and what he'd said, really didn't leave poor Dan any room for manoeuvre.

'Er hum,' Dan cleared his throat and coughed. 'Of course. I didn't mean to suggest...' His discomfiture proved Adam had asserted himself as my partner really rather neatly.

Adam waved this away with an airy gesture. 'Now, who'd like another drink?'

It was an early start for Ted and Walid the following day. Ted was eager to get underway for his train journey to Amarna. Barry had promised to meet him at the station at the other end. As for Walid, he was flying back up to Cairo on the morning flight to collect something from the Museum. He'd need it to take the first step in the plan we'd started to hatch for how we could go about staging the discovery of the tomb.

We'd agreed Adam and I would take temporary custody of the clay tablets. There was no way Ted could take them with him on the train. It was our responsibility to keep them safe from any risk of either discovery or damage. We had a sturdy safe on board the *Queen Ahmes*, so Ted supervised us while we carefully stored them inside it. Then he kissed me, and shook Adam's hand and Dan's, before taking his departure.

After waving them off in a taxi, Adam waited for Khaled to arrive for another day of repair work, and then turned to me with a weary air. 'I'm all done in, Merry. What with all those nights getting the pulley system set up inside the tomb, and then all the excitement over discovering the tablets, I feel as if I could sleep for a week! Do you mind if I head back to bed for a couple of hours?'

It occurred to me to offer to join him. But one look at the dark shadows under his eyes was enough to convince me he really did need to catch up on some missed-out-on sleep. The distraction I had in mind would have to wait. Besides, it was hardly as if he kept me on starvation rations in that department. 'Of course not – you look exhausted. It's been an eventful few weeks. I'll keep Khaled company up on deck.'

He leaned forward and pressed a quick kiss against my lips. 'Don't sit in the full sun,' he advised. 'And wake me with a cup of tea if I haven't surfaced by mid-afternoon. I don't want to sleep the whole day away. And I want to be awake when Walid gets back tonight.' He yawned and stretched. 'But for now, lovely Merry, I'm struggling to keep my eyes open.'

I kissed him back, and watched him enter our cabin, closing the door behind him with a gentle click.

I made a pot of tea, put it on a tray with a plate of peanut crunch biscuits and a couple of mugs, and carried it all up on deck. Khaled had proved himself quite partial to my biscuits. I make them myself from an old family recipe handed down by my grandmother.

I arrived on deck to find Dan already there, deep in conversation with our master boat restorer. 'Ah, Meredith,' he broke off as I approached. 'Khaled here has just been telling me about how this Gamal Abdel-Maqsoud character commandeered your dahabeeyah before setting it alight when you caught up with him.'

I sent Khaled a quick look of disapproval. I wasn't sure I wanted Dan to know all the ins and outs of our short acquaintance with that young opportunist. Khaled bent quickly over his work again. He was re-varnishing the wooden decking boards he'd stripped and sanded down over the last couple of days. The smell of the varnish hung heavy in the still morning air.

'Yes, well; I'm pleased to say he got his comeuppance,' I said shortly. 'Once he realised Adam, Ahmed and Khaled had, all three of them, swum out and climbed on board to put out the flames, he took the coward's way out and jumped overboard.'

Dan took the tea tray from me. Moving away from where Khaled was working, he set it down on the table in the shade at the back of the deck under one of the great furled-in sails on its diagonal pole, and started to pour the tea. He handed one mug to me and set the other down on the floor beside him as he eased himself into one of the charred recliners. I didn't bother attempting to tell him the second mug had been meant for Khaled.

'Yes; but how can you be so confident the chap actually drowned?' Dan selected a biscuit from the plate and crunched into it. "Mmm, I'd forgotten how good these are.'

I smiled briefly to acknowledge the compliment, and then I sat down too. It was clear this was a conversation I couldn't avoid. 'Adam told you; we waited and waited; and scanned both sides of the riverbank. He didn't reappear.'

'Hmm, well I don't like it. Until you know for sure that he's dead, I don't see how any of you can sleep easy in your beds.'

'Ahmed's been in touch with his counterparts in the Cairo police. He's asked them to let him know if any bodies get dragged out of the Nile. The trouble is, there's been so much death and destruction in Cairo during recent weeks, I'm not sure one more dead body would elicit too much attention.'

'And you wonder why I want you home...!' There was no heat in this, only the weary resignation of one who'd said his piece over and over, and finally given up, realising the futility of it.

'Although, really, there's very little he can do even if he somehow survived,' I added.

'But I thought you said he knew about the tomb.'

'Well, yes; but not whose it is, or how to access it.' Then I realised this latter part wasn't strictly true. 'That is, he knows he needs the Aten discs to work the mechanism. But he doesn't have access to them. The replicas Adam made are kept under lock and key in the safe downstairs. And, as you well know, but Gamal Abdel Maqsoud doesn't, the originals are on display in the Cairo Museum, fixed between the horns of the Mehet-Weret couch among the Tutankhamun treasures.'

'But, what if he's got his hands on a copy of the letter? If I remember rightly, it rather stupidly sets out all the necessary particulars.'

'That's because when we wrote it we were trying to protect the tomb from each other. Someone expressed a fear that one of us might try to steal a march on the others if you recall. Walid wanted us each to sign and keep a copy of the letter as a kind of insurance policy.'

'Instead, he succeeded in putting a noose around all of our necks,' Dan said stiffly.

I was instantly defensive. 'He couldn't possibly know that one of us would meet with an untimely end, and leave such a dangerous loose thread hanging.'

Dan sighed. 'Look, Pinkie, I'm not trying to argue with you. I'm just trying to get you to see how much of a risk you're taking by staying here like a sitting duck. Heaven knows, I thought I was simply coming out here to ask you to come home because of the danger of being caught up in the political troubles. Now I find there's possibly someone out there who, if he's still alive, has every reason to hold a very real grudge against you. I just don't want you to get hurt.'

I bit my lip, seeing the genuine concern in his expression. 'You heard what Adam said. He's not going to let anything happen to me.'

To my astonishment, Dan reached out and squeezed my hand. 'Any fool can see that you two are crazy about each other,' he murmured. 'And it's good to see you so happy, really it is.' He let go of my hand. 'I know I never put that light in your eyes or that spring in your step. But that's not to say I didn't care for you. I still care for you. I think I always will.'

Inexplicably, I felt tears spring into my eyes, and had to swallow hard to clear the sudden tightness in my throat. This side to Dan wasn't altogether familiar to me. I was much more used to his high-handedness and to his bluster. And I was more certain of how to respond when he was imperiously bossing me about. This more tender side unnerved me, and left me unsure of what to say. 'But, you're happy with Jessica...?' I ventured.

He smiled and I watched the softness flood into his expression. 'Yes, she's a spiky little thing, and there's no denying she keeps me on my toes. But I know exactly where I stand with her, and I like that.'

I let out a small, shallow breath; relieved this conversation wasn't leading somewhere I didn't want it to go. I'd had a horrible impression for a moment that Dan was going to tell me he'd made a mistake and wanted to break off his engagement to Jessica and give it another go with me. Right here and right now was neither the time nor the place to tell him about the subtle shift in my relationship with Adam since our last entrapment in the tomb. But I sensed there was more Dan wanted to say, so I kept quiet and waited for him to go on when he was ready.

'The trouble was, Pinkie, something seemed to change in you when we came out here on that last holiday together, after you were made redundant. I suddenly realised the person I'd spent ten years of my life with was someone I'm not sure I ever took the trouble to get to know. There's an adventurous side to you that has me running a little bit scared, if I'm honest. I don't think it really surfaced in all the years we were together, perhaps because I wouldn't let it. But once we were out here, and you found those dratted hieroglyphics, it broke through. I recognised then that if you stayed with me, I'd clip your wings. So, I knew I had to let you go. Adam's a great guy, and its clear he's much better suited to you than I ever was. But I can't help but worry about you. You see; you're very much alike, you and Adam. You both get over-excited about the same stuff. And you're both willing to rush in where angels would fear to tread. So far, thank God, it's never ended in disaster. But I have a sneaking suspicion that's been a matter of luck rather than judgement.'

My sense of fair play wouldn't allow me to let that pass. 'On more than one occasion it's because *you've* turned up, just in the nick of time, to rescue us!'

He looked a bit abashed, and then smiled at me. 'Well then; there you go, you see?' That's why I worry – because I can't always be on hand to rescue you and Adam from your latest scrape. Let's face it, your mother doesn't know the half of it.'

I smiled back, suddenly remembering why I'd been attracted to Dan in the first place. His dry sense of humour could sometimes be misplaced, but it was incredibly endearing.

Then he turned serious again. 'If I really thought you and Adam could make a decent fist of this business venture you've been trying to set up out here – and not keep getting yourselves embroiled in all these dangerous misadventures – then, believe me, Pinkie, nobody would be happier for you than me. Truly. But, the trouble is, this time around, it's not just you and Adam who are potentially in it up to your necks. My name is on that letter. And so is Jessica's.'

Knowing he was right, I found myself looking away, unable to maintain eye contact. I watched a fishing skiff drift by on the swift Nile current, the fisherman sitting atop it casting his net across the water. 'But, we don't know where the letter is,' I said quietly.

'No. And that's what worries me,' he said. 'The thing is, there are a lot of lives that could be ruined if it falls into the wrong hands. Ted and Walid might be able to get by on their Egyptological credentials if the proverbial dark stuff hits the fan, but what about Shukura? What about Ahmed?'

I really didn't know what to say, so I kept quiet.

Dan let the silence draw out for a bit, then said, 'So you see, Pinkie; it's all very well for you to resist my pleas for you to come home. I daresay you think it would be the easiest thing in the world for me to simply re-pack my bag, turn around and head back home again, and wait for you and Adam to follow suit when you decide the time's right. But it's not as simple as that. Because, if he's still alive, and whether or not he has a copy of the letter, this Gamal Abdel-Maqsoud potentially poses a threat to me too. It's enough that he knows about the tomb. So I have a vested interest in staying until I can satisfy myself he did indeed drown in the Nile after the fire. Do you understand?'

'You're saying if I'm staying then you're staying too.'

'Correct. At least, until I know what happened to that letter.' Then he grinned. 'And if it means I get another chance to be a hero and rescue you and Adam from another scrape; then so much the better. I have to say, it does my ego no harm at all.'

Walid was due back from Cairo on the late afternoon flight. I left Adam to sleep for as long as I could, knowing he needed it. Dan and I spent most of the day in the shade up on deck, lazily watching Khaled as he worked. Khaled was well acclimatised to the heat, having spent most of his adult life in Egypt, after a Scottish childhood. His only defence against the fierce glare of the sun was the baseball cap he wore with the peak pulled down low over his eyes. I kept him regularly refreshed with cold drinks, and made us all a simple lunch of chicken salad sandwiches.

As mid-afternoon approached, I pulled myself from the dozy lethargy I'd relaxed into. 'Right, time to make Adam his cup of tea and rouse him from slumber.' I pushed myself up from my recliner; collected up the glasses from the chilled homemade lemonade I'd served after lunch, and made my way down the spiral staircase.

I carried the tea into Adam in his favourite mug, and plunked myself down on the edge of the bed, leaning forward to kiss him awake.

He didn't stir.

'Adam, wakey wakey. You've slept all day. Time to get up now.'

He still didn't stir.

'Adam.' I kissed him again, tenderly brushing a lock of glossy brown hair back from his forehead. He looked very appealing, sprawled across our bed, his hair rumpled on the pillow, his cheeks flushed with sleep, all smooth-featured and boyish. It was a Victorian iron-framed bed, in keeping with the décor I'd chosen for the dahabeeyah.

This time when he didn't stir it occurred to me to be concerned.

'Adam?'

And that's when I noticed the strange, sweet, rather cloying smell.

I gripped his shoulder and shook him. 'Adam?'

His lack of response now had me truly worried. I jolted forward and put my ear against his face, listening for the sound of breathing. Hearing nothing, and truly panicked, I leapt up from the bed and yanked the door open. 'Dan!' I yelled. 'Dan! Can you come?'

I felt his movement through the dahabeeyah. In moments he was at my side, looking as if he was the one who'd been wrested none too gently from sleep. 'What is it? What's wrong?'

'I don't think Adam's breathing!' I cried wildly.

With a single glance, Dan took in Adam's inert frame under the single sheet that covered him. He was at the side of the bed in one long stride. Lifting Adam's limp arm, he checked for a pulse. 'Have you got a mirror?' he demanded urgently.

I grabbed my hand-mirror from the dressing table and handed it over. Dan held it against Adam's nose. He let out a sigh of relief.

'He's breathing.'

I felt my knees buckle, and shot out a hand to steady myself against the wall. 'You're sure? Oh, thank God!' I slumped onto my side of the bed and stared at Dan, trying to make sense of what was going on, how sleep could turn into unconsciousness. 'That smell…?'

Dan cocked his head to one side, sniffing the air. 'Chloroform,' he identified it.

'You mean, this was done deliberately? He didn't just pass out?'

Dan's gaze travelled quickly around the room. 'Something tells me Adam didn't hit on the idea of chloroform to guarantee himself a few hours of uninterrupted sleep,' he muttered. 'So, you tell me, Merry. Has anything been disturbed?'

I dragged my gaze away from Adam's face and, this time, it was my eyes that made a slow tour of inspection around our cabin. 'Now you come to mention it...' I got up from the bed. The wardrobe door was partially ajar. I opened it fully and brushed my hand across its contents, a mixture of Adam's smart shirts and jackets and my dressier dresses. 'Yes, it looks as if someone has rifled through here.'

Then I turned my attention to the chest of drawers. The bottom drawer was open by just a crack. I pulled out every drawer in turn. Our collection of everyday clothes – shorts, T-shirts; all the foldable stuff, along with our separate underwear draws – also showed signs of disarray. It was as if someone had felt through each drawer in turn, not removing anything, but checking to see if anything was inside beyond the usual items of clothing.

'Someone's made a search of the room,' Dan translated the evidence of my expression and his own eyes.

'And they wanted to make damn sure Adam didn't disturb them while they did so,' I said bitterly.

'Has anything been taken?'

My gaze flew to my jewellery box, and I quickly lifted the lid. I had nothing of any intrinsic value, but a few pretty bits and pieces that I treasured for sentimental reasons. 'Nothing, so far as I can see.' I let out a little puff of relief.

'And the other cabins?'

I glanced uncertainly at Adam, comatose on the bed. Reading my hesitation correctly, Dan said, 'He'll be fine. I daresay he'll wake up with a headache, but nothing more serious than that.'

'But I thought chloroform could cause heart failure,' I gulped out. 'I thought that's why they stopped using it as an anaesthetic.'

'His heart is still beating perfectly steadily,' he assured me, pressing his fingers against Adam's wrist again. 'I couldn't feel his pulse at first. But that was a deficiency in medical skill on my part, certainly no lack of a heartbeat on Adam's. Now, Pinkie, you need to be the one to check everywhere else. Only you'll know if anything's been tampered with or taken. I'll sit here with Adam and make sure he keeps breathing.'

I nodded and made for the door.

'Just one thing,' he arrested my movement. 'Where do you keep the key to the safe?'

The one at risk of heart failure now was me. His question made the blood freeze in my veins. 'Oh God, the Copper Scroll tablets,' I wailed. 'The Aten discs...'

I darted a glance back at Adam, and almost fainted with relief. The key, along with a crocodile tooth, a memento from a long ago act of bravery, was still safely strung on the bootlace around his neck. I was so used to seeing it there I barely noticed it anymore. Sagging weakly against the door, I took a hold of myself. 'The safe needs a code as well as the key. Adam and I are the only ones who know the combination. I have the spare key here on my bracelet.' I held up my arm to show him the small key dangling like a lucky charm from my wrist.

'Do you want to check, just to be sure?'

I made it along the corridor and into our little wood-panelled reception on legs that seemed to be made of rubber. Crouching in front of the counter and seeing the safe securely locked, my relief knew no bounds. I tested the door just to be on the safe side. It was firmly bolted.

But somebody had been on board our dahabeeyah and made a pretty thorough search of it while Dan, Khaled and I had been up on deck. That much became obvious as I moved from cabin to cabin and then did a quick sweep of the lounge bar. We'd left the gangplank down, attached to the causeway all day, not thinking there was any reason not to. So, just about anybody could have come aboard without us noticing if they were quiet enough about it.

I retraced my steps back to the cabin Adam and I shared. 'Nothing's been taken, so far as I can tell,' I confirmed.

Dan's worried gaze came to meet mine. 'Well, I suppose we should be grateful whoever it was contented himself with simply incapacitating Adam as opposed to anything worse.'

I felt a shudder run through me. Dan's earlier comment about sitting ducks was ringing in my ears. It suddenly struck me how vulnerable and unprotected we were. 'I'm glad you're here,' I whispered shakily.

'And do you have any idea…?'

'Oh God,' I groaned, flopping down on the bed as all the stuffing went out of me. 'Gamal Abdel-Maqsoud. He's alive, isn't he?'

Chapter 5

It was another two hours before Adam, groggily, started to come round. Walid had re-joined us on board the *Queen Ahmes*, having taken a taxi from Luxor Airport. He looked shattered from his long day shuttling to and from Cairo.

His distress and anxiety on learning what had transpired while he'd been gone was painful to observe. 'Allah be praised Adam is alive and that the safe was not broken into,' he breathed, placing one hand over his heart.

'He must have come in search of the Aten discs,' I speculated. 'He knows they're the key to unlocking the tomb. He's only ever been as far inside it as the entrance corridor. But that was far enough to show him the gleam of gold at the other end, beyond the pit shaft. I don't suppose he'll rest now until he's found a way back inside to see it properly.'

Adam groaned with a discomfort that was about more than just his sore head. He was stretched out on the divan in the lounge-bar since he suffered with vertigo every time he tried to sit up. 'I should never have let my anger get the better of me. That's what made me shut him up behind the secret doorway. I wanted to frighten him. Stupid of me. All it achieved was to land us in the mess we're in now.'

Nobody argued. That it hadn't been Adam's finest hour was beyond dispute.

Walid looked around at us all with an urgent expression, shaking off his tiredness. 'We must set about re-discovering the tomb. And we must set about it now. Please! There is no time to lose.'

Adam wasn't recovered enough to embark on the excursion we agreed on for immediate action. I wasn't happy about leaving him alone onboard the *Queen Ahmes* while the rest of us ventured out into the night after the hasty supper of tinned soup and bread rolls I served up.

'We need Ahmed over here,' I muttered.

'Presumably that's a given,' Dan said, 'since I take it Ahmed's the one with the key. Surely he'll need to unlock the place for us, like he did the first time around.'

Ahmed was duly summoned. Thankfully, his shift was nearing an end, so he could pilfer the key we needed and drive directly over to join us.

Dan had been good enough not to crow about the afternoon's events. I'm not sure even he had expected to have his fears for our safety proved right quite so quickly. If he'd hoped to prove a point that Adam might not always be in a position to protect me as he'd so confidently promised to do, it had been done for him; and pretty effectively too. Although I daresay his failure to either sense or avert the danger himself chafed.

I could see Adam was thinking the same. 'I remember hearing a noise in our cabin,' he explained. 'I thought it was you, Merry. I was rather hoping you might have decided to come and join me. But as I turned over and opened my eyes, I felt a hand clamp down over my nose and mouth holding a soaked rag. I remember registering the fact that someone was attempting to asphyxiate me. And that's it. I passed out. God, when I think how much worse...'

I put my finger to his lips and shushed him. It didn't need saying. We all knew that, all things considered, our visitor had probably let us off lightly. In truth, I think we were shocked at how vulnerable we were, even in broad daylight on the riverbank.

Ahmed growled angrily in his throat when we told him what had happened. 'I should have been here to protect you.'

'There's nothing you could have done. If he was able to slip onboard right under Dan's and my noses, I'm not sure your being here would have made any difference.'

'You need police protection,' he asserted. 'I will make it my business from now on to ensure that my colleagues, they add this dahabeeyah to their inspection duties, to see that all it is safe.'

'I'm not arguing,' Adam muttered, pressing the tips of his fingers against his temples.

'Please! We must make haste,' Walid chivvied impatiently.

Ahmed handed him the key. 'You will bring it straight back to me, yes? It must be returned and in its place in the cabinet at the police station before morning. I will remain here and stand guard over Adam. He is still weak.'

I'm not sure Adam needed reminding. But we were all grateful for our police pal's presence and, perhaps more specifically, that of his gun.

Walid and I laced our feet into our walking boots, while Dan donned his trainers. I packed bottled water into a rucksack, and we were ready to go.

'I wish I was coming with you,' Adam said.

'Just take it easy this evening,' I soothed him. 'Hopefully we won't be gone for too long.'

I saw his gaze move to rest on the antique-looking suitcase Walid was holding. I looked at it too and felt a buzz of combined nostalgia and anticipation. 'The scrolls are inside?'

'All present and correct,' Walid affirmed. 'All three of them.'

The battered old case and its contents were the purpose of the museum curator's lightning dash to Cairo and back today. They'd been safely stashed in the museum vault since not long after we'd first discovered the tomb. Nobody was allowed access to the vault without Walid being present, so we'd been confident of their safekeeping while in custody there. Even Walid was required by security protocol never to open the vault unaccompanied.

'I took Shukura with me,' he said.

'Does she know what you're planning?'

'I considered it only fair to take her into my confidence...' he said with a nod, '...since she has been a party to our secret from the start.'

'And you still managed to get away?' I grinned at him.

'I was able to wrest myself free from her constant questions in the end.' His smile acknowledged both Shukura's excitable character and her motor mouth. 'It was important I should not miss my flight back here.'

'Right, we should get going,' Dan urged.

We travelled on scooters. Dan borrowed Adam's. Walid, having secured the small suitcase carefully onto the parcel rack, clambered onto the back of mine, clamping his arms around my waist as we set off.

There's nothing quite so dark as Egypt's night outside of the brightly lit, urban areas. The starlight seemed muted tonight and there was no moon.

We left the scooters hidden behind a low stone wall on the approach to Hatshepsut's temple. We couldn't risk the parking lot. Floodlights illuminated the temple. It wasn't yet late enough for them to have been switched off for the night.

Thankfully, this made the surrounding landscape appear especially dark.

There were security guards posted at the ticket-office-cum-visitors-centre close to the car park. The temple was set against the cliffs some distance away across a broad expanse of open ground. During the daytime trolley buses snaked along a causeway stretched across that basin of open space, ferrying visitors back and forth from the ticket office to the temple forecourt. But tonight everything was still and deserted and quiet. We knew we could give the guards the slip, providing we were quiet and kept our wits about us. We'd done it several times before on nocturnal visits to Akhenaten and Nefertiti's tomb, which was secretly carved into the rock behind the columned Hathor shrine on the first elevation of the southern side of the temple. This is not to disparage the guards by accusing them of laziness or any lack of vigilance. Simply that we've always been extremely cautious, or perhaps extremely fortunate.

But tonight Akhenaten's tomb was not our destination. We struck out to the right of the ticket office, finding the pathway at the foot of the cliffs, which circled in a broad arc behind the temple, and started to climb. We didn't dare use our torches to light the way. This meant we made slow and rather painstaking progress, with our hearts in our mouths the whole time. One misplaced step, or worse, a trip, could send a small avalanche of shale and loose rock chippings cascading down the hillside and give us away or, worse, take us with it.

'Trust the moon and stars to choose tonight of all nights not to come out,' I muttered. But in reality it was a blessing. Our cover was more assured in the pitch darkness.

The climb was long and arduous but we made it. Walid was puffing loudly by the time we made it to the top of the cliff. Even Dan was out of breath, despite his regular use of the gym, and I paused to press at the painful stitch in my side. We didn't have time to stop and admire the magnificent view of Hatshepsut's temple lit up below us. 'Come on,' Walid pressed. 'We're nearly there.'

We scurried forward; moving more quickly now the ground beneath us had flattened out. Once we'd rounded the curve and crested a jutting peak of rock, we knew we were safely out of sight of the guards below and so finally braved our flashlights.

The terrain came to life around us; an expanse of tawny rock stretching away in all directions, looking grey and colourless in the torchlight. It wasn't far along the path until we reached the point where the ancient track across the cliff-top forked in two directions. The left hand branch snaked away across the cliffs, eventually finding its way down the far off slopes towards Deir el Medina, the village of the workers, about a mile-and-a-half away. This was the pathway trodden by the ancient Egyptian tomb-builders and artisans, who'd toiled every day carving and decorating the pharaohs' tombs from the living rock of these hills and wadis.

We took the right hand branch. Switching the beams of our flashlights off again, we carefully slip-slided, on our backsides for some of the way, down the steep slope that dropped us down into the Valley of the Kings. We emerged, dusting ourselves off, close to the entranceway to the tomb of Seti I.

We paused a moment to catch our breath, listening intently. Guards were posted at the gate here in the Valley too. They were tasked with making occasional tours of inspection throughout the night to check all was well. But right now, all was stillness and silence. It was a dense kind of silence, seemingly loud with suppressed sound.

'This place gives me the heebie-jeebies,' Dan whispered.

'Come on then, let's not waste any time. This way.' I set off through the shadowed darkness, leading the way, aware of the cliffs towering on all sides, and listening anxiously to the deafening sound of my footsteps crunching on loose scree as I crept forward.

Our destination lay deep in the easternmost branch of the Valley, cut into the base of the cliff-face. Dan shone his torch on the entranceway, while Walid fumbled with the key to unlock the metal grille fixed across the opening. Standing there while he released it, I knew if we could cut a tunnel straight through the rock, we'd emerge onto one of the ramps of Hatshepsut's temple on the other side of the cliff we'd just climbed. This was KV20, the tomb Hatshepsut had ordered carved for herself once she was proclaimed pharaoh. I felt a thrill run through me. It was some time since I'd been here last. Indeed it was my fervent hope that nobody else had been here since. Our plan depended on the last people to have visited this tomb being us.

KV20 is closed to the public and situated some way off the beaten track. It had been closed up for over a century, since Howard Carter first discovered it in 1903. He and his workmen were forced to dig their way inside through millennia's'-worth of flood infill, dislodging old bat infestations and breathing in the foul air as they went. Conservation work stopped a year later. Beyond an acknowledgement of who its original owner had been, the tomb was of no particular archaeological interest. The walls weren't of good enough quality for decoration because the rock was a soft shale rather than strong limestone. The few texts Carter found were on limestone blocks, which he'd removed. And, in more recent times, the burial chamber had been completely flooded. It was now full of debris and totally inaccessible.

All of this Adam had told me on our one and only visit to this place. I'd remembered his words well. Of course I had. This place held a special place in my heart. For this was where Adam and I had first acknowledged our feelings for each other.

As Dan reached for my hand and helped me step down into the pitch dark of the corridor shaft, I felt myself longing for Adam. He should be here to share with me the nostalgia of this rather bizarre trip down memory lane. Damn Gamal Abdel-Maqsoud and his blasted chloroform, I thought darkly.

Walid switched on his flashlight and shone the beam into the black tunnel carved through the rock. 'So, this is the place Howard Carter hit upon to hide the papyrus he took from Tutankhamun's tomb. Hmm, not a bad location to brick something up and not expect it to be stumbled across by accident.'

'You're sure we can begin to stage the discovery of Akhenaten's tomb from here?' Dan asked as we started to move forward. 'What about all the stuff that led up to Merry and Adam finding this place?'

Walid paused and put down Howard Carter's suitcase so he could reach into his pocket for his handkerchief and mop his perspiring face. It was fearfully hot inside the narrow passageway. There's something about being underground in Egypt that makes the temperature inexplicably even more suffocating. 'Assuming everything goes according to plan; then I think so. I see no need to mention that Merry got locked inside Howard Carter's house.'

'And, having virtually wrecked the place, helped herself to the scrap of paper on which our dear, departed Mr Carter wrote his hieroglyphic message,' Dan added in acerbic tones. 'That's a shame. I think she enjoyed the little treasure hunt it got her started out on, didn't you, Pinkie?'[2]

I sent him a hard look. Although, in all fairness, I'll admit I think I preferred Dan like this. Whilst he riled me, it put things between us back on a much firmer footing. 'Stop calling me that,' I muttered.

'I believe we can safely keep that as Meredith's secret,' Walid said staunchly. 'The world does not need to learn of the puzzles Howard Carter left behind him to be solved. I see no reason for us to explain how his suitcase came to be bricked up in a wall inside this tomb, stuffed full of ancient papyrus. We're the only ones who know he took the scrolls from Tutankhamun's tomb and was unable to return them there...'

'Due to circumstances beyond his control,' I added, feeling a strong need to defend the famous excavator's actions.

'...And, as far as I'm concerned, it can stay that way,' Walid finished.

'I agree,' I nodded. 'If we can keep Carter's reputation intact through all of this, I'd feel much better about the whole thing. He could have come across the papyrus just about

---

[2] Carter's Conundrums – Book 1 of Meredith Pink's Adventures in Egypt

anywhere, and had all sorts of reasons for hiding them away. We can simply plead ignorance.'

Dan seemed to accept this, as he made no further comment. He unscrewed the cap from his water bottle and swigged down a gulp.

We trudged deeper into the tunnel of rock. The shaft was a series of five long corridors, descending into the bedrock beneath the Deir el-Bahri cliffs. The corridors curved in a long, thin semi-circle towards the burial chamber, which we knew was inaccessible. The place we were looking for was approximately half way along the tunnel.

Dan tripped and swore. 'Watch your step,' he advised. 'The floor here is very uneven.'

I stopped to remove my own bottle of water from my rucksack. My T-shirt was sticking damply to my body, and my throat was parched. I leaned against the wall for a moment and took a few long, thirst-slaking swigs. Then I passed the bottle to Walid and he did the same.

Dan flashed his torch beam ahead of us to penetrate into the stygian darkness. 'Look! Aren't those the rocks we're looking for?'

Walid and I focused on the fixed point of light where Dan had his torch beam trained on the ground a little way off. I breathed a sigh of relief. 'Thank God! No one's been in here since us.'

The rocks were lying scattered across the floor underneath a deep gash in the wall. This was the hole Adam had created when he removed them. As we approached with a quickened step, I swung my own torch beam in an arc to the stone roof above us. There, scratched onto the rock face was a line drawing of a female face captured in profile, wearing a feathered headdress with a vulture head rising from her brow. It was small, perhaps ten centimetres square, but unmistakeable.

'Queen Ahmes,' I breathed.

Dan glanced up. 'That's how you found the spot?' he asked. 'That little sketch up there?'

'We guessed Carter had bricked something behind the wall somewhere in here,' I nodded. 'Queen Ahmes sign-posted our way through several of the clues he left us. Why do you think we were so delighted to find the dahabeeyah was named after her?'

Dan rolled his eyes but refrained from comment, for which I was grateful.

But Walid wasn't looking at the drawing. 'Up there?' he queried, staring at the hole set in the upper portion of the wall. 'That's where you found it?'

The hole was above head height but within stretching range. At least, it was reachable if you happened to be fairly tall. It was quite a big hole, probably about the size of a large flat-screen television. It needed to be. It had spent years with a suitcase hidden inside it.

'I'll never reach it,' he added in dismay, pushing himself up onto tiptoes to prove his point. Walid is small in stature and ever so slightly stooped. No doubt the result of years spent bending over the antiquities it's his responsibility to conserve.

Dan stepped forward. 'Ok, give it to me.'

Walid passed Howard Carter's antique-looking suitcase into Dan's outstretched hands. He looked a little bit reluctant to let it go; as well he might considering once this step was taken there was no going back. The papyrus scrolls would be once more outside of our protective custody.

Dan, being big, lifted the suitcase into the hole with no effort at all. 'Ok, start passing the rocks up to me.'

Walid and I took turns to lift them up from the floor and hand them to him. It took Dan a couple of attempts to brick up the hole in the wall to his satisfaction with the suitcase safely stashed inside.

'It doesn't need to be perfect,' I advised him. 'Just good enough that you don't notice it at first glance.'

'Ok, done.' He said at length, brushing his hands together to knock off the dust, and then wiping them on his jeans. I passed him the water and he took a long swallow. Then I trained my torch beam on the wall where he'd been working.

'Well, I'm not sure you'll ever get a job as a brickie,' I murmured. 'But it will do. The important thing is the suitcase is covered up and out of sight.'

In truth, if Howard Carter had shown the same lack of skill as Dan, I'm pretty sure Adam and I wouldn't have needed the little scratched wall sketch of Queen Ahmes to alert us that this was the spot where we should search.

'It doesn't matter,' Walid said. 'Nobody else knows what it looked like before you found it the first time, Merry.'

'Job done.' Dan said with satisfaction. 'Let's get the hell out of here. I need some air.'

We made it back to the dahabeeyah without mishap. I think I'd half expected some knife-wielding maniac to jump out of the shadows and ambush us. That had certainly been our experience the first time around. And it had rather set the template for many of the adventures we'd had since. But tonight, unusually, no one came to waylay us and we emerged unscathed into the still night air. We carefully locked up behind us and arrived home sweat-stained to be sure, and coated in a thick layer of dust thanks to our hands-and-knees scramble back over the cliff top, but otherwise none the worse for wear.

Adam, looking and feeling much brighter now, poured us all a nightcap while we brought him and Ahmed up to speed about the success of our trip into the Valley.

'Mission accomplished.' Walid said with relief. He handed the key back to Ahmed with a small flourish. 'You can put this back, my friend. All is now in readiness, and we can put the next step of our plan into action.'

'When do you propose to do that?' Dan enquired.

'Tomorrow,' Walid said. 'There is no time to lose.'

'Won't we need witnesses?' I frowned.

Adam sat down and immediately leaned forward to join in the conversation. 'I've been thinking about that,' he said eagerly. 'Ahmed's spent the evening telling me all about the trials and tribulations of his last couple of shifts playing nursemaid to a special visitor. It strikes me we have somebody close at hand who could make a very credible witness indeed...'

We all stared at Ahmed, sitting wedged into an armchair in the corner.

He stared back while understanding gradually dawned on his face. Cottoning on at last, he dropped his head forward into his hands and sat holding it. 'Please, no,' he groaned. 'I swear I have done nothing to deserve it.'

Chapter 6

'What is this individual's name?' Walid asked next morning while we were at breakfast.

'Habiba Garai.' Adam supplied. 'Apparently she's some bright young postgraduate working her way up through the ranks in the Ministry of State for Antiquities.'

'Ah yes, her name rings a bell,' Walid nodded, his use of colloquial English sounding quite strange with his Arabic accent. 'I think Director Ismail may have mentioned her to me. She must have made quite an impression. So, she has been seconded here to Luxor?'

Adam nodded. 'It seems she's been sent to oversee the security arrangements the local tourist and antiquities police have in place to protect the historical sites during all this political upheaval.'

'Then I would think she is just about perfectly placed to tag along and play the part we have in store for her today,' Walid approved.

Adam caught my eye. He didn't add Ahmed's reasons for being appalled by the whole idea. He'd told me while we were getting ready for bed last night that this same Habiba Garai had spent the last two days very successfully rubbing our friend up the wrong way.

'Ahmed could talk of little else all evening,' Adam had said. 'Habiba Garai has worked her way under his skin, that's for sure.'

'But she's only just got here,' I'd protested.

Adam shrugged. 'Surely that says it all.'

After such a build up, I'll admit I was very impatient to meet the young woman and find out for myself what the fuss was all about.

We travelled into town by taxi since there were four of us making the journey. I always enjoy the trip into town. The hustle and bustle of Luxor is like nowhere else on earth. Or, maybe I should say the *hassle* and bustle of Luxor, since, as one of the prime tourist spots, the city has a reputation as the hassle epicentre of Egypt. But with no tourists here right now, we had a rare opportunity to see the local people doing their own thing.

'Bloody hell, it *is* quiet, isn't it?' Dan observed.

A few dejected-looking caleche drivers half-heartedly encouraged their horses to trail up and down the Corniche with their carriages in tow. But the drivers' eager shouts for trade were missing, and the jingle-bells they attached to their bridles jangled limply, without their usual merriment. Most of the taxis were empty. The main streets of Luxor seemed sleepy and a bit woebegone. The cracked pavements were littered with men dozing in the shade, or grouped on the ground around game boards, with their galabeyas tucked in underneath them, playing backgammon or draughts, or something similar. Other men sat in open shop doorways; lazily smoking hubble-bubble pipes and watching the world go by with drowsy disinterest.

'If things don't get sorted out quickly, the political situation will choke the life out of Luxor,' Adam agreed sadly.

But as we turned into the back streets it was a different matter. This was the more female domain and the usual housewifely hubbub of grocery shopping and gossip was thankfully still very much in evidence. The women of Luxor went about their daily business looking suspiciously like a flock of crows parading up and down the streets in their voluminous black niqabs.

We arrived outside the police station, thanked and paid the taxi driver, an acquaintance of ours, and got out. The heat immediately hit us with its usual force. The temperature in Egypt in summertime can sometimes feel uncomfortably like a punch in the face.

'Let's get into the air conditioning,' Dan appealed.

We trooped inside, standing back so Walid could lead the way, and felt the immediate relief of the cooler air as the door swung closed behind us.

Walid approached the counter. A uniformed officer looked up from the computer screen he'd been squinting at. He addressed Walid in Arabic so I didn't understand what he said but that it was simply a greeting and a question as to how he might help was fairly obvious.

Walid responded also in Arabic. Even so, I recognised the tone I'd heard him use on previous occasions when asserting his authority. I watched him reach into the inside breast pocket of his jacket and pull out his identity badge, which he handed over. It proved his credentials as Dr Walid Massri, Director of the Antiquities Museum in Cairo.

The officer reached for the telephone on the desk and spoke into the receiver. Moments later, we were joined by a tall, upright man in a crisp white uniform. I recognised him as Ahmed's commanding officer. But even if I'd never seen him before in my life I think I would have guessed from the quantities of gold stitching on his epaulets that he was the senior ranking officer, possibly a superintendent, who was in charge. I'm not sure if Ahmed had ever told us his rank.

He glanced at Walid's identity badge, nodded at him in recognition, and more words were exchanged in rapid-fire Arabic. Walid was standing very straight-backed, looking every inch the important dignitary visiting from the capital city.

The superintendent-or-whatever-he-was glanced around at the rest of us and then motioned for us to follow him.

He used his security card to swipe us through a door; then led us to a meeting room situated at the end of a short corridor, where he invited us all to take a seat.

'This is Chief Superintendent Abdul el-Saiyyid, the commanding officer here in Luxor,' Walid introduced him with a respectful nod. 'You may remember he assisted me to conduct a tour of the Souk after that antiquities thief was killed in the rock fall at Hatshepsut's temple last year.

We all nodded, and Adam thrust out his hand.

'Adam Tennyson.'

'Dan Fletcher.'

'Meredith Pink.'

We all shook hands and smiled politely. I noticed Walid didn't say who we were, but the police commander seemed willing to accept us as Walid's entourage no questions asked, which was a bonus.

'Do you speak English?' Walid asked once the introductions were over.

'A little; enough, I think.' He poured us each a plastic beaker of water from the chiller in the corner, which we accepted with murmurs of thanks. 'Now, how can I be of service?'

Walid sat forward. 'I am here to undertake an inspection of our archaeological sites. Every day I receive reports of looting and wanton digging. I wish to satisfy myself that security measures are in place and that they are fit for purpose. I would appreciate a police escort while I carry out my appraisal.'

Chief Superintendent el-Saiyyid looked confused. 'But the Ministry of State for Antiquities has sent an officer already for precisely this same purpose.'

'Ah yes, that would be Miss Habiba Garai,' Walid said smoothly. 'Director Ismail told me she was here when I was discussing my plans with him. I will be most grateful if you can release her to accompany me, along with the officer tasked with safeguarding her, of course. I have no doubt she will prove most useful to me as I survey the sites. And it will avoid any duplicated effort.'

I was sure I was the only one who could see Walid's crossed fingers under the table.

The commanding officer's brow smoothed out. 'Yes. Of course; Dr Massri. I will do everything in my power to assist you and the Ministry. These are turbulent times, and we must each do our bit to protect our ancient heritage. My division here is sadly under-resourced. I am grateful for your assistance in this matter.'

With protocol or etiquette or semi-political posturing — Dan would no doubt call it brown-nosing — thus observed to everyone's satisfaction, Superintendent el-Saiyyid got up. 'My officer Ahmed Abd el-Rassul is looking after Miss Garai while she is seconded to us. I will fetch them now and instruct them that for the purposes of the Ministry of Antiquities' inspection, they are both to take their orders from you.'

Walid smiled. 'Thank you.'

Habiba Garai was a rather beautiful young woman of about thirty at a guess. It was impossible to tell whether or not she was wearing make-up. She had a smooth café latte-coloured complexion and almond-shaped eyes, with rather startling bronze flecked irises surrounding big black pupils. Darkly lashed and with wide, full lips, she exuded a sultry kind of femininity it was hard to overlook. As her culture dictated, she was wearing a headscarf loosely wrapped to cover her hair. It lacked the flamboyance of the ones favoured by Shukura, who always opted for bright colours and swirly patterns. Habiba's was plain. A deep chocolate brown with gold flecks running through it, it set off her colouring to perfection.

She was a shapely 5'7" at a guess; just a smidgen taller than me, wearing tailored dark brown trousers, walking boots and a fitted white linen shirt belted in at the waist. She managed to pull off the whole ensemble as if this was the latest in desert chic. I looked down at my own cropped trousers, espadrilles and loose fitting top and felt a total frump by comparison.

But her smile was friendly enough, revealing neat, even white teeth and she shook hands with each of us with a bright-eyed interest and lively manner I found quite engaging. I'd feared she might be some uppity postgrad, puffed up with her own self-importance. But she quickly proved me wrong.

As the introductions were performed, I was rather thankful Adam and Dan were both already spoken for. Habiba had a direct way of making eye contact that was almost magnetic. Even I felt myself drawn towards her as she took my hand. Her English was faultless.

Niceties over with, she turned to Walid. 'So, tell me Dr Massri, which sites have you and Director Ismail chosen for us to inspect? I have been trying to explain to officer Abd el-Rassul here that a tour of Luxor's prime historical sites, such as Karnak and Luxor temples, is possibly not the best place to start.'

Her manner was open and guileless, but I felt Ahmed bristle alongside me. 'I did not suggest we should visit the temples of Karnak and Luxor,' he protested. 'I suggested Medinet Habu and the Ramesseum. They are less well guarded as they do not attract so many visitors.'

She smiled disingenuously. 'Even so, I am not sure the temples are our most promising locations if we wish to prevent looting and illicit digging. I'd have thought the tombs would be a better bet.'

I sensed Ahmed biting down hard on another indignant, self-defensive retort, as she looked up at him all twinkly-eyed. It dawned on me with a flash of recognition what his problem was with her. She was teasing him, openly and unmercifully. And Ahmed, who could on occasion take himself a teensy bit too seriously, had no idea at all how to handle it. 'Just because you do not approve of my itinerary...' he said pompously, tightly leashing in his temper, '...it does not give you authority to go off on your own without me. I have been assigned for your protection!'

There was a definite accusation in there. Seeing him all offended while she smiled up at him, wide-eyed and innocent-looking, I felt sure she was guilty of exactly what he'd levelled at her.

Ahmed's dark eyes flashed and snapped, and Habiba's glowed like molten gold. Walid proved himself a braver man than I'd given him credit for by stepping between them. He answered Habina's question at face value as if blithely unaware of the heightened energy in the room. 'That sounds like an eminently sensible suggestion, Miss Garai. I agree we should make a start with the tombs. I would like to inspect those in the Valley of the Kings that are closed to the public. I'm sorry to say I've heard reports of vandals burrowing their way into them just like the ancient tomb robbers did.'

'But surely there's nothing left inside for them to steal?' I said in surprise.

'It is the wall carvings they're after nowadays,' he informed me. 'Unscrupulous dealers will pay large sums of money for sections of painted reliefs chipped from the tomb walls. They command high prices on the black market.'

I gaped at him, horrified. 'I had no idea...'

'These are difficult times,' he said with a sorrowful shake of his head.

Adam and I exchanged a glance. I knew we were both wondering whether the plan to bring Akhenaten and Nefertiti's tomb out into the open was quite such a good idea after all. But then I remembered Gamal Abdel-Maqsoud. We really had no choice. Now we could be sure he was alive and out to cause trouble, staging the discovery of the tomb before he could spring any sort of a trap was imperative. At least then we could ensure it received full military protection and was handed over for safekeeping to the proper authorities. We could only place our faith in them being sufficiently equipped to deal with it.

* * *

'I suggest we start with the tomb of Seti I,' Walid said as we approached the entrance to the Valley of the Kings in the small mini-bus Superintendent el-Saiyyid had put at our disposal since Ahmed's police car was too small for all six of us. 'It's been closed to visitors for upwards of thirty years since the condensation from the thousands of tourists who trooped through it every year was causing untold damage. It's the longest of all the tombs in the Valley, so there are potentially plenty of places for enterprising diggers to break through. And it's fully decorated, with some unique scenes.

Many consider it the most beautiful tomb in the Valley. So it is likely to be high up on the list for those with an eye to the main chance.'

Forget the enterprising diggers; with a build up like that I was just about hopping with excitement to see it for myself. It had been closed up since I was about five years old.

Seti's tomb is located on a branch close to the centre of the Valley, which has a layout a bit like an oak-leaf. We'd scrambled down the steep pathway set close by it on our nocturnal visit here last night. It felt strange to retrace our steps in the blazing heat of the day.

Despite the lack of visitors, the Valley seemed a very different place in the daytime. Bleached by the sun, a sun that, for many months of the year, beats down everything in its path, it was a barren, rather forbidding furnace of a place. The cliffs rising on all sides were like fortresses – imposing, hard, impenetrable. Perhaps that's why the pharaohs chose this spot for their tombs, setting their workmen the near-impossible task of carving sepulchres into the rock.

A guard unlocked the metal gate at the tomb entrance for us, and switched on the electricity supply so the wall reliefs were illuminated by the ambient strip lighting set at ground level.

I stepped across the threshold and caught my breath. 'My God, it's *immense*.' I gazed down the length of a huge corridor carved through the rock, every inch of it painted with the most exquisite wall reliefs.'

'And *beautiful*,' Habiba echoed at my elbow in similarly awe-inspired tones.

'Seti I was an immensely powerful pharaoh,' Walid said. 'He could afford the best.'

'He was the father of Ramses the Great,' Adam added. 'Ruling at the beginning of the 19th Dynasty, when his father, Ramses I, died after only a year or two on the throne.'

'Spare us the history lesson,' Dan said impatiently. 'Now, Walid, what is it we should be looking out for?'

Walid took a few paces forward into the tomb and we all followed. 'Any signs of disturbance or damage on the walls, specifically any missing sections.'

This was all part of the farce, of course, enacted for Habiba's benefit. But we went along with it in good part. We made a slow tour of the tomb. I'm pleased to report there were no signs of any attempts to break in. Its state of preservation was good. And it was absolutely staggering; stretching through ten chambers and seven corridors, carved almost 140 metres into the bedrock.

'I read somewhere that Seti's workers hollowed out something like 1,900 cubic metres of limestone from the rock,' Adam remarked. 'Can you imagine?'

'Frankly, in temperatures like these, I'd rather not,' Dan responded.

'Let's hope they worked in winter,' Habiba said brightly. 'What do you think, Officer Abd el-Rassul? Would you fancy hacking out chunks of rock from the hillside on the pharaoh's command at this time of year?'

Pressing his shirtsleeve against his damp face to remove the beads of perspiration, Ahmed frowned at her. 'I would not.'

As usual, it was getting hotter the deeper we penetrated into the tomb. The little squares of cardboard the guard had handed us at the gate to fan ourselves with were sadly unequal to the task.

She sent Ahmed a coy look. 'No. Of course not. A clever man such as yourself. You would not have been given such an unskilled job. I imagine you'd have played an important role among the pharaoh's private entourage. Perhaps his personal bodyguard, or something like that.'

She was ribbing him again, and it was clear Ahmed didn't like it one little bit.

'I am a police officer,' he said solemnly. 'Not a bodyguard.'

She treated him to a long sideways glance from under her dark lashes. 'But I thought you said earlier you'd been assigned to protect me. So you're not a bodyguard then? Ah, that is a shame.'

I watched Ahmed fingering his gun and took pity on him. It was hard to say if she was teasing him or flirting with him. Either way he was out of his depth. 'Come on, let's get back outside and ask Walid where he wants to go next.'

We trooped in and out of half a dozen tombs, all of them closed to the public. 'The visitor's ticket permits access to three tombs,' Adam explained. 'Although, you can add those of Ramses VI and Tutankhamun if you're willing to pay extra. It means the authorities can rotate those tombs that are open, so they can regulate the numbers of visitors.'

'Next year the first facsimile tomb will open,' Habiba added. 'It will be a replica of Tutankhamn's tomb, perfect in every detail, even down to the mould on the walls.'

Dan raised an eyebrow. 'So eventually tourists will end up visiting carbon copies of the tombs rather than the real thing? Sounds a bit Hollywood to me.'

'If it protects and preserves the originals, it will be worth it.' Walid said emphatically, managing rather nicely to have the final word on the subject. He glanced at his watch. 'Now, we have time to inspect one more tomb before I think we should call it a day.' He made a play of studying his guide showing the topography of the tombs. 'Ah yes; KV20, I think.'

Habiba frowned at him in confusion. 'But Dr Massri; that is Hatshepsut's tomb. It is in a very poor state of preservation, has no wall reliefs and has *never* been open to the public. I don't think it fits your brief at all.'

109

Walid tilted his head to one side and regarded her through his sunglasses, as if he was thoughtfully turning over what she had said. 'What you say is true,' he said at last. 'But it is carved in a series of long corridors into the cliffs directly behind Deir el-Bahri. That is to say, directly behind Hatshepsut's temple. As we all know, Hatshepsut's temple has some of the most remarkable and best-preserved wall reliefs in all of Egypt. It is well protected by the guards on the gate…'

I nearly choked when he said this.

'…But if I were an inventive and resourceful young criminal, intent on stealing some carvings I could sell for the highest possible price, might I not be looking for other ways I could perhaps find a way into Hatshepsut's temple without necessarily presenting myself at the ticket office?'

Habiba was staring back at him with renewed respect. 'Sir; you think they might try to burrow a way into the temple from one of the corridors of KV20?'

Walid smiled at her. 'We know the rock there to be of soft shale rather than hard limestone,' he said guilelessly. 'Put it this way: I would like to satisfy myself it is intact and thereby rule it out.'

Listening to this exchange, Ahmed stepped forward and pulled himself up to his full impressive height. 'I told you we should inspect the temples as well,' he declared imperiously.

For the second time in less than twenty-four hours I found myself approaching the metal grille fixed across the entrance to Hatshepsut's tomb carved into the rock in a remote branch of the Valley. This was what everything else today had been leading up to. I know Walid didn't want to leave it any longer. All the time Howard Carter's suitcase was bricked up behind the wall, there was a risk looters would indeed dig their way inside and perhaps steal a march on us. There was no room for further delay.

'So, what are we looking for, Dr Massri?' This time Habiba's innocence was genuine; while the rest of us were complicit in the little game we were playing.

'Any sign that the rock has been disturbed inside. Anything to suggest there is a hole in the wall that has been hastily bricked up. Something of that sort.'

I looked at him admiringly. If I were a screenwriter I couldn't have scripted it better.

Once we were inside the passageway that tunnelled into the rock there was very little to distinguish this visit from last night's. It was pitch dark and sweltering. Electricity had never been installed here. So once more we were forced to resort to flashlights.

Adam slipped his hand into mine as we trudged forward across the uneven stone floor. 'I don't know about you, Merry; but I've got goose bumps. Does this feel quite hopelessly nostalgic to you?'

'Well, the first time around it was just the two of us,' I said wistfully. 'It's not quite the same with all these hangers-on.'

'Do you remember the nervous anticipation of knowing we were so close to the end of solving Carter's conundrums? We were pretty certain we were going to find whatever it was he'd hidden in here.'

'I remember being terrified.'

He squeezed my hand. 'Well, you were right to be when that awful Youssef Said jumped us.'

'Do you remember that bone chilling moment when we thought Ted might be a villain?'

'I remember how badly I wanted to kiss you.'

'You said my boyfriend would just have to understand.'

He flashed his torch at Dan, walking a few paces ahead of us. 'Thankfully he's not your boyfriend anymore. That all sorted itself out rather nicely, don't you think?'

'Thanks to Youssef and the cobra,' I smiled.

He pulled me into his arms.

'I'm not sure I tell you often enough how much I love you, Meredith Pink. But just for the record, I do. Very much.'

His mouth descended onto mine. 'This is what I wanted to do the first time around,' he murmured against my lips, and kissed me with a conviction I found quite thrilling.

We broke apart at a discreet cough from Walid. We were nearly there.

By some unspoken agreement we hung back so Habiba approached the spot first. She swung her flashlight this way and that sending wide arcs of yellow light across the uninspiring walls. Suddenly she stopped abruptly and caught her breath. 'Dr Massri! Come quickly! Look!'

We all ran forward, dutifully shining our flashlight beams onto the wall where Habibia was pointing, and let out what we deemed the appropriate volume of gasps.

'But it makes no sense!' she frowned. 'Why would looters choose to start to dig a tunnel so high up on the wall?'

'They'd need a stepladder to get to it,' I agreed, eager to add the correct level of verisimilitude to the moment. 'Dan; can you reach up and pull out a few of the loose rocks?'

'Stop!' Walid commanded, freezing us all in our tracks. 'We must take photographs before we disturb anything. We may need them as evidence.'

From that point onwards it was pure theatre. Dan and Ahmed shared the task of pulling the rocks form the wall since they were the biggest and strongest among us. Adam recorded every movement on the movie setting of his iPhone. Walid, Habiba and I kept our torch-beams focused on the hole the men were opening in the wall so there was enough light for the camera to record everything properly.

Once the space was large enough to shine a flashlight into, Walid spoke up. 'Officer Abd el-Rassul, are you tall enough to see inside? Do we have a tunnel or a shaft of some description?'

Habiba was standing on tiptoes trying to train the beam of her flashlight through the opening. But she lacked the necessary inches. She caught hold of Ahmed's arm in her eagerness to be the first to look into the hole. Perhaps she wanted the kudos of being the one to report this possible sign of a breach in security back to her bosses at the Ministry of Antiquities. Or maybe she was just caught up in the moment. Either way, her plea to Ahmed lacked her usual provocativeness. She sounded simply excited. 'Can you lift me up so I can see?'

Ahmed hesitated, looking uncertain and uncomfortable.

'Go on,' I encouraged him. 'Let the poor girl take a look.'

He remained torn. Then, at a nod from Walid, he visibly steeled himself. Reaching forward, he placed his big square hands around Habiba's narrow waist and, maintaining as much bodily distance as possible, lifted her up.

Tensely, we watched Habiba shine the beam of her torch into the dark gap in the wall. I counted heartbeats. And then, very gratifyingly, she shrieked.

Ahmed dropped her as if she'd scalded him, and suffered the ignominy of having to help her up from the floor, apologising profusely.

'What is it?' We all clustered around, clamouring for information.

'There's something in there!' She didn't bother to brush herself off, just darted back towards the hole.

'What is it? A snake? The way you screamed...?'

'No. No.' In her excitement she was trying to scale the wall, since it was abundantly clear there was no way on Gods green earth Ahmed was going to offer to lift her up again. 'Nothing like that; it was an object; something flat and rectangular... Can you help me reach it?'

Walid was standing back. 'An object, you say? Are you sure?'

'Yes sir.'

'Adam, are you capturing this?'

'Yes sir.'

Dan was the one who stepped forward and reached up with both hands. Moments later he lifted Howard Carter's suitcase out of the hole.

Chapter 7

'So, the first stage in the drama has been successfully enacted,' Ted approved.

Adam, Dan and I were clustered around the telephone in the lounge-bar back on board the *Queen Ahmes*. Adam had pressed the speakerphone button, so we could all hear Ted and participate in the conversation.

We'd invited Habiba to join us on the dahabeeyah for some refreshments. She'd declined politely, saying she'd taken a room at the Nile Palace hotel and would prefer to make the telephone call she and Walid had agreed on, and then return there to let everything sink in. She said she was still in shock; as well she might be after all the hullaballoo.

Ahmed agreed to drop her off after returning the minibus to the police station and collecting his car. He'd taken Howard Carter's suitcase with him, so he could lock it away securely until we could make our pretence of studying the scrolls properly. Walid had gone with them. He wanted to supervise the safe storage of the papyrus within police custody. And of course he wanted to be there when Habiba made the call to her boss at the Ministry of Antiquities. I wasn't sure quite how he intended to square his self-appointed inspection duties with Director Ismail, and do so without arousing Habiba's suspicions. But, knowing Walid, he would find a way.

'We all tried to behave exactly as we did the first time around, and act as if we'd never seen the papyrus scrolls before in our lives,' Adam said. We hadn't quite finished telling Ted the story.

I smiled, remembering the spectacle we'd staged. 'Walid dropped forward onto his knees when we opened the lid on Howard Carter's suitcase in exactly the way you did, Ted,' I told him. 'He looked as if he was going to have a heart attack! It was an Oscar-worthy performance.'

'I was rather disappointed when nobody attempted to jump us with a knife,' Dan interjected. 'That would have topped it all off nicely. I wouldn't have minded a quick punch up.'

I frowned at him. 'There are some parts of our first experience much better not repeated. Adam still bears the scars, you know.'

'Amen to that,' Adam said firmly. 'I don't mind admitting I've spent most of the day looking over my shoulder, just in case Gamal Abdel-Maqsoud should have taken it into his head to spy on us, and was following us around.'

'You mean; he's alive?' Ted's startled voice filled the room.

It gave us no choice but to fill him in on the events of yesterday.

'I don't like it,' he said when we'd finished retelling the tale. 'I don't like it one little bit. It strikes me that all the time you're moored up there on the riverbank you're exposed and vulnerable.'

'That's why we decided Ahmed should take Howard Carter's suitcase with the scrolls to the police station.'

'Our safe's a sturdy, metal one,' Adam started. 'But...'

'...But it's not if we aren't already weighed down with quite enough priceless relics from antiquity,' Dan interrupted acerbically.

'...But if Gamal Abdel-Maqsoud should happen to be prowling around with a box of matches at the ready, it's a risk not worth taking,' I finished.

'Besides,' Adam went on. 'We thought Habiba might smell a rat if we all piled back here with our new discovery. She seems to have accepted that we're Walid's friends and he's staying with us while he's here in Luxor carrying out his *"inspection"*. Put it this way, she hasn't raised an eyebrow about us trailing around with him today. But we don't want to look too complicit. The girl's no fool.'

'Still, I'll feel happier if you can get away from Luxor as quickly as possible. I'd be delighted to have you here with me.'

'Khaled's making great progress with the repairs,' I said. 'And I've ordered replacement recliners and cushions. We should have everything done in a few days.'

'Good. I'll sleep easier when we're all together again.' He paused, and then returned to the subject of today's adventure. 'So, setting the scene for finding the papyrus was the first step towards staging the discovery of the tomb. Thankfully that seems to have gone without a hitch this afternoon. What comes next?'

Adam leaned towards the phone. 'Well, as you know, there are three scrolls in that suitcase: the text written by Ay to Tutankhamun; the transcription of the prayer to the Aten; and the scale architect's drawing of Hatshepsut's temple with the Hathor Chapel highlighted and the annotation "*Aten is key*"...'

'Not forgetting the scrap of paper Howard Carter sewed into the lining of his suitcase with the drawing of a key and the clue about Mehet-Weret,' I added. 'We carefully re-stitched it back inside before we bricked the case behind the wall the other night.'

'Basically, it's all set up and ready to go,' Adam nodded. But we need to get hold of a damn good philologist who can translate everything.'

I smiled. 'Sadly for us, the best philologist in the business is already on an important assignment in Amarna, for all that he's supposed to be retired. Part of Walid's plan is to ask Director Ismail to send someone from the Ministry who can do the job.'

'Shame,' Ted said, 'I'd have enjoyed another opportunity to study those papyri.'

'You have a whole fresh set of scrolls to get your teeth into now,' I reminded him. 'So, come on! I've been breathless with anticipation to find out what we unearthed in that cellar. Is it anything exciting? Because somebody obviously went to considerable lengths to hide those documents away in what looked like wine jars.'

Ted allowed a long pause to draw out. 'I thought you'd never ask.'

Adam and I exchanged a hopeful glance, while Dan let out a long sigh.

'It does indeed appear to be a very significant discovery,' Ted said at length. 'Unless I am very much mistaken, what we stumbled across in that wine cellar at Panehesy's house is a body of correspondence.'

'Correspondence? Letters, you mean?' Dan preferred plain English.

'Well, one half of a body of correspondence if I'm to be accurate,' the professor qualified. 'The letters – yes, you are absolutely right, Dan; that's what they are – are all addressed to a woman by the name of Nebt-Het. It's an ancient Egyptian name meaning Mistress of the House. She appears to have been Panehesy's wife.'

'Are the letters from Panehesy?'

'They are signed simply "your husband", so I believe so. It looks as if he sent them from his travels. Panehesy was a powerful and wealthy man. As well as being the Chief

Servitor of the Aten, his titles also include Second Prophet of the Two Lands and Seal Bearer of Lower Egypt. He could obviously afford to pay a runner to carry his letters back to Amarna from wherever he happened to be.'

I swallowed hard. 'Wherever he happened to be? Professor! That box Nabil found in the same cellar was also transcribed by Panehesy... it said he would follow his Lord on every step of his journey to lead their people out of Egypt. Are you saying he sent letters home from that journey?'

'That's my reading of what I've been able to translate so far; yes.'

I gaped round-eyed at Adam. 'So am I right in thinking...?'

I trailed off, not knowing quite how to put it into words. Adam, staring back at me with no less astonishment on his face, managed to find them and finished for me, albeit rather haltingly.

'We know "his Lord" was the High Priest Meryre... We suspect Meryre may have been Moses... Are you suggesting...? Might we have uncovered...? Oh my God...! Do we have a written record of the Exodus?'

'It would seem so, my boy! Yes.'

* * *

Our call was abruptly severed at that point. There was a knock on Ted's door at the other end of the line, and he said he had to go.

We said a hasty goodbye and then Dan, Adam and I stared at each other.

'Did he just say what I thought he said?' Dan asked.

Adam and I both nodded, speechless.

'Great!' Dan exclaimed. 'I always wanted to know how dear old Moses went about parting the Red Sea! Maybe we'll find out from someone who witnessed it at first hand.'

Adam got up. 'I don't know about the two of you, but I could use a drink right now. Beer?'

He fetched three bottles from the chiller cabinet underneath the bar and flipped off the caps. None of us bothered with a glass; just took long swigs directly from the bottle.

Adam smacked his lips together. 'That's better.' He sat down again, slumping onto one of the sofas. 'Well, at least it's starting to explain why all those nobles' tombs in Amarna were found empty. Egyptologists have often remarked how strange it is that all of the key officials at Akhenaten's court seem to "disappear" when he dies. If they all upped sticks to follow Meryre when he led Akhenaten's people out of Egypt, the fact of their tombs all standing empty and their remains never having been found would start to make sense. They all died elsewhere.'

Dan was sipping his beer and frowning. 'Who exactly were these people Moses, or this chap Meryre, is supposed to have led out of Egypt? I thought they were a bunch of Hebrew manual workers being freed from slavery. But now you're going on about nobles...?'

Adam sat forward. 'I think there were certainly Hebrews among their number, although it's debateable as to whether or not they were slaves. If Nabil Zaal is right, then Akhenaten was descended from Joseph, who was the son of Jacob; who, according to the Bible, came to Egypt from Canaan with his sons...'

'...Forming the twelve tribes of Jacob' I added. 'They settled around the city of Goshen in the Nile Delta. The Bible also gives Jacob the name "*Israel*", so his people would have been the "*Israelites*".'

'More to the point, they would have been Akhenaten's kinsfolk,' Adam went on. 'If you think about what the Bible says; Egypt is a place for the Hebrews to flee to – a place of sanctuary. That was the case for Abraham, Jacob; even Jesus. Or it is a place to flee from, as in the case of Moses and the Exodus.'

I sat forward to explain, putting my beer bottle on the coffee table. 'Nabil believes the reason the Hebrews, or Israelites, were persecuted was because Akhenaten took their belief in one god and elevated it above the Egyptian Pantheon, effectively wiping out centuries' worth of traditional belief in favour of the religion of his own people; who were foreigners.'

'But I thought Akhenaten worshipped the sun?' Dan said, his brows drawing together again. 'Surely that's not the same thing as the god of the Hebrews, is it? I mean, it's not the same as *our* God?'

'Lots of religious writers of both Jewish and Christian faith have said the same,' Adam said. 'But I'm not so sure it's fair to dismiss Akhenaten as a 'heretic' and simple worshipper of the sun. I think he held a much deeper set of spiritual beliefs.'

I wrinkled my brow. 'But he did represent the Aten figuratively as the sun disc, with outstretched hands giving the power of life and goodness to the world,' I said. 'Isn't that a classic case of sun-worship?'

'Perhaps,' Adam admitted. 'But Akhenaten's prayers and texts, of which we have numerous examples, make it clear the god he believed in was not the sun, but an unknowable Supreme Force that had power over everything in the universe.'

'And you believe he instilled this belief, the belief of his Hebrew forebears, in his followers, that is, his priests and his nobles?' Dan said.

Adam nodded.

Dan went on, working it through in his head by speaking his thoughts aloud. 'So that, when he died, or a little while afterwards, they decided to leave Egypt along with the descendants of the tribes of Jacob, rather than stick around and face persecution from the pharaohs who followed and sought to obliterate all memory of Akhenaten and his heresy. Is that right?'

'If Nabil is correct, then that would be my take on it; yes.'

I was working things through in my mind too. 'You know, I think what Akhenaten attempted was incredibly brave. In something like the seventeen short years of his reign, he tried to turn back the tide of several thousand years of history. Ok, so in Egypt he failed, and was labelled a heretic and a criminal by those who came after him. But, looking at our beliefs today, I'm sure there are many people who would say he was enlightened; just born a millennia or so before his time.'

'I agree,' Adam said with a slow nod. 'Some historians argue that Akhenaten's religion was of little consequence in overall history as it was "ephemeral".'

'Ephemeral?' Dan queried.

'Fleeting. Short-lived.' I supplied.

'But I think the fact it didn't survive here in Egypt after his death is to misunderstand its significance,' Adam went on. 'Akhenaten's priests didn't die with him. His writings and works didn't suddenly become obsolete. His ideas lived on. Assuming his followers did indeed pass down a version of his beliefs through the generations to the Qumranites who wrote the Dead Sea Scrolls ...'

'...Then it's possible to see Akhenaten's influence in all of the major religions of the world today.' I finished.

* * *

Walid was back in time for dinner. I'd made a simple pasta carbonara for supper since it was quick and easy. I served it with a nice crisp salad, all the leaves washed in the special water purifier Khaled had installed for us. We ate up on deck, enjoying another velvety Egyptian evening.

'Director Ismail swallowed it,' Walid announced with satisfaction. 'I managed to talk over the top of him when he expressed surprise at my being here to check on security. I said with everything so quiet at the Museum in view of the lack of tourists, and with the on-going protests in Tahrir Square, I was grateful for the permission to take up my duties on behalf of the Ministry here. Anyway, he didn't argue.'

'And Habiba?' I asked. 'She didn't notice anything amiss?'

'I don't think so. And she played her part to perfection, even without knowing it.'

'You let her be the one to tell Director Ismail about the discovery of Howard Carter's suitcase?'

'Yes; although, remember, we're not supposed to know it was Howard Carter's case. So far as any of us know at the moment, we have no idea who it belonged to or how it came to be bricked up in a hole in the wall inside Hatshepsut's tomb. Ok?'

'Of course,' I said quickly. 'I hadn't forgotten. I just…'

He smiled at me and then carried on filling us in on the call he and Habiba had patched through to Director Ismail at the Ministry for Antiquities. 'She was bubbling over with excitement. I stepped in to explain that naturally we would resist the temptation to unroll the scrolls until we were under controlled conditions where they could be properly conserved.'

'So, is he sending a philologist to translate them?'

'He suggested we should take the papyri to the Luxor Museum. He is contacting the curator to be there to greet us tomorrow. He said he'll decide what kind of additional expertise we may need once we know exactly what it is we've found. And, of course, I had to be satisfied with that as I'm not supposed to know exactly what it is we've found.'

'We were very lucky to have Ted with us when we discovered them the first time around,' I said.

Dan harrumphed. 'Yes; although perhaps not quite so fortunate that he was there with the sharp-end of a bloody great knife pointed dead centre in his back!'

'Hmm, we do seem to attract an unsavoury bunch of characters,' Adam agreed.

'Speaking of which; is there any sign that other young ruffian has been snooping around here again today?' Walid asked. 'After all, the coast has been clear with us all out of the way. He could pretty much have ripped the place apart if he chose to.'

I winced at the images his turn of phrase sent flashing before my eyes. 'Khaled has been up here on deck all day, and we told him to keep the gangplank raised and the door locked. I don't think anyone could have jumped on board without him noticing.'

'And you've checked the safe?'

'It was the first thing we did when we got back. We unlocked it just to be sure. Nothing's been tampered with. The Aten discs and the clay tablets are still safely stored inside.'

'And you can be assured we locked it up again,' Adam said, fingering the small key hidden behind the crocodile tooth on the bootlace at his throat.

'Even so, I'll be relieved when we no longer have need of those Aten discs. Gamal Abdel-Maqsoud knows we have them on board, and he knows how to use them. Now I've decided to bring the tomb to light, I'd really like to get on with it as quickly as possible.'

Since there was nothing we could do on that score until our visit to Luxor Museum tomorrow, we let the subject drop.

'So, tell me, how is Ted getting on in Amarna with those scrolls that turned up in the wine jars? Do they appear to be anything of interest?'

He spotted the electricity in the atmosphere straight away.

'What is it? What do they say?'

We told him as much as we knew and he slumped back in his chair, looking stunned. 'Letters home from the Exodus,' he breathed. 'Oh my goodness! It has the potential to knock even Akhenaten and Nefertiti's tomb into the shade.'

'Well, if you're looking to attract visitors back to Egypt, I would think we're uncovering stuff that will prove an irresistible draw,' Adam said.

'Humph, even if only to the world's collective Press.' Dan added. 'Be careful what you wish for is my motto. You'll soon have the place swarming with journalists like flies around carrion.'

Walid looked uncomfortable. 'Each new discovery takes me further and further out of my depth. I am in over my head, and the water is hot.'

I couldn't help but smile at his mangling of our English metaphors. It was reminiscent of Ahmed at his finest.

'I will not rest easy until I am in a position to hand everything over to my superiors in the Ministry,' he continued. 'They can be the ones to make these decisions and perhaps allow the world's Press to descend on us in droves. I should never have taken it upon myself to play God. This... this is too big for me. I'm terrified half out of my wits!'

I felt for him. But I wasn't sure I could wholeheartedly agree with his desire to pass everything over. The tomb; yes – but I wanted to know what those letters to the Mistress of the House Nebt-Het said before the rest of the world got to hear of it. Still, Barry was in charge of things at Amarna. I felt quite sure Ted would report his findings to the field director as he made them. So I wasn't suffering any pangs of guilt over what we had discovered in that wine cellar. Quite the reverse; I was thrilled to bits. We'd had a bunch of Egyptologists on the scene within moments, and everything had been properly recorded and catalogued. As a bona fide archaeological find, I felt we could take a genuine if vicarious pleasure in unlocking the secrets those scrolls contained. And, let's face it; Barry had invited Ted to be the one to undertake the translations. Ok, so he may not have known Ted would share his discoveries with us. But I say friendship has to count for something. We'd proved we were good at keeping secrets. And it was a simple fact we would never disclose anything we learned beyond the small group of us who were already in the know. So, any insights from the Exodus were safe with us. They would stay that way until Barry, or Director Ismail, or Abdel Fattah el-Sisi, the Military Commander himself, should choose to go public.

'You know, I'd like to know a bit more about this Meryre,' I said as my thoughts carried me forward.

Adam was already reaching for his iPad. He swiped it on and started tapping on the screen. 'Meryre,' he read aloud. 'He was a senior nobleman at the court of Pharaoh Akhenaten in Amarna, ancient Akhet-Aten.'

'This much we already know,' Dan muttered.

Adam took no notice and kept on reading. 'His unfinished tomb was found among the northern tombs in the cliffs surrounding the city. It is lavishly decorated with scenes of local life. Had it been completed, it would have been the largest of all the nobles' tombs found in Amarna, no doubt reflecting his importance as one of the foremost officials at Akhenaten's court. He was not interred there and his remains have never been found.'

'So, tell us something we don't already know,' Dan muttered again.

Adam flashed a quick glance at him, but didn't let him put him off his stride. 'As well as being the High Priest of the Aten, his other titles were "Fan-bearer at the right-hand side of the King", "Hereditary Prince", "Royal Chancellor"... And that's just to name a few! The list goes on.'

I zoned out for a moment and stared out across the dark waters of the ever-shifting Nile. The talk of Meryre's tomb stirred a memory of something Nabil Zaal had told us when we were with him in Amarna recently. 'Do you remember there were two tombs Nabil wanted to visit in Akhet-Aten as well as the Royal Tomb?'

They all looked at me enquiringly.

'Yes, those of Panehesy and Meryre.' Walid said.

'Do you remember why he chose those two in particular?'

Adam and Walid both frowned, but it was Adam who replied. 'Not especially; beyond his mission to prove that they were never buried there.'

'He said these two men were Akhenaten's two highest priestly officials at the temple,' I reminded them. 'Meryre was the High Priest of the Aten and Panehesy was the Chief Servitor of the Aten.'

'Yes,' Walid said slowly. 'So…?'

'So, he also said the two highest priestly officials under Moses had names that were very similar, remember?'

'Merari and Pinehas,' Adam supplied. 'Whose names translate into Egyptian as Meryre and Panehesy.' He looked at me with a dawning comprehension in his eyes. 'So, you're saying…?'

'I'm saying if Meryre himself was Moses, who was the priestly official Meryre? Surely he can't have been both!'

Walid sat forward. 'There was another nobleman in Akhet-Aten whose name was Meryre. He has come down to us as Meryre II, probably to distinguish him from the High Priest.'

Adam was swiping the screen on his iPad again. 'Meryre II,' he read. 'His titles were "Royal Scribe", "Steward",

132

and "Overseer of the Treasuries". His tomb contains the last known scene recording Akhenaten and the royal family all together at Amarna – dated to year twelve of the king's reign. Once again, it seems he was never buried there and his remains have never been identified.'

'I'm starting to wonder if anyone was actually buried in any of tombs they took so much trouble to carve out of the cliffs in Amarna,' Dan said, sounding as if his credulity was being stretched to the limit. 'Surely they can't *all* have buggered off on the Exodus once crazy old Akhenaten popped his clogs! Didn't *any* of them decide life was more comfortable in their nice new city and decide to stick around, even if it did mean converting back from Atenism to the worship of that other bunch of weird animal-headed deities?'

'I think you're underestimating the strength of religious conviction,' Walid said quietly. 'Just because much of the Western world has lost what we might call "*faith*",' He made speech marks around the word to emphasise his point; 'it does not mean it is not deeply felt by those who are believers. Wars are still being fought in the name of religion. Sadly it is often in the name of Islam.' He shook his head regretfully. 'But it proves people are willing to die for their beliefs.'

'People were burnt at the stake in the name of religion in our own not-so-distant past,' Adam nodded. 'And, looking down this list, I'd have to conclude that very few of Akhenaten's followers seemed willing to stay put once the king was in his sarcophagus. There are at least another half-dozen officials named here who had tombs they were never buried in carved into the cliffs around Amarna. Perhaps they felt motivated by some divine purpose in taking the dead pharaoh's beliefs out of Egypt and passing them on to future generations.'

'So, if he left Egypt as part of the Exodus, then Meryre II could possibly have served as one of Moses/Meryre's officials,' I mused, bringing us back to the point. 'And my ears pricked up at something else you read out,' I added. 'Didn't you say Meryre II was "Overseer of the Treasuries"?'

Adam tapped the screen and glanced down. 'Yes, that's right.'

'So, he had access to all the wealth of the nation – gold most probably; vast quantities of gold. And didn't you say he was also a "Royal Scribe"?'

Adam looked at the screen and nodded again.

'So, I'm wondering if perhaps he was the individual who transcribed those clay tablets that are sitting in the safe downstairs. Maybe we've identified the author of the first draft of the Copper Scroll!'

Chapter 8

The Luxor Museum, set overlooking the east bank of the Nile along the Corniche, is one of a handful of places in Egypt that holds a special place in my heart. The Museum has the distinction of being where I first clapped eyes on Adam or, more accurately, where he clapped eyes on me.

On that occasion, I'd been there alone, just in the company of my guidebook, since Dan, my boyfriend at the time, had elected to stay back at the hotel to top up his suntan by the pool while I went out sightseeing.

Adam, similarly on his own, was there to gen up on his Pharaonic knowledge for his online Egyptological studies.

I'm not sure it's fair to say that our eyes met in front of the exquisite statue of Thutmosis III, and certainly not that it was love at first sight. But at some time during the encounter he must have looked at me, and I daresay I must have looked at him.

As I recall it, we had one of those polite stranger-to-stranger conversations; just a few words in passing, commenting on the strength and prowess of Egypt's finest warrior pharaoh. I think it may have been the first time Adam likened himself to a walking guidebook, but I couldn't say for sure.

I just know I came away with a vague impression of a good-looking man with a rather self-deprecating sense of humour. Enough anyway that the next time I saw him, on the forecourt of Hatshepsut's temple, I took more notice.

Now, I slipped my hand into his as we came through the security kiosk onto the narrow grassy bank in front of the Museum. 'This is where it all began.'

He squeezed my hand to acknowledge the memory, hazy though it was. 'If we could only have known then... huh?'

Dan broke the spell. 'I presume we're not required to look at all the exhibits. I've seen enough stone pharaohs to last me a lifetime!'

Walid led the way through the entrance into the thankfully air-conditioned interior. 'No. This is not a pleasure trip. We're here to meet Mr Ibrahim Mohassib, the curator.'

I saw Dan's raised eyebrow. 'I'd have to take issue with the word *pleasure*!' But he said no more, and dutifully followed Walid into the Museum.

Ahmed stood back to allow Habiba to enter ahead of him. Something seemed to me to have changed between those two. Ahmed appeared unusually deferential, and I had not heard a single provocative remark pass her lips on the journey over here, with Ahmed once more at the wheel of the minibus.

I hung back so I could exchange a few words with our police buddy while everyone else went on ahead. 'Is everything alright with you and Habiba?'

He cast me a quick look from his dark, snapping eyes. 'Alright?' he queried. 'I'm not sure that I understand.'

'It's just, well, yesterday everything seemed quite...' I groped for a suitable word, '...prickly... between you two. I wasn't sure if you'd exactly hit it off. But today, well, let's just say I've seen the way you keep glancing at her. I wondered what had changed.'

This time, the look he gave me was steadier. 'You miss nothing, Meredith.'

I didn't allow his perfect pronunciation of my name to distract me. 'So, has something happened?' Honestly, it was like drawing blood out of a stone.

He hung back even further to be sure we were out of earshot, and spoke in a low, conspiratorial tone. 'Last night after Dr Massri left the police station, I offered to take Habiba to her hotel in my car.'

'You gave her a lift after she and Walid made their call to Director Ismail,' I nodded. 'It was very decent of you, Ahmed; especially after she'd spent the day pulling your leg.'

'Pulling my leg,' he repeated, no doubt filing away this rather lovely colloquialism for future use. 'Yes. I thought she would just get out of the car when we got to the hotel and tell to me goodbye. But instead, she asked me to join her there for dinner.'

I tried not to look too surprised. After all, Ahmed is a very handsome man; especially now he's had his teeth fixed. And Habiba is a beautiful young woman. Still, there was something about lambs to the slaughter that flashed uncomfortably through my mind. 'But I thought she said she wanted to be alone to let it all sink in. She was in shock. She declined our invitation to come back to the *Queen Ahmes* for a drink.'

Ahmed nodded. 'All of this, it is true, exactly as you say. But she said to me that she was too excited still to be on her own. She wanted to talk to me about the miracle of what we had discovered.'

'So, you joined her for dinner,' I concluded, deciding to cut to the chase.

'I did,' he said, his dark eyes gleaming. 'I thought she wanted to talk about way that we finded the papyrus,'

'Found,' I said automatically.

'But instead, she wanted to know about me. She asked me lots of questions – all about my job in the Tourist and Antiquities Police. She wanted to know about the most exciting things I had done.'

For the first time I felt a frisson of alarm. Ahmed is a man who does not lack an ego – show me one who does. And ... a pretty woman ... appealing to that side of him ...

there were all manner of things he could have let slip ... Let's face it; Habiba worked for the Ministry of State for Antiquities. 'I hope you stuck strictly to the things that have been firmly within your remit as a police officer, not outside of it,' I said sternly.

'Of course!' he said, looking injured. 'I telled to her that I was hurt while trying to capture an escaped antiquities thief last year.'

'But not how, where or why, I trust.'

'No. Only that he lost his life in the rock fall behind Hatshepsut's temple. This, it is common knowledge, is it not?'

It was, so I subsided. 'And you let her assume you were hurt in the same rock fall?'

'I was silent on this matter.'

'Anything else? Oh, and it's *told*, by the way; not *telled.*'

He nodded. 'I told to her that I received a Military commendation for my quick action during the demonstrations against President Morsi in Cairo when a man he was killed.'

'But not why you were in Cairo?'

'No. This, it was not relevant to the story.'

I smiled. So basically he'd regaled her with all the incidents that showed him to be big and brave and strong. 'I hope she was suitably impressed,' I said mildly.

'It was a most enjoyable evening.'

I'll bet it was, I thought. Seeing as you were with an attractive woman who seemed happy to sit back and let you talk about yourself the whole time. But I wasn't unkind enough to say this. 'I'm sure it was,' I soothed. 'Just be careful, Ahmed. Remember, she's here to check up on police security at the archaeological sites. She may hope that in a relaxed moment you'll let your guard down and tell her something that might make your department seem a bit lapse. Not that it is, of course!' I added hurriedly.

He managed to look both mollified and anxious. 'You think that she was testing me to look for weak spots?'

'I'm sure she just wanted to spend an evening in your company. What young woman wouldn't? I'm just advising you to watch what you say, that's all.' I glanced across at the others a few feet away and lowered my voice even further. 'We're playing a bit of a game with Habiba, as you know. She's ideally placed to add credence to what Walid is doing. Just remember the stakes are high, that's all.'

Ahmed nodded. 'I will tread with a careful step.' He said seriously. 'And not allow myself to be pushed onto the wrong foot.'

Mr Ibrahim Mohassib, the Museum curator, was a helpful, mild-mannered man, whose English was, to use his own word, inadequate (which seemed to me to prove quite the reverse). He asked if we would permit him to speak to Walid and Habiba, as the two representatives of the Ministry of Antiquities, in Arabic. Of course we acquiesced. But I was frustrated not to be able to follow every word that was said. I decided I really must make more of an effort to learn the language.

We were shown through a security door into the private part of the Museum behind the exhibition rooms. It was clean and clinical, with a long corridor lined with closed doors. I presumed they led to storerooms or workshops where conservation work was undertaken on the antiquities, or something of that nature.

Walid was carrying Howard Carter's suitcase. He'd been gripping it ever since we left the police station, so tightly his knuckles showed white. Considering how light it was, with only three papyrus scrolls inside, I thought this said much about the state of agitation he worked himself into whenever the precious artefacts were unprotected. I imagine he feared Gamal Abdel-Maqsoud might appear out of the woodwork at any moment and snatch the case away from him. I could have told him he wouldn't get very far if he tried it. With Dan, Adam and Ahmed on hand, I'd say the ancient scrolls were pretty well guarded.

We reached a large, square room set up as a laboratory.

Walid and Habiba approached a workbench where a glass-plated mechanism was set up with metal clamps at each of the four corners. Above it, attached to the ceiling on a long, jointed mechanical arm, was something I took to be a type of state of the art microscope.

'Wow,' I whispered to Adam. 'That equipment looks amazing. I've only ever seen stuff like that in a hospital.'

'No expense was spared fitting this place out,' he agreed. 'It's one of the most modern facilities in this part of the world. I daresay the new museum being built in Cairo will outstrip it when it finally opens. And, of course, it will be huge by comparison. But, yes, it's pretty impressive, isn't it?'

A breathless hush descended over us as Walid unclipped the locks on Howard Carter's suitcase and lifted the lid.

Mr Ibrahim Mohassib donned a pair of soft white gloves and carefully lifted the papyrus scrolls, one-by-one from the silken lining. He handed gloves to Walid and Habiba and they put them on and dutifully stepped forward to assist him.

Carefully and with painstaking slowness, they unrolled the first scroll. It was the transcription of Akhenaten's hymn to the Aten. They positioned it on the lower glass plate, unscrewing the clamps, so they could slide the scroll between the bottom and top plates.

The second scroll cracked loudly as they unfurled it. We all gasped as small flakes of the ancient paper drifted to the ground. It was the oldest of all the scrolls, the scale drawing of Hatshepsut's temple, possibly drawn by Senenmut, the female pharaoh's famous architect. We all held our collective breath while Walid and Ibrahim Mohassib inserted it between the two glass plates, alongside the other one.

Finally, it was the turn of the largest of the three scrolls, the transcription authored by the pharaoh Ay, who succeeded Tutankhamum to the throne. It unrolled with comparative ease, and the two museum curators slid it carefully onto the lower glass plate.

At a word from Ibrahim Mohassib, Ahmed stepped forward to help with the clamps. With one of our Egyptian acquaintances on each corner, they were screwed firmly back in place, so the three papyrus scrolls were protectively sandwiched between the two plates of glass.

Last year we'd used a rather less high tech version of the same basic procedure, securing the papyri between the glass from two poster frames taken from the wall in Adam's flat, and weighting the corners with books. It made me quite nostalgic to think about it.

Ibrahim Mohassib took off his glasses and leaned forward over the glass plates to study the papyrus. I could see he was holding his breath. Walid, no less breathlessly, did the same. This was the first time he had seen them unrolled. I was quite sure all his scholarly fires were alight. Habiba was looking as if she might faint, swaying where she stood as she gazed at the scrolls. She sucked in a loud gasp and spoke a single word in English. 'Wow!' Then she switched back to Arabic and addressed the two men.

'She asked if they're genuine,' Adam translated.

Ibrahim Mohassib stood straight again and replied in his native tongue.

'He said he will arrange for samples of the papyrus and ink to be analysed. But, at first glance, he thinks the answer is yes.'

Walid also straightened. He spoke a few words to the other curator, then motioned for Adam, Dan and I to approach the bench. We all gazed at the mounted papyrus with the requisite amount of wonder. In truth, my reaction wasn't something I found it necessary to fake. Seeing the three scrolls displayed alongside each other was genuinely breathtaking. We'd only dared to look at them one at a time last year and, in the case of Ay's scroll, section-by-section, never the whole thing in one go.

I frowned and feigned ignorance. 'Do you have any idea what they say, Dr Massri?' We'd agreed it was best to use his professional title in front of others.

He gazed at the scrolls again. 'This one; I recognise as the Hymn to the Aten. I studied it at university. And this one,' he pointed to Senenmut's drawing. 'Well, it appears to be an architect's plan of some sort, but I would not like to say where...'

Adam caught his breath very convincingly. 'Sir! I think I can suggest where it might be. See those lines? They look like ramps to me. And these small, evenly-placed circles? I'd hazard a guess at columns. I'd say we're looking at an aerial-view of Hatshepsut's temple.'

Ibrahim Mohassib either knew enough English, or deduced enough from hearing the name *Hatshepsut*, to follow what Adam was saying. Adam made it easy for him, pointing as he went. Either way, the Luxor Museum curator started nodding his head excitedly. 'Deir el Bahri,' he exclaimed. 'It is Djeser-Djeseru indeed.' This was the ancient name Hatshepsut herself had given her temple. It translated as "the holiest of holy places".

Then he frowned and continued in English, 'But I don't understand…?'

I thought Adam had pushed things forward very helpfully. But it wasn't for us to point out the key features on each of the scrolls. We didn't want to appear too knowledgeable. This was the first time any of us were supposed to have seen the papyri. And the truth was, there was no obvious link between Akhenaten's Hymn to the Aten and Senenmut's drawing of Hatshepsut's temple. We needed Ibrahim Mohassib to turn detective and puzzle it out for himself, in the same way we had done. Although, I'm sure we could be prevailed upon to drop hints along the way should it prove necessary.

Habiba had followed this exchange with bright-eyed interest, looking almost impossibly excited to be part of this miraculous find. What might have seemed to her like a dull and perhaps routine visit to Luxor had certainly taken an unexpected turn. 'And the other scroll? The big one? Can I take a closer look, please?'

We all stepped backwards so she could get up close to this section of the glass-plated workbench. She leaned forward, squinting at the ancient lettering with a focused concentration. 'It's written in hieratic script,' she said.

'That's the abbreviated form of hieroglyphics,' I said for Dan's benefit. 'Ancient scribes used it to write administrative documents, letters and the like.'

'Can you read any of it?' Adam asked.

'I'm no philologist,' she said apologetically. 'But look! Does this say *"Nebkheperure"*? That was one of Tutankhamun's throne names! So, is this something to do with Tutankhamun?'

Clever girl, I thought. You've hit on the most important thing.

Adam obviously thought the same and took it upon himself to help her along a bit. 'And what's this?' he pointed at the oval stamp with hieroglyphs drawn inside it. 'Is that Tutankhamun's cartouche?'

Habiba frowned at it and hesitated. 'Er, no, I don't think so. I'm struggling to read it. Dr Massri, can you make it out?'

146

Walid leaned forward so their heads were alongside each other above the glass, his shiny balding pate next to her carefully wound headscarf. Any closer, and they'd be touching. He sucked in a long breath. 'It reads "*Kheperkheperure*". And here, underneath, it says "*it-netjer*".

Adam's breath quickened alongside me. 'Those are the *nomen* and *prenomen* of pharaoh Ay,' he said in a strangled voice. I wasn't sure if he was so much acting for Habiba's benefit or dragging up from his memory banks the words he'd spoken the first time around and repeating them.

Whatever, they had the desired affect. Ibrahim Mohassib clasped his hands together and rocked up and down on his toes. 'This would seem to be a very important find indeed,' he said in careful English.

'Yes,' Walid agreed. 'A document bearing the royal titles not just of one pharaoh but of two. We must get it authenticated and translated with all possible speed.'

Ibrahim nodded emphatically, clearly understanding every word. 'I will make the necessary arrangements right away. You permit that I should keep these papyri within my care, here at the museum?'

Walid let out a long sigh of relief. 'Nothing would give me more pleasure.'

Habiba sidled up to me after we'd said our goodbyes and emerged into the hot sunshine.

'Congratulations,' I said to her warmly. 'You must be absolutely thrilled to be the one who made the discovery.'

'Yes,' she said, her unusual bronze-flecked eyes sparkling. 'I am lucky indeed. It seems almost too good to be true.'

I sent her a swift, searching glance. She appeared completely unaware her turn of phrase might have a more subtle meaning, walking along beside me with a quick, light step. Reassured I could take her at face value – it was a common enough expression after all – I quickly shared her enthusiasm. 'I know. It doesn't seem quite real to me, either! One minute we were inspecting the tombs for any signs of break-in, and the next we were making a discovery that could rock the world!'

'Do you really think we've found something as important as that?' she asked breathlessly.

I wondered if I'd overdone it a bit, and tried to be rather more circumspect, mentally kicking myself for not taking the advice I'd dished out earlier to Ahmed to watch what I said. 'Well, that big scroll, assuming it's for real, mentions both Tutankhamun and Ay,' I reminded her. 'I'm no Egyptologist, but even I know those are names to stir up a storm of interest. Put it this way; I'm daring to hope.'

'Dr Massri and Mr Mohassib both seem to think all three scrolls are genuine,' she mused.

'Yes,' I said. 'Which is why I'm so optimistic.'

'Then it is probably just as well the scrolls are now being looked after at the Museum instead of in the police station,' she remarked.

I sent her a surprised glance. 'What on earth do you mean?'

She was looking at Ahmed's broad back. He was walking with Dan a few paces ahead of us, deep in conversation. 'I had dinner with Officer Abd el-Rassul last night,' she confided. 'I am familiar, of course, with the name, and asked him about it. The Abd el-Rassul family were quite infamous in their day, back at the turn of the last century. They were notorious tomb-robbers, you know.'

'Oh, he regaled you with that old chestnut of a story, did he?' I smiled. 'Yes, he's quite proud of his dodgy heritage.'

She plucked at my arm, looking concerned. 'But these things are in the blood,' she said earnestly 'He still has that same blood of his ancestors flowing in his veins.'

This showed her to be a true Egyptian, for all her Westernised appearance and impressive educational attainments. They can be an irrational and superstitious lot on occasion.

I smiled at her, 'No doubt it's what makes him such a good police officer. He's channelled his instincts in a more constructive direction.'

This didn't seem to reassure her as I had hoped. She gazed sideways at me as if trying to read my thoughts. 'You seem to be on friendly terms with him. Is he to be entirely *trusted* do you think?'

Now she had gone too far. I stopped stock-still and looked her full in the face. 'Ahmed Abd el-Rassul is the finest of men,' I said staunchly. 'Anyone who thinks differently needs their brains tested!'

'She chose not to speak to me after that,' I admitted to Adam, telling him the story later when we were back on board the dahabeeyah.

'Do you think she smells a rat? Have we overdone it?' he asked.

'I don't think so. I sincerely hope not, anyway. I sense a bit of an undercurrent between Habiba and Ahmed. I think they're attracted to each other, and both afraid to admit it. Maybe she was just trying to sound me out about him.'

'Well, let's hope it's that. Walid needs her to believe in this little charade we're acting out so she can play it straight down the middle with her superiors.'

Dan had offered to knock up something tasty for supper. He was quite a dab hand in the kitchen. Walid had gone to his cabin to rest. I daresay the quantities of nervous energy he'd expended in the last few days were taking their toll. So Adam and I headed up on deck to see how Khaled was getting on with the repair work.

150

He was wiping his hands on a rag soaked in some chemical-smelling liquid as we came up the spiral staircase.

'One more day, and I think I'll be done,' he said in his soft Scottish brogue. It was always a surprise to hear him speak. Apart from his unusual blue eyes, Khaled is Egyptian through and through to look at.

I inspected his handiwork, impressed. He'd stripped, sanded and varnished the charred wooden floorboards so well it was impossible to tell they'd ever been burnt.

'They need one more coat of varnish,' he said. 'I'll do that tomorrow after this last one is fully dry. And then another coat of the calico paint over there, a bit of polish on the handrails, and I'll be out of your hair. Oh, and there was a message this afternoon from the retailer to confirm the new seating and cushions will be delivered tomorrow. We'll have the *Queen Ahmes* back to her old self within twenty-four hours.'

I gazed about the deck with tears in my eyes. 'Thank you, Khaled; you've done a wonderful job. I'm not sure we can ever thank you enough.'

'I'm grateful for the work, and the pay.' he admitted. 'Besides, I love this old boat. It broke my heart when that young devil set a match to her. I'd cheerfully have throttled him with my bare hands, if he hadn't spared me the effort by jumping overboard. Put it this way; if I see him skulking around here, I'll ask not to be held responsible for my actions.'

'Granted!' Adam said emphatically. 'But let's hope it won't come to that. He's been conspicuous by his absence over the last couple of days.'

We waved Khaled off home. Then Adam glanced at his watch and slung one arm around my shoulders. 'Just time to put a call through to Ted and bring him up to speed before supper I should think.'

We wandered through to the lounge-bar and punched out the number. But there was no answer so Adam picked up his iPad from the coffee table. 'I'll ping him a quick message to let him know we called and we're about for the evening if he's able to call back. Oh! Hang that. He's beaten me to it. There's an email from him sitting here in my Inbox.'

'What does he say?' I leaned across him to see the screen.

Adam grinned, lifting it teasingly away from me. 'D'you know what? This feels quite like old times, Merry. Getting emails from Ted translating ancient documents...' And he started to read aloud.

"Dear Merry and Adam – there was one thing I wanted to tell you before we had to cut our call short yesterday. As I was unable to do so, I've decided to set it as a little challenge for you. I know how much you both enjoy a puzzle. So, work this one out ...

Take a look at Meryre's titles and tell me what you think his relationship was to Akhenaten. It's been staring

Egyptologists in the face for years. But nobody has ever seen it. I know I didn't. But these letters... Well, let me constrain myself to saying this: these letters explain a lot of things that were previously unclear. I am privileged indeed to have the task of translating them. Let me know when you think you've cracked it. Yours, Ted x"

Adam and I gazed into each other's eyes for a long moment as he lowered the iPad onto his lap.

'You started to read us Meryre's titles from that website last night,' I said. 'I think I zoned out when you were only half way through. Can you load it up again?'

Adam was already swiping his way through various screens. 'Here!' he said. 'Ok, here goes; are you concentrating?'

I nodded.

'Right. "High Priest of the Aten", "Fan-bearer on the right-hand side of the King", "Royal Chancellor", "Hereditary Prince", "Sole Companion", "Friend of the Great King", "Sometime Prince", "High Noble'. Crikey! It's an impressive list by anyone's standards! So, tell me, Merry; is there anything in amongst that lot that makes your ears prick up or catches your eye?'

This time he allowed me to lean across him so I could read the list for myself. My gaze did indeed catch, and my senses started to fizz.

'Prince!' I gulped. 'The titles "Hereditary Prince" and "Sometime Prince".'

Adam stared back at me and his eyes seemed to deepen from blue to an intense violet. This was a certain way to tell he was excited. 'As I understand it, the term "hereditary prince" was a term sometimes used to denote a royal bloodline through the maternal side. If that's right, then these aren't just ceremonial titles. As Ted suggests, they denote a genuine familial relationship.'

'Through the maternal line? Adam, that would suggest Queen Tiye, Akhenaten's mother, had another son.'

He gazed at me. 'Which would mean what?'

I stared back. 'That Akhenaten had another brother. Oh my God, Adam! Meryre was Akhenaten's brother!'

He went very still. 'Well, thinking about it, Merry, it's always been said that Moses was a Prince of Egypt!'

Chapter 9

'Nabil Zaal is going to freak out when he hears about this!' I prophesied.

We'd just come off the telephone from Ted, who'd called us straight back when we texted to say we believed we'd solved his little test. Dan had served up a hearty meal of chicken and artichoke casserole into which he'd chopped a generous handful of fresh coriander. We were sitting around the table outside on deck, mopping up the juices with hunks of fluffy white bread, and trying to assimilate this latest revelation. The sun had set and the stars were beginning to pop in the sky.

'If Moses wasn't Akhenaten himself, as Nabil hoped, he certainly turned out to be the next best thing.' Adam said. 'You were wrong, Dan, when you said Meryre as Moses wasn't of the same blood as the Hebrew Patriarchs.'

'Another son born to Queen Tiye?' Walid questioned. 'But not fully royal? Not Amenhotep III's son?'

'Born the wrong side of the blanket, was he?' Dan said bluntly. 'A royal bastard.'

'Yes; by the sound of it,' I confirmed. 'But, unusually, it sounds as if it was the queen who strayed rather than the king.'

155

'Amenhotep had a reputation as a rampant ladies man, with a harem stuffed full of foreign princesses and concubines.' Walid said. 'Maybe Queen Tiye got sick of his womanising and decided to take comfort in the arms of another man.'

'That was potentially a very dangerous strategy for a Great Royal Wife,' Adam remarked. 'I mean; Amenhotep had already stuck his neck out by marrying her in the first place. Those marriage scarabs he issued suggest she wasn't exactly a popular choice. She had two black marks against her, being both a commoner and, worse, a Hebrew.'

'There's evidence to show Queen Tiye was an extremely powerful woman,' Walid said musingly. 'She's been described as something of a power behind the throne. Even to the extent of foreign dignitaries and ambassadors addressing diplomatic correspondence to her. Perhaps Amenhotep felt he had no choice but to look the other way if she indulged in a bit of extra-marital activity.'

I smiled at his turn of phrase; then turned serious again as an idea struck me. 'Or maybe he didn't know.'

'How do you mean?' Adam asked.

'Well, it occurs to me that it would certainly help explain the "Moses in the bulrushes" story – although it puts a slightly different slant on it.'

'I'm not sure I follow…?'

156

I could feel my excitement mounting as I thought it through. 'Well, let's just say Queen Tiye found herself pregnant knowing the child could not belong to her husband. I have no way of knowing how easy or difficult it would be for her to conceal a pregnancy...'

Walid interrupted me. 'There's evidence to suggest Queen Tiye spent a lot of time in the Delta region, at the frontier city of Zarw. Amenhotep built her a pleasure lake near there. Egyptologists have identified Zarw as Biblical Goshen, where the tribes of Jacob settled after their descent into Egypt. So, it would make a certain kind of sense for the Queen to spend time there, since that's where her family was situated. If Amenhotep was running the country from either Memphis or Thebes, there's every chance they could have spent several months apart.'

'Possibly enough time for her to conceal the latter months of a pregnancy,' Adam speculated.

'We know that Amenhotep and Tiye had daughters,' I continued, slotting pieces together as I spoke. 'At least three of them, in addition to their sons Thutmosis, who died young, Akhenaten, who became pharaoh, and Smenkhkare, who somehow escaped the historical record until he succeeded Akhenaten very briefly as pharaoh. I think it's possible to run a scenario whereby Queen Tiye concealed her pregnancy, gave birth among her relatives, the Hebrews living in Zarw...'

'And asked one of them to float the baby along the river towards the royal palace in a reed basket?' Dan snorted derisively. 'Come on, Pinkie; it's far-fetched even for you! Wasn't the river supposed to be teeming with crocodiles and hippos in ancient times? They'd have gobbled him up in no time!'

I glared at him. 'We're back to whether or not you choose to take the Biblical stories at face value. Seeing as you consider the Old Testament to be a work of fiction from start to finish, all I'm suggesting is it might be where the germ of the idea came from. I'm quite happy to accept there was some literary embellishment.'

'You're saying one of the princesses brought the baby back with some story about finding him in the bulrushes as a way of Queen Tiye being able to bring up her illegitimate son within the royal palace...' Adam concluded.

'I'm saying it's a possibility,' I nodded. 'Nothing more than that.'

Adam nodded, looking intrigued. 'It would certainly explain how Amenhotep might be persuaded to accept him and grant him the ceremonial titles "hereditary prince" and "sometime prince" even if he wasn't fully royal; although of course it's possible Akhenaten was the one to bestow those honours.'

'The Bible is quite clear in stating that Moses was brought up within the palace as a royal prince adopted by the pharaoh's daughter.' Walid nodded. 'Ted is convinced from the way Meryre is referred to in the letters he's translated so far that the High Priest was Akhenaten's brother. So it follows that Queen Tiye must have been his mother.'

'It also explains why Meryre was such a proponent of Atenism, as its High Priest,' Adam commented. 'Tiye instilled the beliefs of her Hebrew ancestors in all her children, perhaps in Moses/Meryre most of all.'

I nodded. 'For all we know, he had a Hebrew father and was therefore fully descended from the Patriarchs. The Bible tells us Moses was Hebrew.'

Adam collected up our plates. 'Well, I'm certainly starting to see how some of the pieces might begin to fit together. You're right, Merry; Nabil Zaal will have a field day when all of this comes to light.'

* * *

I was quite glad of the opportunity for some quiet time at home the following day. After all the excitement and activity of recent weeks, a bit of a break was more than welcome. The replacement deck furniture and cushions were due to be delivered at some point during the morning. It would give me the chance to help Khaled put the finishing touches to the repair work. And, all in all, I felt the opportunity to rest was probably much needed and long overdue.

Walid arranged another early appointment for himself at the Luxor Museum. Ibrahim Mohassib had promised to have his best people working through the night performing the laboratory tests necessary to authenticate the three scrolls. Walid was eager to check on progress and keep everything moving along apace. He'd suggested Habiba might like to accompany him. He wanted to ensure her involvement throughout since we'd had the good fortune to have her unexpectedly drop into our laps as a wholly independent set of ears and eyes. Better still, as a voice that could speak directly to the head honchos in the Antiquities Service. He'd arranged to pick her up en route and departed after downing only a bowl of cereal and a cup of coffee for breakfast.

So, all in all, a quiet day beckoned on board the *Queen Ahmes*. 'Dan, you know, you really don't need to stick around today if you don't want to. There's not much for you to do. If you'd prefer a day by the pool of one of the local hotels, we really won't mind. And I'm sure they'd be absolutely delighted to have you as it's so quiet. Why don't you let me call the Guest Relations Manager at the Jolie Ville and let her know you're coming?'

Actually, I thought it might be a relief to have a bit of respite from him too. His company could be abrasive; a bit like having a human brillo pad on board, which chafed and scratched each time you brushed against it.

160

'And what if that Gamal Abdel-Maqsoud character should show up again?'

'We'll keep the gangplank raised, the door locked and our wits about us,' I promised.

'Hmm, well I think I'd be happier if you could float out to the middle of the Nile and drop anchor there.'

I smiled sweetly. 'That also can be arranged.'

So, he packed a holdall with his swimming stuff, some suntan lotion and a spy novel he'd brought with him, and was persuaded to leave us.

Adam put his arms around me, 'If it weren't for Khaled, it would be quite like old times, Merry. I'm struggling to remember the last time we had the dahabeeyah to ourselves.'

I hugged him back. 'But, look on the bright side, darling. Once he's all finished today, there's nothing holding us here in Luxor. We can head on up to Amarna to join Ted. Personally, I can't wait! I want to see those letters we found for myself!'

The new deck furniture was perfect. I'd ordered a selection of traditional Victorian-style steamer chairs and more upright recliners, all in teak, which looked fabulous with the newly varnished decking and polished brass railings. New rugs and brocade cushions completed the look of an outdoor space, under its wide canvas awning (thankfully spared by the fire) that was a throwback to the heyday of Victoriana and luxury Nile cruising for wealthy turn-of-the-twentieth-century travellers. The whole idea of our fledgling business enterprise was to offer up-market sailing trips along the Nile for discerning travellers. Our target market was people drawn to Egypt by the lure of nostalgia for this bygone age, as well as the chance to view the treasures of antiquity in the fabled land of the pharaohs.

But as I adjusted the braiding on the scatter cushions and stood back to admire my handiwork, I wondered if Adam and I were living in cloud cuckoo land. Our website had been up and running for months. I'd sent the glossy leaflet I'd designed to all the major travel agents back at home in an attempt to get a listing in their holiday brochures. But so far we'd had not a sniff of a booking. Not even a request for more information or a visit from anyone in the travel industry to check us out. The only people who'd stayed onboard as fee-paying guests had been Ben Hunter back in the spring, and Nabil Zaal.

And now the British Foreign and Commonwealth Office had slapped a ban on non-essential travel to this part of Egypt. The only region to have escaped this tourist embargo was the Red Sea holiday resort zone around Sharm el Sheik and Hurghada. The News still reported daily clashes in Cairo between the Military and supporters of the toppled president, who were fighting for his reinstatement.

I let out a long sigh. With things as they stood, it was hard to imagine a time when my beautiful new deck furniture would ever be used by anyone outside of Adam, myself and our friends. Realistically, I didn't know how much longer we could hold out. Our savings wouldn't last forever, and the income I received from my rented-out flat back at home wasn't enough to live on, as it had to cover the mortgage. We were only able to afford to pay Khaled for the repair work because Nabil Zaal paid us such a generous fee for his recent trip.

I lifted my gaze and let it drift first along one bank of the Nile, then the other. I had a great view of both from this position anchored in the middle of the mighty river. The east bank was lined with modern tourist hotels, all deserted. In the distance I could see the smudge of Luxor city in the heat haze. I could make out row after row of cruise boats moored up and chained together in banks sometimes up to fifteen deep. On the west bank, I had a more rural view of children splashing about in the shallows, donkeys and cattle on the banks and, in the distance, glowing bronze in the sunlight, the distinctive shape of the Theban hills rising above the flatlands, where the cultivated agricultural fields gave way to the desert. The temples and tombs would be standing emptily bereft of visitors today.

Reluctant though I was to accept it, Dan, and even Adam, had it about right. The writing was on the wall. Standing with the hot sunshine scorching through my cotton top, I knew the time was fast approaching when we'd have no choice but to read it.

Adam and I were going to have to leave this country we loved, admit defeat or, at the very least bad timing, and go home. A trip to Amarna might delay things by a few days. But it couldn't prevent something that was looking increasingly, distressingly, inevitable.

It was a bitter pill to swallow.

I heard Adam's mobile phone ring as I was coming back inside to prepare lunch. He'd left it on the coffee table in the lounge-bar. Adam was in the engine room with Khaled. I could hear the murmur of their voices. Khaled had arrived early this morning to complete his last few jobs before the heat became too aggressive to work in comfortably. Adam had come below deck to give him his last payment, then steer us back to the riverbank so Khaled could hop off the dahabeeyah and make his way home for a well-earned siesta. I was looking forward to a lazy afternoon with Adam floating in the middle of the Nile. He was right when he said we'd had almost no time alone together. Walid and Dan wouldn't be back for a while yet. The afternoon was rich with romantic possibility, and I was determined to make the most of it.

I hesitated before picking up his phone. But in the end I pressed the button to accept the call and pressed it to my ear.

'Hello?'

'Merry, is that you? Oh, thank goodness!'

'Walid? Why are you whispering?'

'Is Adam with you?'

'Yes, of course. Is everything alright?'

'No. A man has muscled his way into the laboratory at the Museum. He's holding Habiba at knifepoint and demanding that Ibrahim Mohassib hands over...'

The line broke up. 'Walid? Are you hurt?'

'No. I just slipped out to use the toilet. The break-in happened while I was out of the room. There are others...'

The line crackled again.

'Walid, where are you now?'

'I've locked myself back in the toilet. But I can't see what's happening.' His voice gave way in a frightened choke.

'Ok, just sit tight and don't move. I'm going to call Ahmed and get the police over there right now. Adam and I won't be far behind. Please don't try anything reckless. We're on our way.'

Darting a glance through the window, I could see we were already easing up against the riverbank ready to dock. Khaled leapt off the dahabeeyah and secured one of the long ropes around the docking posts on the causeway.

'Oh, thank God,' I breathed. 'Adam!' I was already scrolling to find Ahmed's number on Adam's phone. I ran through to the engine room as I made the call. Adam looked up from the instrument panel in surprise as I hurtled into the small space. And Ahmed answered the call almost immediately, so I was able to gabble out Walid's message to them both at once.

'It must be Gamal Abdel-Maqsoud,' Adam said in alarm.

'Walid said there are others… Maybe a gang…!'

'He's sure to have friends,' Adam said darkly.

'I am on my way,' Ahmed's deep voice resonated in my ear.

'Ahmed, for God's sake take back-up.'

By the time we got there on our scooters it was all over of course. Ahmed and his team had successfully stormed the building and brought the situation under control.

Ahmed had thrown himself bodily against the man holding Habiba at knifepoint. Ahmed is a big bloke so this was a reasonably safe bet, and he'd succeeded in sending the fellow sprawling. But not without earning himself a long gash in his upper arm in the process. Thankfully, the knife hadn't penetrated deeply into his flesh. Nevertheless he'd shed copious amounts of blood.

His colleagues had carted Habiba's assailant and his two accomplices off to the police station, leaving Ahmed behind to be patched up. Habiba was bending over him securing the knot on a bandage she'd retrieved from the Museum's First Aid box and wound around his arm. She was making small, wordless sounds of comfort, while Ahmed sat bolt upright as still and stiff as a statue. He looked completely uncomfortable at being ministered to like this. But there was an odd little gleam in his eye I found telling. I felt quite sure secretly he loved all the attention.

We rescued Walid from the toilet cubicle and gathered in the laboratory to conduct a post mortem on what had happened. A cleaning lady swathed from head to toe in Egyptian robes had already worked around us with a mop and big metal bucket, cleaning up Ahmed's spilled blood from the floor. The papyrus scrolls were thankfully still secured untouched between their glass plates, and the crisis had been averted. Even so, I wished we'd offered to accompany Walid today. I'm not sure we could have prevented what happened. But I was as frustrated as hell not to have been where the action was taking place. A quiet day on board the *Queen Ahmes* was all very well, but not when our friends were in danger. We were stupid to think the dahabeeyah was the only target for our enemy.

'Was it Gamal Abdel-Maqsoud?' I demanded.

Walid shrugged. 'I have never met him, so could not identify him even if it were he. In actual fact, I did not stick around long enough to see if I recognised anyone. When I opened the door and realised what was happening, I quickly closed it again and hurried back to lock myself in the toilet and raise the alarm. I am just grateful I was not spotted.'

I turned my attention on our police pal. 'Ahmed? Was it him?'

'I could not say for sure. When I catched sight this man with his knife pointed against the throat of Hab... I mean, of Miss Garai, well I... I... That is to say, my vision...'

'You saw red,' Adam finished for him. 'And decided to hurl yourself at him, rather than simply unsling your gun and ask him politely to drop the knife.'

'But you do not understand... I could not take the risk...' he started energetically to defend himself.

'It's alright, my friend,' I smiled. 'I think we understand perfectly.'

'What Officer Abd el-Rassul did was very brave,' Habiba said staunchly. I smiled to myself. The perfection of my understanding was purer than they knew.

'So you didn't recognise him at all?' I persisted, still looking at Ahmed.

'You forget,' he said solemnly. 'Gamal Abdel-Maqsoud was only within the line of my sight on one occasion before today.'

'When he stole the dahabeeyah and we pursued him along the Nile in Cairo,' Adam recalled. 'You started to swim out to ambush him as soon as we caught him up. And then when he set fire to the deck, you were so busy trying to flatten him, you probably didn't stop to get a good look at him.'

Adam was making fun of him very gently and Ahmed knew it. Full of wounded pride, he pulled himself even straighter, tilted his head back and looked at us imperiously down the length of his nose. 'On this occasion, to flatten him, it is exactly what I did.'

'And very successfully, too,' Habiba backed him up. 'Just before you slapped a pair of handcuffs onto him.'

Ahmed nodded with satisfaction. 'And now he is in police custody, and we can interview him in our leisure time.'

'At our leisure,' Adam corrected automatically. 'You're right, Ahmed. Good job. We'll know soon enough if he's our man. Merry and I can come along to the police station and identify him. Police custody is just about the best place for him right now. It gives us some breathing space without having to keep looking over our shoulders.'

Now she was recovering from her shock, and had patched up Ahmed's arm and defended his bravery, Habiba was starting to take notice of what we were actually saying. 'Are you suggesting that you might actually know the people who broke in here? Or one of them at least?'

I realised I'd thoughtlessly blurted out the name Gamal Abdel-Maqsoud without stopping to think. It was too late to call it back. Adam and I exchanged a glance of dismay. We had no choice now but to offer up some sort of explanation. To be fair; she probably deserved one. He could have killed her with that knife.

I let out a sigh while my mind raced trying to think up a story that would satisfy her. There was no way we could tell her the truth: that he'd ambushed us while we were in Akhenaten's secret tomb, and was now dogging our footsteps trying to find a way back inside.

'I'm sorry to say we were responsible for the young man losing his job,' Adam stepped in smoothly. 'It was quite a good job with the Ministry for the Preservation of Ancient Monuments in Luxor. I daresay he bears a grudge and wants to even the score. That's no doubt why he took it into his head to set our dahabeeyah alight. I don't think we exactly endeared ourselves to the young man.'

'You made a complaint against him?'

Adam sidestepped a direct answer. 'Let's just say we found him somewhere he wasn't supposed to be, and made life a bit difficult for him.'

I toyed with the idea of telling her about his attempt to rob us on the *Queen Ahmes* the other day, but decided it begged too many questions. So I restrained myself. 'We think he may have been following us around. It's possible he saw us inspecting the Valley of the Kings yesterday. If he watched us go into KV20 empty-handed and emerge a little while later with that suitcase, it may have aroused his suspicions.'

'And then if he observed us bring the same suitcase here yesterday...' Habiba finished for me. She was a bright girl, and it didn't take her long to cotton on.

'Exactly,' I nodded. 'So, I think we need to know precisely what happened here today.'

I'd addressed myself to Ibrahim Mohassib, wanting to take the focus of the conversation away from Habiba before she could ask more questions about our association with Gamal Abdel-Maqsoud. But the museum curator folded his hands together, looking uncomfortable. Whether this was because the conversation was taking place in English or because he felt responsible for not preventing the breach in security that had allowed armed men to break in to the off-limits parts of the Museum was anyone's guess. Anyway, he pressed his lips together in much the same way as his hands, so Habiba was given no choice but to tell the story.

'The first we knew was when the door flew open and three men rushed in wielding knives. The first man grabbed me and held his knife against my throat, as you know. The second man stood just inside the door with his knife at the ready, should anyone attempt to enter from the corridor. Luckily the toilets are through that door over there,' she pointed towards the back of the room. 'So he did not see Dr Massri when he attempted to re-join us. And the third man threatened Mr Mohassib, and said his friend would kill me if Mr Mohassib didn't do as he said.'

'But how did they get in? We had to go through a security check posted with guards when we were here yesterday,' Adam frowned.

Ibrahim Mohassib untwisted his hands and decided to contribute to the conversation at last. 'There is a back entrance. My staff step outside sometimes to smoke their cigarettes.'

'And you think these three thugs jumped one of your people while they were taking a quick break?'

Mr Mohassib looked a bit sick. 'When the police arrived, they found my laboratory assistant lying on the floor outside in a pool of blood. He was stabbed in the stomach. He has now been taken to the hospital to receive treatment. Thankfully, the wound does not appear to be life-threatening.'

Habiba looked at the wet floor where Ahmed's spilled blood had been washed away. 'You see, this is exactly why I am here in Luxor. Security is woefully lapse. With their income gone as the tourist industry collapses, people grow desperate.'

Grateful to have this oblique confirmation that she accepted our story about Gamal Abdel-Maqsoud losing his job, I asked, 'Won't the government – I mean the military – step in to offer any help?'

Habiba levelled her gaze on me. 'We don't have a welfare state in the way I think you are used to in the UK. Our government provides subsidies on low-cost staples such as

172

bread and fuel, but with our exploding population and sinking economy, it is not enough to reach everybody. Even this scanty provision is uncertain after the political unrest of recent weeks. For now, people must fend for themselves. So we must do everything in our power to protect our nation's precious heritage while our people go hungry.'

I was left unclear whether her concern was more for the people or the heritage. I gave her the benefit of the doubt by concluding it was both. But then she seemed to swing towards the latter, turning to Ahmed and saying,

'Officer Abd el-Rassul, you see now why we must demand that the police patrols on our museums and historical sites are doubled. I did not realise our treasures were also at risk as a result of your – er – friends here, making enemies of some of the local people...'

'...*One* of the local people,' I corrected.

'So I can only be thankful that your swift action has placed this person...' she glanced at me, '... *and his associates* behind bars.'

That told me, I thought. But as it also put Habiba and Ahmed more fully on the same side even than before, I decided a dignified silence was my best response.

After a pause, I concluded we'd strayed away from the point long enough, and said so. 'But I'm not clear what Gamal Abdel-Maqsoud and his merry men, always assuming that's who they were, hoped to achieve by breaking in here today. What were they after?'

'While one of them held his knife against my throat, the other one threatened Mr Mohassib and demanded to be given the gold.' Habiba said.

'The gold?' I questioned. 'Not the papyrus?'

'What gold?' Adam asked.

Habiba frowned. 'I got the impression it was any gold. Just something portable and valuable that they could take away to sell.'

'So, what on earth have we been wasting our breath arguing back and forth about for the last ten minutes?' I demanded. 'If this was just an opportunistic would-be robbery by a bunch of local amateur crooks, why have we been frightening ourselves silly with images of Gamal Abdel-Maqsoud walking off with the papyrus?'

There was a pregnant pause. Finally, it was Adam who said, very quietly, 'Merry, my love; I think it might have been *you* who put the idea in our heads that he might be the villain of the piece.' Then he no doubt saw the look I gave him, and corrected himself. 'You and *me*, that is. We both thought it.'

I'm sorry to say this little flash of insight went from bad to worse when Adam and I accompanied Ahmed back to the police station. We found three perfect strangers staring back at us from behind the bars of their cells.

174

Chapter 10

Dan was unimpressed we'd left the dahabeeyah unguarded at the riverbank and wasted no time in saying so. 'I suppose the only saving grace,' he huffed, 'is that since I found it impossible to find a way onboard, I daresay your chum Gamal would have found it bloody difficult, too. What the hell do you think you were playing at, disappearing off like that without a by your leave, or a telephone call, or a note pinned to the door, or anything?'

It was quickly told and the called-for apologies readily made. 'But, it leaves me wondering what Gamal Abdel-Maqsoud is up to,' I said worriedly. 'There's been no sign of him at all since he came onboard the other day and attempted to asphyxiate Adam.'

'Perhaps he was behind the break in at the Museum today,' Walid suggested, 'even if he didn't carry it out himself. Maybe he feared he would be recognised.'

'You're saying he put a bunch of his buddies up to it?' Adam questioned. 'Then I don't think much of the company he keeps. I'm not sure I could persuade any of my friends to go and hold up the staff at a museum at knifepoint.'

'Maybe he's promised them riches beyond their wildest dreams,' I mused. 'You heard what Habiba said about people living on the bread line. He's seen the gleam of gold inside the tomb. He knows all he has to do is get hold of the Aten discs to open the hidden doorway and find his way back inside.'

'Then I don't understand why those thugs didn't use their threats against Habiba's life today to get to us and demand we open the safe. Better still, why not storm us here onboard the dahabeeyah, stick a knife to one of our throats and do the same? It doesn't make sense.'

'We've had the *Queen Ahmes* chained up and bolted like Fort Knox for the last couple of days. And we've all been on our guard. Maybe he knew he had to try a different tack to get to us.'

'But that's what I don't understand,' Adam frowned. 'He hasn't got to us. And those three unsavoury characters Ahmed has in the slammer deny all knowledge of a Gamal Abdel-Maqsoud.'

'They're hardly going to cough out a full confession within their first five minutes in custody,' I argued.

'Why not?' Adam asked reasonably. 'If Gamal Abdel-Maqsoud put them up to it, I'd have thought they'd want to divert police attention onto him at the first opportunity.'

'But we don't know what he may have threatened them with ...'

'A moment ago you said he'd enticed them with the gleam of gold,' Adam pointed out.

'Maybe they think it's all too fantastical now they've been caught, and think their best chance lies in keeping schtum. Perhaps they hope the police will let them kick their heels for a few days then let them go.'

'Not much chance of that, I should think,' Walid interjected. 'They may not actually have stolen anything, but they stabbed that lab technician and left him bleeding in the doorway.'

I nodded my agreement. 'And with the Ministry of State for Antiquities breathing down the police's necks, I should think Commander el-Saiyyid will be more determined than ever to keep them off the streets. You heard what Habiba said. This is exactly the sort of security breach they've all been so het up about.'

'If you ask me,' Dan said, even though we hadn't, 'you lot need to concentrate on keeping your own noses clean. From what you've told me, you've already let the cat out of the bag to this Habiba. You want to watch that she doesn't start putting two-and-two together. The last thing you want is for her to invite her superiors down here to interview you. I should think that might prove rather uncomfortable, to say the least. I doubt Egyptians uphold the nice friendly interrogation techniques we've all come to expect back home, with lawyers present and that sort of thing.'

I bit my lip, knowing he was right, and that I was the guilty one who'd almost given the game away. 'I was stupid to blurt out Gamal's name in front of her,' I admitted. 'I was just so sure it had to be him.'

Adam came to my defence. 'We all thought it,' he said. 'Personally, I still think it. I sure as hell didn't imagine that hand clamping a rag soaked in chloroform over my face. I'm just wondering if he's a bit more intelligent than we've given him credit for, and is playing a rather clever game of cat-and-mouse with us.'

'Well then, it strikes me you need to stop skulking nervously about jumping at your own shadows, and go on the offensive,' Dan said bluntly.

'What do you mean?' I stared at him.

'I mean you need to get to him before he gets to you.'

'We need to find him,' Walid nodded.

Adam's gaze slowly came to meet mine. 'How difficult can it be?' he asked.

We made a plan of sorts and took a break from the conversation while Adam and I prepared a couscous salad served with pan-seared salmon fillets for supper. We ate up on deck under the stars as was becoming our habit. Everybody admired Khaled's repairs and complimented me on my choice of replacement deck furniture as we enjoyed our food and Adam, Dan and I shared a rather pleasant bottle of Egyptian white wine. It was fresh and fragrant, and very palatable. I felt the cares of the day start to ease away as the dusk softened to darkness around us. Walid drank iced tea in deference to his religion.

'I'm pleased to say one good thing came out of our visit to the museum today,' Walid remarked, wiping the corners of his mouth with his napkin and sitting back.

'Yes?'

'Mr Ibrahim Mohassib has confirmed the authenticity of the scrolls. They are genuine Pharaonic documents, without any shadow of a doubt.'

'Yes, well, we already knew that,' Dan said a bit dampeningly. 'We've all seen the proof in that improbable tomb.'

Walid chose not to be baited. 'And now the stage is set for others to discover for themselves what you call *that improbable tomb*. Mr Mohassib has asked for a philologist to be sent from Cairo to translate the large scroll. His team locally is not skilled enough in hieratic script to take on such an immense task and guarantee accuracy.'

'We were lucky to have Ted on hand,' I said. 'Even so, it was no simple task. He transcribed it passage-by-passage into his notebook. It took him several days.'

Walid sipped his tea. 'Time is a luxury we can ill afford. Not without knowing what Gamal Abdel-Maqsoud may have up his sleeve. For this reason, Habiba and I made a start on a loose translation of the scroll this morning. She is a bright young lady, that one. She has clearly made a study of the hieroglyphic language. Between us, we were making a rather decent fist of it until those thugs broke in and brought everything to a standstill.'

'Perhaps that's it!' I interrupted. Everyone's gazes swung towards me enquiringly. 'Perhaps Gamal suspects us of exactly what we are doing: staging the discovery of the tomb! Maybe his objective today was simply to slow things down to buy himself a bit more time.'

Dan arched his eyebrows. 'So, now you'd have us believe the man is telepathic?'

But Adam wasn't quite so quick to dismiss my conjecture. 'What's the one thing those men did achieve today? They got inside the laboratory. They were able to see for themselves that you were studying papyri. Perhaps that's all Gamal wanted to know.'

'So why the demand for gold?' Dan sneered.

'Perhaps that was just to throw us off the scent.'

I frowned, seeing the gaping holes in my own theory. 'But they're not in any position now to get the information back to him.'

Adam looked at me. 'I daresay they may be allowed visitors – maybe their wives or girlfriends, who could carry a message.'

'If the objective was to slow things down,' Walid said, 'they certainly achieved it. But I'm pleased to say the morning was not a complete write-off. Ibrahim Mohassib had already translated that line of text on the architect's drawing of Hatshepsut's temple.'

'*Aten is key*,' I murmured. It was branded on my memory.

'That's right. And Mr Mohassib is a good enough Egyptologist to ask why Aten would be key in a temple dedicated so ostentatiously to the rival god Amun.'

'The fact of Akhenaten's Hymn to the Aten being discovered inside the same papyri cache is another big clue,' Adam added.

Walid nodded. 'Mr Mohassib is scratching his head about why three such different scrolls should all be bricked up together, and apparently during the first half of the last century, given the style of the suitcase they were found inside.'

'We need him to believe they are linked,' I said with quick concern. 'Not just a random assortment that some early twentieth century collector happened to hide away together.'

Walid smiled at me. 'Then you will be relieved to hear that he is already speculating that the scrolls came from a royal tomb during the years the Valley was being excavated by either Theodore Davis or Howard Carter. Luckily for us, his theory seems to be that an archaeologist or site workman employed by one or other of these famous excavators stole the papyri and bricked it up, planning to return for it at some later date which, for some reason or other, he was prevented from doing.'

'Phew,' Adam said. 'That takes the heat off us a bit.'

'All the time we keep quiet, they'll be forced to find an explanation that fits the evidence,' Dan said. 'And it seems to me the one Mr Mohassib has dreamed up is preferable – and certainly more plausible – than the reality. Our silence has served us well.'

'And, more importantly, kept Howard Carter's reputation intact,' I said with feeling.

Walid smiled at me and brushed his wispy hair across his balding scalp in the sudden breeze. 'We'd already established the link to Ay and Tutankhamun through the cartouche and titles Habiba recognised yesterday. Today, with my prompting, we were able to take things a little further.

'Did you get to the part about the *'precious jewels'*?' I asked excitedly.

Walid's eyes gleamed back at me in the candlelight from the hurricane lamps Adam had lit across the deck. 'We did. If I remember rightly, the text says, *"that which was hidden by us remains hidden".*'

'There was definitely something in that early passage about *sacred shrines* and *golden images*,' Adam said.

'*Our precious jewels shall persevere throughout all eternity.*' Walid quoted. 'And I'm delighted to say Habiba has cottoned on that the scroll is referring to buried treasure.'

'But not a royal burial?' I probed. 'She hasn't made the leap that the *precious jewels* are actually Akhenaten and Nefertiti?'

'Give the girl a chance,' Dan said.

Walid shook his head. 'We have not progressed far enough yet with the translation. That's why we need the philologist from Cairo here quickly. We need a full translation of the scroll as soon as possible. In the meantime, I have proposed to Habiba that we should visit Hatshepsut's temple tomorrow. I am keen to help her find an answer to the question of why Aten should be key within Amun's temple.'

* * *

Walid's professional clout was such that we knew we would be granted access to the off-limits parts of Hatshepsut's temple with no questions asked. But we presented ourselves at the administration building next door to the ticket office anyway. This is where Gamal Abdel-Maqsoud worked after he was promoted to fill Mustafa Mushhawrar's shoes at the Ministry for the Preservation of Ancient Monuments here in Luxor. His tenure had been cut short thanks to his brief acquaintance with us. It was his own fault. He should never have tried to ambush us and muscle his way inside the tomb. My shoulder was still stiff where he'd kicked me. And Adam's bruises were yet to fully disappear.

Walid and Habiba presented their credentials to the new guy, a smartly attired young man whose name badge announced him as Nasser Saady. He addressed them respectfully and willingly handed over the key to the Hathor Chapel. (Strictly, this was unnecessary since we still had the copy key Adam had taken and had cut – but we wanted to keep up the pretence in front of Habiba). They went ahead of us to stand outside to await the hastily mobilised trolley bus that would transport us across the open desert plain to the temple forecourt. It was preferable to trekking across the rocky dust-bowl on foot in the savage mid-morning heat.

Ahmed hung back with Dan, Adam and myself. He was in uniform, and addressed a few curt questions to Nasser Saady in Arabic. I watched the young man shake his head with a rather bewildered expression.

'He doesn't know anything,' I concluded as we moved to join Walid and Habiba outside.

'He never even met Gamal Abdel-Maqsoud. He's only been in post for a couple of weeks. He was transferred from the ministry office at Karnak. All he has been told is that the previous post-holder was involved in an accident and has not returned.'

'Ah yes, we persuaded Gamal to phone his boss and say he'd fallen off his moped,' Adam explained for Dan's benefit.

'And they haven't checked up on him?' Dan said with raised eyebrows. 'Then I don't think much of their duty of care as employers.'

'They're possibly relieved to have one less person on the payroll,' I said. 'Afterall, they're not so much guards as pen pushers. If I've understood the job correctly it's about coordinating the teams of archaeologists and conservationists who apply to work at the monument sites. It's more administrative safeguarding than standing about with a rifle in hand. There are proper security guards for that.'

Adam nodded, 'And at this time of year it's low season for excavation due to the heat, and there are no visitors thanks to the political situation.'

'But there must be someone who knows where he lives,' Dan said. 'It's one thing for him not to have returned to work after his little encounter with you lot and the tomb. But surely he's been back home. He must have friends and relatives we could use to track him down.'

Ahmed pulled himself straight. 'Leave these matters with me. I will investigate.'

'I was rather afraid he'd say that,' Dan mumbled.

The symmetrical beauty of Hatshepsut's mortuary temple never fails to make me catch my breath with wonder. Set against the rugged Deir el Bahri cliffs, which rise steeply behind it, it has my vote as the finest example on earth of a manmade structure set in perfect harmony with its natural surroundings. But in the searing heat of mid-July I was less inclined than usual to stop and admire it.

The Hathor chapel is set on the left-hand edge of the first terrace as you look at the temple full on. This makes it the southernmost part of the structure; which faces the Nile. The river is not visible until one reaches the upper terrace. It's possible to discern it, with lots of squinting against the glare of the sun, off in the distance beyond the desert and narrow strip of cultivated land. Despite our ride out on the trolley bus, we were all fanning our faces and swigging thirstily from our water bottles by the time we crossed the southern portico and ducked eagerly into the sanctuary, out of the direct sunlight.

The Hathor chapel is an inner room set behind a pillared shrine also dedicated to the goddess of dance, fertility and jubilation. Each of the pillars, which provided welcome shade, is topped with a female-headed capital of the goddess who was the ancient guardian of the Deir el-Bahri area.

Walid pointed upwards. 'See; Hathor is represented as a cow, with bovine ears, topped with a crown.'

We all shielded our eyes and studied the architecture.

'Why a cow?' Dan asked.

'The association is one of fertility,' Walid explained. 'Hathor is often shown as the goddess of motherhood. She absorbed this role from another cow goddess 'Mehet-Weret', who was the mother of the sun god Re in a creation myth and carried him between her horns.'

Dan went quiet. I daresay he wished he hadn't asked. His interest in this stuff was paper-thin at the best of times. I think the only reason he'd come along with us today was to keep a watchful eye on us, and a weather eye out for Gamal Abdel-Maqsoud.

Walid was still pointing. 'See the central section of the crown...? It depicts a shrine with two rearing cobras surmounted by sun discs.'

'Sun discs, did you say?' Adam leapt into the conversation, suddenly animated.

'You mean, as in the Aten?' I added. This was the cue we had agreed on. It was time for us to start carefully following the script we'd prepared.

Habiba stepped forward. 'Hathor was usually depicted with the sun disc on her head set between her upraised horns.'

Bingo, I thought.

Walid hesitated. 'I think the sun disc in this instance is more likely to represent the sun-god Re.' Then he allowed excitement to sweep across his expression. 'Hang on a minute. Are you suggesting...?'

'That line of hieratic script on the architect's drawing of this temple reads *'Aten is key'*,' Habiba said breathlessly. 'Aten was always represented as a sun disc. But it makes no sense for Aten to be worshipped here. As we said yesterday, this temple was dedicated to Amun, Akhenaten's rival god. Akhenaten set out to destroy the cult of Amun, persecuting its priests and defacing its temples.'

'But look!' Adam said, matching her breathless tone to perfection, and pulling out his iPhone to take photographs. 'This place is plastered with images of the sun disc, for all that they're disguised between Hathor's horns.'

'There are even more inside,' Walid said, unlocking the stable door fitted into the back wall as he spoke.

We followed him into the dim interior of the shrine itself, carved into the rock behind the temple. The heat inside was oppressive as is so often the case with interior spaces in Egypt in high summer.

While Adam busied himself taking photographs, I tried to look as if this was somewhere I was unfamiliar with, pretending a sense of privilege in being invited to join Walid on this visit. I hope my gasps and expressions of awe sounded convincing. The truth was, of course, I was intimately acquainted with this place. Although, it's fair to say I was more used to seeing it in pitch darkness with just a torch beam for light, and with my heart hammering in my chest for fear of being discovered trespassing into this inner sanctum in the dead of night. With daylight streaming through the door we'd left open behind us the life-sized carvings of Hatshepsut worshipping before various deities etched into the walls didn't seem half so nerve-shredding.

Everywhere we looked, it seemed, there were wall reliefs showing the circular sun disc set between the upturned horns of Hathor, whether she was depicted in human or animal form. It was an effort to keep my gaze away from the deep gash in the wall beneath the most impressive carving of them all. This was the 'keyhole' into which the Aten disc fitted as a 'key'. Once pressed into the gash – which looked like a large slot on a gaming machine – it worked a secret mechanism fitted inside the wall. There was a hidden panel in the rock at just-above-knee-level, which shifted aside, revealing the entrance to the secret tomb carved into the cliff side.

Our proximity to Akhenaten and Nefertiti lying mummified on the other side of that wall, among their almost unimaginable riches, sent shivers down my spine and goose bumps pricking across my skin.

'*Aten is key... Aten is key...*' Habiba was repeating to herself, gazing around her at the various sun discs. She stood still and tilted her head to one side, deep in thought. 'We need to think clearly about what we have found,' she said. 'A papyri with Akhenaten's Hymn to the Aten transcribed on it. An architect's plan of this temple, with this chapel highlighted and a tantalising line of script that reads, "*Aten is key*"...'

'…And a lengthy scroll which mentions *"precious jewels"*, *"golden images"* and *"sacred shrines"*…' Adam put in. At a quick, suspicious look from Habiba, he explained himself hurriedly. 'Walid was kind enough to tell us about your stab at translating the first portion of the papyrus yesterday.'

'…All of which items we suspect to have originated in a royal tomb…' Walid added.

'I'm guessing at buried treasure,' Habiba breathed.

We all stared at her, silently willing her to make the next mental leap… to reach the conclusion we must be within touching distance of it. All the clues were pointing right here to where we were standing. She couldn't know yet that it was a tomb rather than a cache of golden objects. But we could forgive her that for now, while we waited for the papyrus scroll to be fully translated. What we needed was for her to realise, or guess at least, the significance of this place.

'You know what I think…?' she asked, softly serious. She looked very beautiful in the semi-light, with her brow furrowed in concentration, her eyes sparking with the idea her train of thought was leading her towards, and her shirt clinging damply to her body.

'What…?' Ahmed asked with a slight catch in his voice.

'I think… I think this might all be pointing us towards the Copper Scroll.'

You could have heard a penny drop in the shocked silence that greeted this assertion.

I flashed an urgent glance at Ahmed. It silently demanded: *have you let something slip?*

The look he darted back was absolute in its denial. I could almost hear him saying: *No Meredith; I swear that not a word has passed my lips.*

Adam and I also darted a lightning look into each other's eyes. This time it said: *She can't possibly know...can she...?*

'The... The Copper Scroll...?' I stammered.

She leaned one shoulder against the wall and crossed her feet at the ankle. It was a relaxed pose; not the stance one was likely to adopt if about to start levelling accusations. Even so, I felt my cheeks redden and my eyes slip sideways.

'You haven't heard if it?' she smiled. 'I'm not surprised. Few people have. It was discovered among the Dead Sea Scrolls in the caves in Qumran by the Dead Sea.'

'I may have read something somewhere,' I mumbled.

'I wrote my thesis about it,' she said conversationally. 'I've always found it fascinating. You see, it is unique among the Dead Sea Scrolls.'

Walid nodded. Like me, I daresay he could feel the conversation and our purpose in being here slipping away from us. But as a scholar himself, he could hardly plead ignorance of such a momentous discovery. 'Not only was it engraved unusually onto copper pieces but it was not a religious or literary text like the others. Still, I fail to see...?'

'No.' Habiba cut him off, eyes shining. 'Far from being a theological text, it is apparently a list of buried treasure! So, it strikes me…'

'Hang on,' Adam interrupted, making a desperate attempt to regain a hold on the conversation. 'Are we in danger of veering off onto all sorts of wild tangents here? A devout, secretive Jewish sect wrote the Dead Sea Scrolls at about the time of Christ. How on earth can they be relevant to the papyri we found bricked up in that wall, especially if they came originally from a royal Pharaonic tomb?'

Oh Bravo, I thought. He was proving himself Ted's protégé in more ways than one.

Habiba met each of our gazes in turn, looking as pleased as punch with herself. 'What you may not know, is that many of the characteristics of the Copper Scroll are actually Egyptian in origin. The use of Copper itself is extremely unusual. The only place in the Middle East where copper was used in antiquity, albeit rarely, was Egypt. There is clear evidence that engraving lists on copper was being practised as early as 1200 BCE, and relatively pure copper was available from the Bronze Age onwards, which coincides with the 18th Dynasty of the New Kingdom here in Egypt. Indeed, the weights and numbering system is typical of that in use in Egypt around 1300 BCE – the time of Akhenaten!'

We all fell silent.

'In my thesis I concluded the Copper Scroll must be a list of treasure that originated in Egypt and was somehow passed down through generations until it reached the care of the religious community living on the shores of the Dead Sea. Since then, other scholars have gone further. They claim a direct link between the Copper Scroll and the pharaoh Akhenaten. Don't you see what this means?'

We all gazed at her in silence, unwilling to follow where she seemed to be leading us.

She uncrossed her ankles and looked around at us in earnest. 'I think the papyri are pointing us towards the location of some buried treasure from antiquity, which may or may not have survived until today.'

I was more than willing to place a tick in that particular box, since her conjecture was entirely accurate.

Habiba waved her hand in an expansive gesture meant to incorporate the place we were standing. 'This chapel seems to be significant in some way. And yet we are told Aten is key. And we have the Hymn to the Aten, plus a document mentioning both Ay and Tutankhamun. So we're slap bang in the middle of the Amarna period. Don't you see...? It's all pointing towards Akhenaten!'

Well, I wasn't going to argue with that one, considering whose tomb we were standing within a stone's throw of.

'But...' Adam started.

She silenced him with a gesture. 'Wait! I think I've got it!'

We all stared at her in a breathless hush of trepidation.

'We know Akhenaten set out to destroy the cult of Amun. He defaced Amun's temples and threw his priests out on the street. There is no temple more lavishly dedicated to the worship of Amun than this one built by Hatshepsut. I think Akhenaten's henchmen came here and confiscated the temple treasures. I think they took them back to Akhet-Aten and put them in the royal treasury.'

I could feel the sense of defeat settling over us. The brighter and shinier Habiba's eyes became, the duller and more hooded did ours.

Habiba swept on, her excitement mounting. 'I'll bet the Copper Scroll is a list of where Amun's treasure was buried after Akhenaten's death. His priests would have wanted to bury the evidence before the Theban priesthood regained power and elevated Amun back to prominence. I think we'll find the large papyrus is a transcription written by Ay, as the last pharaoh of the Amarna period, telling us where to look!'

I'll say that for the girl; she had an alert brain and a vivid imagination. One or other might have been acceptable. The combination was devastating.

'So, what are you suggesting...?' I asked weakly.

'It's obvious, isn't it?' she demanded. 'We need to go to Amarna! Dr Massri, I think we need to ask permission to undertake our next security inspections in the remains of Akhenaten's holy city!'

Chapter 11

'My goodness! It's an intriguing hypotheses,' Ted said on the telephone. 'Who can say how Akhenaten amassed his treasure? All I can tell you is he had plenty of it!'

I raised my eyebrows. 'You think it's possible he gave orders for the treasures of the Amun temples to be collected up and stored in his treasury?'

'I couldn't rule it out.'

'Then no wonder the Amunite priests were so set on vengeance,' Adam remarked. 'Not only did Akhenaten's Hebrew beliefs challenge centuries of tradition, but he also closed their temples, stole their treasures, and deprived the priests themselves of their livelihoods. I imagine the sense of personal grievance ran deep. When he died they decided it was time to settle the score.'

'The death of Akhenaten proved a disaster for his followers,' Ted agreed. 'But they at least had a forewarning the Theban priesthood might try to regain the upper hand when General Horemheb led his army against the new Pharaoh, Akhenaten's brother Smenkhkare.'

'Smenkhkare ruled only briefly,' Adam said.

'That's right.' Ted confirmed. 'While he was on the throne, the priests and followers of Akhenaten's Hebrew-based theology were able to live on in an uneasy sort of limbo. But as soon as Horemheb crushed Smenkhkare they knew it was over and scattered. Luckily for them, they had the resources to make good their escape... and to bury some of the treasures of the Great Aten Temple and from the Treasury that they could not carry with them. Their plan – since Ay had been wily enough to marry off the young prince Tutankhamun to Akhenaten's third daughter and set him on the throne – was to sit things out while the boy king grew to maturity, and wait to see which way the religious wind was blowing once he was able to take full power.'

'They always hoped he would revert back to Atenism?'

'Yes, but sadly he died before having complete royal authority.'

'Horemheb again,' I muttered.

'Maybe, maybe not.' Ted said. 'We have no proof Tutankhamun was murdered.'

'Just circumstantial evidence and suspicious timing,' Adam said.

Ted continued. 'Ay, possibly in a last desperate bid to hold Horemheb off, mounted the throne himself. He could claim a relationship to the previous three pharaohs even though he was not of royal blood himself. He was uncle to Akhenaten and Smenkhkare and great-uncle to Tutankhamun. But he was an old man by now and couldn't keep the winds of change at bay for long.'

'And when he died after only four years on the throne, there was nothing stopping Horemheb from seizing power.' I deduced.

'Quite the reverse,' Adam agreed. 'His marriage to Ay's daughter legitimised his claim.'

'Horemheb had one other big advantage,' Ted said. 'He was fully Egyptian. He didn't have any royal blood in his veins but neither did he have any Hebrew blood. He was the first fully Egyptian Pharaoh since Amenhotep III contaminated the royal bloodline by marrying Tiye, Joseph's daughter.'

I let this sink in. 'You think that's why Horemheb was allowed to seize the throne without any apparent uprising?'

'That, and his military strength.' Ted said.

Adam nodded. 'And, with Horemheb as pharaoh, the Atenist priests in hiding knew their days were numbered.'

'Worse than that,' Ted said. 'This is when Horemheb's men started hunting them down proper. All the time an Amarnan pharaoh was on the throne, they were left in hiding in relative peace. But not any more.'

I felt the stillness come over Adam alongside me and watched the colour of his eyes deepen from blue to an intense violet. 'Ted, there's a strange note in your voice. Are you surmising all of this... or do you know it?'

'Oh, I know it.' Ted said a trifle airily. 'The letters Panehesy sent home to his Mistress of the House Nebt-Het have proved incredibly illuminating so far. The good lady had the intelligence to number the storage jars. So I have been able to translate them in sequence.'

'Then, please can we start from the beginning?' Adam appealed. 'You said Akhenaten's priests and followers scattered when Smenkhkare was murdered. Where did they go?'

I heard the smile in Ted's voice. I think he'd been waiting for this invitation to tell the story. 'Panehesy's letters tell us the priests fled, fearing the vengeance of the old Theban guard. Under cover of darkness, and heavily laden with the most portable Temple and Treasury treasures – gold, jewellery, lapis lazuli, malachite, fine spices and unguents, cloth – all they could carry, they stole away into the night. They took with them the knowledge of the locations where they had already buried the bulkier treasures. And, of course, they carried something they considered more precious by far: the theological beliefs of Akhenaten's new religion.'

'Where did they go?' I repeated Adam's question.

'Meryre, or Moses, as we should perhaps start calling him, fled north to Heliopolis with Panehesy and a small band of priests, among others.'

'Heliopolis was up near the Delta region, north of modern-day Cairo.' Adam said. 'Probably not a million miles away from the Hebrew stronghold in Goshen, or Zarw as the Egyptians called it.'

199

'That's right.' Ted affirmed. 'Heliopolis was a traditional centre for sun-associated worship. It's where the first Temple to Aten was built. As such, it was somewhere the priests could rely on as being sympathetic to refugees of Akhenaten's new religion.'

'Did all Akhenaten's followers from Akhet-Aten go with them?' I asked.

'No.' Ted replied. 'Meryre II, the chief treasurer and scribe, led a different group of followers loyal to the dead king south.'

'Was he the author of the clay tablets we found in Akhenaten's tomb?' I interrupted. 'The prototype Copper Scroll?' I was eager to test my theory.

'He was.' Ted confirmed. 'Reading the writing on the wall, Akhenaten's men spent the short years of Smenkhare's reign burying the heavy treasures while Meryre II kept a record of where they were hidden.'

'Which he was able to secrete inside Akhenaten's sarcophagus before its reburial by Tutankhamun,' I surmised.

'That's correct.'

'So, where did Meryre II and his band of followers go?' I asked.

'They travelled south to the Elephantine Island.'

'The island in the Nile in Aswan?' I queried.

'Yes. In ancient times it was a remote part of southern Egypt. Even today the island has the remains of monuments to Amenhotep III, Akhenaten's father, on it. There were priests there sympathetic to Aten worship.'

'So the two groups of Atenists sat out the reigns of Tutankhamun and Ay in Heliopolis and Elephantine Island,' Adam nodded. 'They lived in relative safety. And then Horemheb seized power and everything changed. Suddenly they feared for their lives.'

'That's right,' Ted agreed. 'Horemheb clearly knew where to look for them, and he wasted no time. Of course, the one he wanted was Meryre.'

'Because he knew Meryre was Akhenaten's half-brother, the "hereditary" and "sometime" Prince.' Adam concluded.

'Exactly. Meryre posed a huge threat. Horemheb knew he couldn't afford to leave him alive. And there's more. Among the group Meryre fled north with was the youngest daughter of Akhenaten and Nefertiti. Her name was Setepenre.'

I felt my eyes widen with surprise.

'And while they were in hiding among the priests of Heliopolis, Meryre took her as his wife.'

I watched the expression of Adam's face become speculative. 'Which made him even more dangerous to Horemheb,' he said. 'Any child of the union could stake a claim to the throne.

'Exactly. And so the hunt was on.' Ted concurred.

'Did Horemheb find them?'

'Well, put it this way; Panehesy's next letter home to Nebt-Het was brought to her from Sinai.'

'Sinai?' Adam and I repeated in unison.

'Horemheb's troops marched into Heliopolis, slaughtering those who'd shielded the refugees from Amarna as they went. Meryre and his men fought back, and Meryre killed an Egyptian soldier.'

'The Bible says Moses slew an Egyptian before fleeing to the Sinai,' Adam murmured.

'They knew they had to get out of Egypt.' Ted said. 'They became fugitives, and settled in a place we now know as Sarabit-el-Khadim in the Sinai Peninsular.'

'I remember Nabil Zaal mentioning a place with that name in the lecture he gave at the Egyptian Museum in Cairo last month,' I said.

'Archaeologists have unearthed evidence of a settlement, including symbols of Aten worship.' Ted affirmed. 'Meryre was there alright.'

'So that was the start of the years Moses spent in exile,' Adam said on a note of enlightenment.

'Yes, and I think we can surmise that back in Egypt the treatment of the Hebrews under Horemheb went from bad to worse. For possibly the first time in its already long history, Egypt saw real slavery. Horemheb sentenced those born of the twelve tribes of Jacob to harsh labour. They were deprived of the food and medical care previous pharaoh's had provided for their conscripted workers.'

'So, Horemheb was the Pharaoh of the Oppression.' I breathed.

'Yes, Merry; he was.'

'So, was he also the Pharaoh of the Exodus?'

'I will have to read on to find out.'

Adam looked up as Dan came into the lounge-bar, but didn't allow Dan's presence to distract him. 'Ted, have you told Barry all of this?'

'Not as yet,' Ted's voice echoed through the speakerphone. 'He knows it will take me some time to translate all of the scrolls. He's been kind enough to say he'll wait until I've finished. Then I can tell him if the scrolls offer up anything useful.'

My breathing nearly stalled. 'Anything useful! Only the facts of the most explosive story in history! I should think he'll have some kind of seizure when he hears all of this!'

We said our goodbyes to Ted and cut the call.

'It sounds as if you've had an illuminating conversation,' Dan remarked from the other side of the room, flipping the lid on a bottle of beer from the chiller as he spoke.

'You won't believe it!' I murmured.

'You can try me later,' he said. 'I really only came in to ask whether you're really willing to set sail for Amarna with the whole Gamal Abdel-Maqsoud situation unresolved.'

***

Ahmed arrived early and unexpectedly the following morning. 'I have news!'

I broke off from pouring coffee and stared at him as he barrelled into the kitchen.

'I have discovered Gamal Abdel-Maqsoud where he lives.'

While Ahmed's pronunciation was vastly improved, he still mangled his sentence structure. 'You've discovered Gamal himself or where he lives?' I sought to clarify.

'His home. But he is not there. His family have not seen him for several weeks. They believe he went to Cairo to see his friend Abdul Shehata and to join in the protests. They fear he met with some accident while there.'

I raised my eyebrows. 'That's one way of putting it.'

'But wait! There is more.'

I put down the coffee pot to give him my full attention.

'The chapel in Hatshepsut's Temple... Where the tomb it is located... Last night... This chapel, it was broken into...!'

'What?' I promptly forgot the half-poured coffee and gaped at him.

'The guards, they found the door hanging open this morning. Somebody, he had picked the locks! It must be him! It must be Gamal Abdel-Maqsoud!'

I was already heading outside and up the spiral staircase. 'Adam! Walid! You need to hear this!'

Ahmed loves nothing so much as telling a story. It took him longer to recount his news this second time around as he added embellishment throughout. 'The guards, they think it was looters trying to steal sections of the wall reliefs,' he finished. 'There is a section where there is damage. But perhaps something disturbed him. The wall reliefs, they are intact.'

'Allah be praised!' Walid exhaled.

Adam and I exchanged panicked glances. 'It must be Gamal. He must've been testing to see if there's a way to get the hidden mechanism to work without the Aten discs.'

'We need to go and take a look,' Walid declared.

A scant twenty minutes later we were there. Dan shared Adam's scooter and Walid shared mine. As before, we presented ourselves at the ministry administration building. Adam, Dan and I looked on as Walid exchanged a rapid-fire conversation with Arabic with Nasser Saady, the young official who'd taken Gamal Abdel-Maqsoud's place. This time he wasn't quite so accommodating nor nearly so deferential as before.

'He says he must accompany us,' Walid explained.

'Doesn't he speak English?'

'Not with any great accomplishment.'

'Then the Ministry must be lowering its standards,' I said. 'Both Mustafa and Gamal spoke perfect English.'

'I try.' Nasser Saady said, evidently wishing to be helpful. In truth, his two words were more helpful than he might imagine. They proved he could understand our language, even if he couldn't speak it. We would need to be circumspect.

'Watch what you say in front of him,' I whispered to Adam and Dan. 'The last thing we need is for a *third* member of the Ministry for the Preservation of Ancient Monuments to get wind of things.'

The stable door leading into the Hathor Chapel had been re-locked. Nasser Saady opened it with a small flourish and stood back so we could enter ahead of him. I was so jumpy I half expected him to slam the door behind us, locking us in. But he followed us inside readily enough.

It came as no surprise when he pointed out the damaged section of wall. Naturally, and as we'd feared, it was the most impressive relief showing Hatshepsut worshipping in front of Amun. Directly beneath it was the gash in the wall containing the hidden mechanism that worked the secret doorway leading to the tomb.

'Rather ambitious, even for looters,' I murmured, looking at the sheer size of the carved section.

'Walid, can you distract his attention for a bit?' Adam said softly. 'We need to check out the gash.'

To be fair to Walid, he made a game attempt. But Nasser was watchful and alert. I don't think he was suspicious of us. But there'd been a serious breach in security at the temple he now held some responsibility for. I daresay he was watching our every move so closely because he didn't want us to find anything that might reflect badly on himself, considering how recently he'd taken up his new post.

In the end it fell to Dan to feign heatstroke. He collapsed in impressively melodramatic fashion. His loud groan was finished off to perfection with a profound silence.

'Water!' I cried urgently. 'Pour some water on him and make him drink!' I made a big show of fanning him with my battered straw hat. 'Nasser! Please can you help me get him outside? He needs air! It's suffocating in here!'

Poor Nasser Saady could hardly ignore a direct appeal from a damsel in distress, an English one to boot. How much he understood of what I actually said, I couldn't be sure. But I made sure my gestures were wildly expressive and my voice pitched at just the right note of panic. My performance was eloquent enough and got him moving. Between us, Walid, Nasser and I heaved Dan (a conveniently dead weight) outside, setting him in the shade of one of the Hathor-headed columns. It was enough to give Adam a few precious moments alone.

He didn't push his luck and was quick to join us outside, rather over-doing his solicitude for my ex-boyfriend. 'Is he ok? Should we take him to hospital?'

Dan revived remarkably quickly at the mention of hospital. He sat up and groaned. 'God damn this inferno of a country!'

'We need to get him to some air conditioning,' I appealed.

Between us, we helped Dan to the forecourt where the trolley bus was waiting.

Once we were back at base, Nasser took charge manfully for one so young. 'Taxi?' he said.

I gathered from this suggestion he felt Dan would not be capable of travel by more direct means.

'He'll be fine,' I reassured him. 'He just needs a few moments here in the cool.'

Adam pulled me aside while Nasser and Walid continued to fuss over Dan. 'There are definite signs of someone trying to force something into that gash in the wall. The plaster is scratched and scraped.'

I looked at him in alarm. 'Gamal is no idiot. He's seen our Aten discs. Maybe he hit on the same idea you did and tried to fashion a disc of his own.'

Adam met my gaze. 'The same thing occurred to me.'

We stared at each other in a tense, anxious silence.

'You're thinking the same thing I am, aren't you?' I said at length.

'He might have been successful,' Adam said. 'He might be inside.'

'There's only one thing for it,' I said to Walid when Dan was sufficiently "recovered" to think about making a move. 'One of us will have to stay here to keep watch.'

'But there's no guarantee he hasn't been inside and already made good his escape,' Dan argued.

'The guards found the door standing open at first light,' I said. 'You're right, of course. But we have to be sure. Adam has volunteered to hole up somewhere he can keep an eye on the chapel – the ruined temple of Montuhotep next door is a pretty good vantage point. If Gamal Abdel-Maqsoud is still inside the tomb and tries to leave, Adam will spot him.'

We thanked Nasser Saady for his assistance, assured him we did not hold him in any way responsible for the break-in, and made a bit of a show of leaving. As soon as we reached the open road beyond the car park, Adam hopped off his scooter and Dan slid forward to take the handlebars. We watched Adam double back on himself on foot then veer off to the left, ducking behind an outcrop of bleached rock so he could skirt the temple perimeter and take up position without being seen. I hoped he would be able to find a nice shady spot from which to keep his vigil. The sunshine was blistering, the heat a physical force pressing in on all sides making it difficult to breathe.

Dan, Walid and I made our way back to the dahabeeyah, where all we could do was wait.

'Walid, why don't you head over to the Museum,' I suggested. His incessant pacing was stretching my nerves to breaking point. 'You can check the philologist from Cairo has arrived and see how he's getting on translating the large scroll. No doubt Habiba will be keen to accompany you.'

'She will want to know when we can leave for Amarna,' he frowned, anxiously twisting his hands together as he always did when worried. 'But, how can we leave with this hanging over us...?'

'If Gamal Abdel-Maqsoud has made a replica Aten disc and managed to get inside the tomb then he'll have to leave again at some stage.' I pointed out sensibly. 'The number of guards patrolling the temple has been doubled. Security has never been tighter. If he's there and he attempts to break free, they'll capture him. And if they don't nab him, Adam will. Please Walid, try not to worry. If he's inside the tomb then he's cornered. We'll catch him for sure.'

'This is exactly what I have feared all along.' Walid's voice was plaintive and he was wringing his hands even tighter. It was clear he was in no mood to be reassured. 'I should never have delayed announcing the tomb. He will rob it or he will blow the whistle on it. Either way, it will be my fault. What if he has already made good his escape and carried off some of the treasures? The tomb I have sought to protect I have instead exposed to the worst sort of villainy. I am not worthy of the position I hold. I should resign immediately.'

'Walid, now you've got to stop being so defeatist.' I said firmly. 'Everything you've done has been for the very best of reasons, and we will all testify to that effect, should it ever prove necessary. For all we know, Gamal attempted to get into the tomb last night and failed. We've never left scrapes and scratches on the wall whenever we've used the replica Aten discs Adam created. I'll bet Gamal got the size and weight wrong. He's probably gone away to have another go at getting the scale right. And if he makes a second attempt to break in, he'll be caught.'

'Then where is he?' Walid moaned. 'Why can't we find him?'

'We've barely started looking,' I reminded him. 'We know he hasn't been home, and we know he hasn't attempted to report for work – which, let's face it; might have been his best bet if what he wanted was a chance to study the Hathor Chapel. Ahmed is working on it. If he's holed up somewhere, Ahmed will find him.'

In truth, I needed to hear myself say all these things out loud so I could start trying to believe them. Gamal's attempt (successful or not) to break into the tomb had me seriously rattled. If he'd truly stolen the march on us before we could stage the tomb's discovery then Walid wasn't the only one in trouble. Even if he wanted to, I didn't see how he'd be able to keep Adam and me out of it when the difficult questions started to be asked.

Our best bet might be to plead ignorance altogether. But if Gamal Abdel-Maqsoud started pointing fingers and mud slinging we didn't stand a chance. Our only hope might be to make a completely clean breast of things and throw ourselves on the mercy of the authorities.

Dan's prophesies about it all ending in disaster were starting to look uncomfortably accurate. He'd been predicting they'd toss me into an Egyptian jail and throw away the key right from the start.

As the afternoon wore on, I decided I really couldn't take any more of Dan's *I-told-you-so* silence and Walid's pacing of the deck. At this rate he'd undo all Khaled's good work and wear away the fresh varnish.

We'd agreed it was a bad idea for him to go to the Museum. His anxiety was such he'd give the game away for sure. Instead he placed a call to Habiba, asking her to supervise work on the translation, and promising to make a decision on whether or not we could take time out for a visit to Amarna once she'd reported back on progress. He managed to sound like his usual self on the telephone which, given his state of barely repressed panic, was to his great credit.

I retreated to the cabin I share with Adam and tried to take my mind off things with a good book. But the words kept scrambling on the page and the storyline failed to hook me out of the drama of my own life, so I gave up.

Supper was a simple affair. I was in no mood to cook so Walid and Dan had to be content with chicken portions and salad, which were the only things I could be bothered to transport from the fridge to our three plates. Even so, more of the chicken ended up being thrown onto the causeway for the stray cats to fight over than found its way into our stomachs.

At last, as the huge ball of the sun was clinging to the horizon, sending a liquid shimmering light across the Nile, the longed-for call from Adam came through. The mobile reception on the west bank was notoriously hit and miss but he'd found a spot where he could pick up a signal. I pressed the speakerphone button so we could all hear him.

'Nothing,' he announced. 'Other than the regular guard patrols, there's been no movement on or around the temple at all. No visitors; nothing.'

'Then perhaps he was successful in getting in and out last night without being seen.' Walid said dolefully

'Or he didn't get inside at all,' Dan suggested. 'Maybe he tried and gave it up as a bad job.'

'Ahmed has been scouting about all afternoon,' I said. 'He's tracking down everyone who's ever known Gamal Abdel-Maqsoud. But so far he's drawn a blank. Nobody has seen him. He's gone to ground. But Ahmed is keeping up the search.'

'Then there's only one thing for it,' Adam's voice echoed from the phone. 'Merry, you're going to have to bring one of those Aten discs out here tonight and you and I are going to have to pay a visit to the tomb to check he's not still inside.'

Chapter 12

Before I could put this plan into action, I was forced to have something close to a stand up row with Dan over which of us should go.

'It's not safe, Pinkie,' he protested. 'How could I live with myself if something happened to you? Worse; how would I tell your mother?'

'Dan, this is down to me. I got us started on all this. And I've got to see it through. Adam and I are in this together. Besides, he asked for me, not you.'

'Perhaps the alternative didn't occur to him. You two are too used to being a double-act. But he's not thinking of your safety, and I'm sure if he were here now he'd change his mind and back me up. You've already told me this Gamal has a nasty streak. If you think I haven't spotted the marks on your shoulder, you're mistaken. I presume the bastard kicked you while you were down?'

My obstinate silence spoke volumes.

'I thought so,' he said grimly. 'Look, Merry; if it turns into an out-and-out fight, I'm better equipped to back up Adam than you are. You're letting your emotions cloud your judgement.'

'And you're letting your *me Tarzan, you Jane* sensibilities get the better of you!' I snapped. 'Dan, this isn't your fight.'

'But...'

'Think about Jessica.' I pressed on. 'You're getting married at the end of the year. What's she going to say if I allow you to go off on some macho crusade and you wind up getting caught? As things stand, you're an innocent bystander to everything that's happened so far. If I let you go and Gamal somehow turns the tables, then you're in it up to your neck. If you love Jessica, and if you retain some affection for me, then you won't ask this.'

I saw his indecision and knew I had triumphed. I wasn't proud to emotionally manipulate him. But the truth was, he'd come to Egypt to look out for me. I wasn't prepared to see him hang (even if only metaphorically) for something I had done. None of us knew what the outcome of tonight's little jaunt would be. But it was an outcome waiting in store for me, not Dan. Of that much, I was certain.

Point won, argument over, I waited for the cover of full darkness. The temple floodlights were switched off earlier now to conserve energy. Since Luxor was bereft of visitors, I daresay the authorities questioned the value of having the monuments artfully lit up at night. Power-cuts were still a common occurrence, so it made sense not to waste electricity.

216

I took the key from my bracelet and removed a single Aten disc from alongside its twin inside the safe with a deep sense of trepidation. Locked up inside the safe, I could vouch for their security. Outside of it, it was down to me to be extra vigilant.

I secured the disc inside the storage box on the back of my scooter with shaking hands, took a deep breath and readied myself for the off.

'Don't try anything stupid,' Dan admonished. 'If you find Gamal inside the tomb then I rely on Adam having sense enough to tie him up and leave him there. Leave your key to the safe with me. If you're not back in a couple of hours, I'm bringing the other disc and I'm coming to get you, like it or not.'

It was a big enough threat to guarantee my determination to be back quickly. Even so, I wasn't daft enough to set off without a rucksack bursting with flashlights, fresh batteries, bottled water and biscuits. Our previous encounters with the tomb demanded no lesser precaution.

Not wishing to attract attention, I left the scooter behind a wall at the roadside about half a mile from Hatshepsut's temple, and went the rest of the way on foot. I wedged the Aten disc on top of my provisions, secured the buckles, hoisted it onto my back and half-walked, half-ran along the kerb.

I heard Adam's low whistle as I approached the rendezvous point we'd agreed on. 'There you are,' he said in relieved tones, stepping out of the shadows to greet me. 'I was beginning to think you weren't coming.'

'Just waiting to ensure the coast was clear after the temple lights were switched off,' I murmured, opting not to tell him about Dan's energetic protests.

'You may as well not have bothered,' he muttered archly. 'The moon's like a damned searchlight tonight.'

I gazed up at the bright white orb dangling in the sky and saw what he meant. The full moon bathed the entire landscape in silvery light. The graceful terraces and porticoes of Hatshepsut's temple looked especially magical picked out in monochrome tones against the graphite starkness of its mountainous backdrop. But we weren't here to admire the aesthetic beauty of the temple by moonlight. The visibility was a disaster for what we had in mind. Any movement would show up sharply as a sudden displacement of the shadows.

'Still no sign of Gamal?' I questioned.

'Not a whisper. I've had my eyes glued to the chapel and my backside welded to the same spot for hours. I'm as stiff as a board and suffering with eyestrain. But if he tried to slip out of the tomb and away, there's no way I could've failed to spot him.'

'So, we really are going to do this? We really are going to check out the tomb?'

'I don't see we have any choice. But we'll have to be quick. The guards are running their patrols on a relay system every fifteen minutes. Look; there they go now.'

I focused where he was pointing and caught the movement of two guards descending the lower ramp and striking out across the vast area of open space between the temple and the guard post next to the ticket office. They were frighteningly plain to see in the moonlight. I could even hear their boots crunching on the loose scree of gravelly rock as they walked and the low hum of their conversation. Every sound carried at night. Both guards had their rifles unslung and were patrolling with them held loosely at their sides.

'They're not taking any chances, are they?' I murmured, feeling my nerve and bravado start to desert me. 'Adam, do you really think this is such a good idea? If they catch us they're more likely to shoot first and ask questions later. We're taking one hell of a risk.'

'So, what's the alternative?' he asked simply, looking into my eyes in the darkness. 'We have a responsibility towards that tomb, Merry. If it weren't for us, it would still be hidden away, undisturbed and undamaged.'

I bit my lip and shifted uneasily from foot to foot, feeling torn.

'Look, if you're having second thoughts, I can go in alone,' he suggested. 'Maybe it would be for the best in any event. That way you can keep watch and make sure I come out again.'

'No way,' I vowed. 'After what happened last time, if Gamal's in there you're not facing him alone. That's final.'

'Right; come on then,' he urged, taking my hand and pulling me with him as he moved. 'It's now or never.'

I swallowed down hard on my misgivings, deciding I had no choice but to go through with it now I was here. I knew I couldn't return to the dahabeeyah and sleep easy wondering if Gamal was even now inside the tomb packing up the most portable items for removal. The thought of facing Dan was even worse.

We crept forward, crouched low to take advantage of the cover afforded by the crumbling ruins of a temple that pre-dated Hatshepsut's by several centuries. Adam led me on a circuitous route. There was no way we could risk running across the more open ground. It meant we approached the temple broadside from the south, and necessitated a frantic scramble up the lower cliff-face and over the boundary wall, but finally we made it.

'Phew!' I panted, leaning weakly against a pillar and wiping sweat from my brow with the back of my hand. My heart rate didn't show any sign of slowing down and I was out of breath, but we'd eluded the guards, reaching the chapel without being spotted, so I was daring to believe it might just be possible to pull off this suicide mission.

Adam glanced at the little illuminated dials of his watch. 'No time to rest, Merry; we need to get inside. The next patrol will be setting off any moment now.'

We hastened between the pillars and I played lookout scout while Adam unlocked the door with the copy key he'd taken a few weeks back. It creaked slightly as he opened it and we sucked in our breath, ears straining. All remained still and quiet. Adam grabbed me, pushed me inside, threw himself in after me, then closed and hastily relocked the door behind us.

He placed one finger against my lips. 'No talking,' he whispered.

I unhooked the rucksack and felt through its contents for a flashlight. Moving away from the door, I dared to switch it on. It brought the figures carved into the walls leaping to life. But I was sensitised to them by now and certainly happier to be in here with the creepy wall reliefs than outside with the guards and their loosely slung rifles.

I handed the Aten disc to Adam and we moved deeper into the chapel, approaching the gash in the lower section of the opposite wall.

'Ready?' he murmured.

'As ready as I'll ever be.'

I held the flashlight trained on him while he fitted the disc into the gash and pushed down on it with all his strength. There was the usual agonising moment when it seemed the disc was stuck fast, refusing to budge. Despite the number of times I'd witnessed this phenomena, it still managed to take me by surprise when suddenly it disappeared into the wall.

Adam reached silently for my hand, the one that wasn't holding the flashlight, and we gripped each other tightly while we counted heartbeats.

At last, we heard the familiar rasping sound, almost a low groan, and watched the hidden panel shift sideways in front of our knees. Adam immediately dropped onto all fours and peered through, cocking his head sideways listening for any tell-tale sound to indicate someone was already inside. After a moment, he took the flashlight from me and shone it through the hole into the yawning darkness beyond.

I crouched low beside him and followed the penetrating torch-beam. And promptly froze. I felt Adam go similarly rigid alongside me. 'What was that?' I whispered, terrified.

Adam flicked the switch on the flashlight. Everything plunged into darkness. 'Stay very still, Merry,' he murmured. 'It came from behind us. The guards are outside.'

My breath caught painfully in my throat, almost choking me. I bit back a strangled gasp of fright and put every ounce of energy into holding my breath and keeping myself motionless and silent. If the guards unlocked the door, opened it and swung a flashlight inside now we were done for. The tomb was gaping open and unprotected in front of us. There was no excuse on earth imaginative enough to account for our presence here in the dead of night and not a penny between us to offer as a bribe.

I've been told one's whole life flashes before one's eyes when death comes on swift wings. Crouching there, paralysed with fear, wondering if we were about to succumb to the pharaoh's curse, I had a similar experience. Except it wasn't my whole life – just the part of it I'd spent in Egypt. I saw a kaleidoscope of images starting with myself inside Howard Carter's house, trying to break free; and finishing up with Gamal Abdel-Maqsoud leaping from our flaming dahabeeyah into the Nile. Had every moment been leading towards this one – to suffer the ignominy of being caught red handed exposing the one thing we were trying so hard to protect?

I heard the doorknob rattle and closed my eyes, every nerve ending taut and screaming. Any moment now the beam of a flashlight would land on me, shouts of discovery ringing in my ears. In my head I was already crafting a carefully worded confession. But, after a moment that felt like a lifetime, the doorknob stilled. I heard an exchange in Arabic, and then the voices receded along with the footsteps.

Adam pulled me against him. I could feel his thundering heart as I clutched him back. 'My God, that was close,' he breathed. 'I thought our number was up, for sure.'

I gave in to the crazy desire to kiss him, suddenly feeling insanely euphoric and wildly alive.

'Enough of that,' he grinned, setting me gently away from him. 'There's only so much control a man can be expected humanly to exert over himself, you know.'

We waited until the silence was stretched almost to breaking point, then Adam snapped the flashlight on again. 'If Gamal's inside, then he's as silent as the grave itself and can obviously see in the dark,' Adam muttered.

But I think we both knew already that he wasn't there. We went in anyway, crawling through the narrow opening into the corridor beyond.

I swallowed down on the big lump that sprung into my throat as we stood up inside. This was the spot on which Adam and I had exchanged our impromptu marriage vows in the private ceremony Adam had concocted for us *à deux* when Gamal shut us in here in the pitch dark. Adam squeezed my hand, and I knew he was remembering too.

A few paces forward and we were able to step onto the little bridge Adam, Ahmed and Walid had constructed over the deadly pit shaft below. 'You realise we're going to have to come and dismantle this pretty damn quick if Walid goes ahead with the staged discovery,' I murmured. 'I think this might just give the game away that someone else has been here first.'

'The same thing's true of the burial chamber,' he nodded. 'We need to get rid of the pulley system. Damn! I'd forgotten all about our little adaptations.'

'Not to mention the quantities of rock dust Mustafa Mushhawrar exploded in here,' I muttered.

He squeezed my hand again. 'Hmm, it's not the beautiful pristine place it was the first time we were here, is it?' he said regretfully.

'I think it's safe to say we've made our mark,' I agreed with no less remorse. 'Perhaps it would have been better if we'd left well alone. I'm not sure Akhenaten and Nefertiti deserved the devastation we've wrought to their final resting place. Tutankhamun and Ay must be rolling in their graves.'

'Be thankful for one thing, at least,' Adam said. 'It doesn't appear that Gamal Abdel-Maqsoud has found a way in here. Our fears were unfounded.'

'That may be only a matter of time,' I said pessimistically. 'If those scrape marks are anything to judge by, the chances are he misjudged the size of the Aten disc and has gone away to correct his miscalculations.'

'Then we will catch him on his next attempt,' he vowed.

We stopped just inside the treasure chamber. Adam stood just behind me, with his hands resting on my shoulders. 'Take a moment, Merry,' he whispered against my hair. 'Soak it all in. If that villain Gamal does beat Walid to it before he can stage the discovery, this will be our last chance to experience the wonder of this place. Even if Walid is successful, we may not get another chance to be here alone.

I'm not sure our previous visits have really lent themselves to sightseeing. It really is staggering, don't you think?'

Looking around in the broad arcs of the flashlight beam, words failed me. A little slice of the Amarna period, the most fascinating of them all, was laid out before us. To think that Akhenaten himself, Nefertiti, Tutankhamun lived with these objects… touched them… took them for granted, was wonder enough. To know Moses, that towering figure from the Old Testament and other holy works, may also have left his fingerprints on these chairs, chariots and gaming boards took my sense of star-struck awe to a whole new level. I gave way to the shudder running through me and leaned back against Adam, just for the warm, reassuring feel of him.

'I promised you a ring,' he murmured.

'No, Adam; there's nothing I want to take from here; nothing but the memory. It's worth more to me than any amount of jewellery.'

Very slowly, he turned me into his arms and kissed me. 'You know, Merry, that's why I love you so much.'

'That, too, is worth more to me than any amount of jewellery,' I whispered against his lips.

We stayed as long as we dared, drinking in the fabulous treasures with our eyes and imprinting every last detail on our memories. 'Every time I come in here, I see something new,' Adam said, running his fingers across a golden pectoral exquisitely inlaid with jasper, carnelian and turquoise. 'Do you think Akhenaten wore this?'

'I'd be willing to place the shortest of odds on it.'

'In here, I feel as if the past is within reach,' he said.

'As time capsules go, it's pretty hard to beat,' I smiled.

'But with great reluctance, Merry, I think it's time to go.'

Even so, we lingered. We retraced our steps at last only because we knew if we delayed any longer our friends would come looking for us.

'Do you think on this one occasion the gods might look favourably upon us and let us leave without any drama?' Adam asked.

'Fingers crossed,' I murmured, fitting the action to the words.

We crept along the corridor, crossed the bridge and crawled on all fours through the opening in the wall. I half expected to see two pairs of big black boots waiting on the other side, then look up to see the guards with their rifles trained on us. But thankfully it was just my imagination running away with me.

Adam helped me to my feet and, collecting up the Aten disc, I watched with the flashlight while he pressed it into the gash. The moment it disappeared into the wall, Adam flung himself back through the entrance hole so he could collect it on the other side. This was a precision manoeuvre. He had literally five seconds to get through the hole, scoop up the disc and get back again. He'd always made it before. But this time he misjudged it. As the panel shifted closed with its usual low groan of ancient rock scraping against ancient rock, Adam's foot got caught. He let out a cry of pain and the Aten disc rolled out of his hand towards me.

His cry seemed to ricochet around the room, echoing from the walls. I let out a yelp of horror.

'Quick! Merry! The disc! You need to press it back into the gash! Now! Quickly! The damn panel's crushing my foot!'

I snatched it up and shoved it into the slot, forcing it down with all my might, while Adam groaned on the floor beside me, trying to yank his foot free. But it was caught in a vice of stone. I'd swear I could hear his bones crunching.

I didn't think it was going to happen for me, but just as I was starting to sweat and panic, pressing down with every last ounce of energy I possessed, the disc went weightless and dropped into the wall, out of sight. 'Oh, thank God!' I sagged, feeling my knees turn to jelly.

I dropped to the floor and pulled Adam free the moment the panel shifted sideways again. We lay there slumped together on the hard stone floor, panting with shock, and trying to get our breath back. Seconds beat by. I'd swear I could still hear Adam's anguished cry echoing from the walls. And then I heard something else. Something that made my blood congeal in my veins. Voices outside. The guards were back.

Of course they were. They could hardly fail to have heard us with all the noise we'd been making.

'Adam! We need to move.' I whispered urgently.

There was only one place we could hide. I scrambled back through the opening, pulling him with me into the entrance passage to the tomb. I grabbed my rucksack and the torch at the last moment. Pressing the switch, I plunged us once more into darkness. We were curled against the inner wall, next to the opening.

'Adam! If I shove the disc back into the slot from this side, we're trapped in here. What do I do?'

'We're dead whatever happens,' he murmured. 'If they see the disc lying on the floor, it won't take any great leap to spot the gash directly above it. They'll find us either way. Let's just sit tight and keep quiet.'

Clutching each other in the pitch-blackness, we heard the key turn in the door lock on the other side of the chapel. A moment later the door creaked open and a narrow torch beam split the darkness.

Adam and I both stopped breathing. The only sound from our side of the wall was our hammering hearts. To my straining ears, they were loud enough to wake the dead. I heard a single sentence spoken in Arabic. 'كان فارغا'. Then, unbelievably, came the sound of the door swinging closed again and being re-bolted.

'What did he say?' I choked, forcing the words past the blocked breath caught in my throat.

'He said, *it is empty*.' Adam provided the translation.

'But how the hell did they fail to spot this bloody great hole in the wall?'

'The guard swung the flashlight round at head height. He was looking for a person, not to see if there was something resembling a large cat-flap cut into the wall at just above skirting board height.'

'You mean, we're free? We haven't been caught?' I didn't dare believe it.

'Let's call it a reprieve,' he said. 'We've still got to get the hell out of here, and I don't think I can run with a broken foot.'

Very slowly, our breathing shallow, we pushed ourselves up from our position hunkered down on the floor and crawled through the hole. Adam grunted, attempting to put pressure on his foot as we got up on the other side, back inside the chapel.

'It's no good, Merry, you're going to have to go without me.'

'I'm not leaving you here, and that's flat.'

'But I'll slow you down.'

'Then we'll move slowly.'

But first, we had to close up the tomb entrance again. There was only one thing for it. With Adam injured, I would have to be the one to fling myself back through the hole, collect the disc from the floor inside and throw myself back again. I was never much good at gymnastics at school. But I was lithe and supple, and I'd just had an agonizing demonstration of the consequences of getting it wrong.

'I'm not sure we should risk it,' Adam said. 'Maybe it's best to just leave the disc inside the tomb, let the panel slide closed and get the hell out of here.'

I won't deny I was tempted. If I got hurt too our chances of getting away were almost non-existent. 'But we need both discs,' I argued.

'Do we?' he challenged. 'We've managed tonight with only one. The second one is just an insurance policy.'

That swung it for me. 'Exactly. And, given our experiences so far, it's an insurance policy we can't afford to be without. We must come back here at some stage because we've got to dismantle the bridge and the pulley system. I, for one, don't want to take the chance of getting trapped inside again. It's happened once too often already for my liking. Gamal Abdel-Maqsoud is on the loose and dangerous. And I doubt Walid's ability to bring the genuine Mehet-Weret discs from Cairo for a third time. Adam, I'm not leaving here without that disc.'

He looked unhappy, but I knew I'd convinced him. 'Ok; but you'd better be quick.'

He limped to the wall, wincing with pain and inserted the disc into the gash, pressing down hard. I crouched down by the opening ready to spring forward the moment the stone panel started to move. When it happened, I barely waited for the hole to be wide enough; just launched myself through it, felt about in the darkness for the disc, scooped it up from the floor and threw myself bodily back through the hole, pulling my legs up tight behind me.

Home and dry, I lay flat on the stone floor for long moments, catching my breath.

Adam let out a raggedy sigh of relief. 'Well done.'

I rolled over and pushed myself up. 'Right, time to go.'

I edged towards the doorway and leant against it with my ear pressed against the panelling. Listening intently, I heard only silence from the other side, if indeed it's possible to hear silence. Perhaps I should say I heard an absence of sound.

'Go easy,' Adam murmured. 'The guards may not have gone far.' He took the key from his pocket and handed it to me. He was leaning against the wall, keeping the weight off his foot.

I eased the key into the lock, stopped; listened again. Silence. Cautiously, painstakingly, moving the key by millimetres, I turned it sideways until I felt the lock catch. With a swift flick of my wrist I twisted the key through its full rotation, catching my breath at the deafening crunch of it turning in the lock. I froze, motionless, listening again. Nothing.

'Ok, have we got everything?'

Adam hopped towards me, holding his damaged foot up off the floor with his knee bent. I wedged the Aten disc and the flashlight back inside my rucksack and secured the buckles, then slipped my arms through the straps and shrugged it onto my back in the dark.

'This is suicide,' he muttered.

'Funny, I was thinking the same thing earlier, but our luck has held so far.'

'Then perhaps it's best not to push it. Merry, my foot's killing me. You should make a dash for it and leave me here.'

'Adam, if I lock you in here, it will be like playing Russian roulette. They only need to open the door once to find you.'

'You could lock me back inside the tomb?'

'After everything we've just been through to close it up!' I gaped at him. 'If you think I'm leaving you incarcerated in there, you've lost your mind. What if I don't make it back to the *Queen Ahmes*?'

'Then Dan and Walid know where to start looking. They've got the other disc; remember? I thought that was your whole point about the insurance policy.'

'You're mad! Adam, we've got to stay together. What if Gamal comes back? If he finds you here, he'll kill you.'

'He'd be taking a chance with all the guard patrols out there.'

'So did we, and we made it without being spotted. Now come on! Stop talking. We've got to get out of here.'

He joined me at the door.

I gripped the handle and... slowly... slowly... started to pull down on it. The hinge creaked and I went rigid. No sound from outside. So I dared to push the door open by just a crack. A narrow strip of pale moonlight illuminated the floor at my feet. After the dense darkness it seemed as bright as day out there. I eased the door open inch by careful inch. The pillared Hathor shrine was deserted. I listened for the crunch of boots on gravel, the low hum of conversation; but heard nothing. All was emptiness and silence.

'What if they're lying in wait for us out here?' I whispered.

'They'd have jumped us by now. They have guns, remember?'

Sucking in a deep breath and stealing myself to be brave, I stepped across the threshold. My eyes were everywhere at once, frantically scanning the space between the columns for any sign of movement. My ears hurt with the effort of listening for any small sound in the gaping nothingness. Every one of my senses was alert, every fibre stretched to the limit.

'Ok, coast's clear,' I breathed at last.

Somehow we made it to the perimeter wall. I shunted myself up under Adam's shoulder so he could use me like a crutch as he limped alongside me. I clambered onto the wall, dragging him with me; then dropped down onto the other side, pulling him as I went. He collapsed in a heap beside me, grunting with exertion and pain.

'The scooter's about half a mile from here,' I whispered. 'If we stick to the shadows of the ruined temple, we should be fine. Can you make it?

'I've come this far,' he muttered.

I knew his foot hurt like hell. His face was grey in the moonlight, with a damp sheen of perspiration across it. His breathing was ragged and shallow. I didn't want to hazard a guess at how many bones were broken, impacted or crushed in his foot.

'Ok, stay low and hang on to me.'

We moved in fits and starts. Progress was slow, but gradually I started to breathe a little easier as we put more and more distance between ourselves and Hatshepsut's temple behind us.

We'd almost reached the roadside when the sound of footsteps brought us to a heart-stopping standstill.

I heard a match flare. Moments later I caught a drift of cigarette smoke carried on the night air. Adam and I clung to one another, silent, watchful, nerves stretched taut. A crumbling ridge of rock hid us. Just as well, because the guard was within spitting distance. He'd obviously wandered away from his colleagues for a hasty smoke.

Not being a smoker myself, I really had no idea how long it took to finish a cigarette. But our unseen companion was taking forever about it.

I was propping Adam up, shouldering almost all of his weight. As one interminable moment dragged into the next, I wasn't sure how long I could keep it up. Every muscle protested the enforced paralysis and I could feel my strength giving out.

Lifetimes later, I heard a sound I took to be the guard crushing his cigarette stub underfoot into the gravel. I sagged with relief. Adam let out a long breath, and I felt the rigidity go out of his body. 'Phew! That was close.'

We waited until the footsteps receded, then jolted forward again. But we mistimed it. As we started to move, I heard a shout.

I may not speak Arabic, but even I could translate the universal demand for us to stop and show ourselves.

Adam shot a panicked look into my eyes. 'Run, Merry!'

'But...'

'Please... Stick to the line of this ridge and *run*!' He gave me a hard shove as he spoke, and collapsed to the floor, leaving me no choice. If I hesitated, attempted to haul him back to his feet, we would both be caught.

Chapter 13

I have no recollection whatsoever of how I made it back to the *Queen Ahmes*. My inner self remained with Adam behind that ridge, frantic about what might be happening to him. Everything else functioned on a mechanical sort of automatic pilot that delivered me to the riverbank above the stone causeway; shaking, sweating, panting; but in one piece.

'At last!' It was Dan who crossed the gangplank first. Walid hovered just behind him.

I stumbled down the stone steps and collapsed into Dan's arms, choking out a sob.

'Where's Adam?'

'The guards caught him,' I wailed. 'His foot! He broke his foot! The tomb doorway crushed it!'

'Pinkie! Slow down. You're not making any sense.'

Dan was forced to half-carry me inside. My legs didn't seem capable of holding me up anymore.

He took me through to the lounge-bar, deposited me on the divan, barked out an order for Walid to pour me a glass of brandy, and pressed it into my hand. 'Now, start from the beginning.'

With the liquid warming me through, I was able, haltingly, to get the essential facts out in some semblance of order. 'We've got to get back there!'

'It's the early hours of the morning,' Dan pointed out. 'If we go haring back to the temple now, we'll only make things worse. Adam did the right thing, getting you out of there. Let's not undo all his good work. He's a quick-thinker. He'll come up with some clever story or other; you mark my words. You say you weren't caught in the temple precinct itself?'

'No; at the roadside.'

'Then I'd place some faith in Adam's ability to spin a yarn, if I were you. In the meantime, I suggest you put in a call to your chum Ahmed.'

Ahmed, as luck would have it, was already on the scene. 'I am on my night duty,' he announced as I finished stumbling and stuttering my way through my urgent need for his help. 'I have Adam right here at this very moment. Would you like to speak with him? Here, I will pass the phone across.'

'Hello, Merry! Glad you made it back ok.'

I nearly fainted clean away. '*Adam?*'

'Merry, did our police pal here ever let on to you that he was a closet smoker? And I don't just mean hubble-bubble pipes!'

'*What?*'

'Yes! It was Ahmed all along! He was posted here to reinforce the guard patrols tonight as a result of last night's break-in. They decided an overnight police presence was necessary. I've told him he needs to kick the habit or his pristine set of new teeth won't stay that way for long. The occasional hubble-bubble pipe is one thing, but cigarettes...'

I was grateful to be already sitting down, and to have a glass of something alcoholic in my hand. I wasn't sure I dared believe it. I'd been suffering tortuous visions of Adam carted off in chains, or worse. Hearing him safe and well and apparently full of beans, was more than my fevered brain could take in. 'But, even so, how did you explain... I mean, what did you say... That is: what about the guards...?'

I heard Adam's grin come down the phone, even though I couldn't see him. Some may say it's impossible to hear a grin. They would be wrong.

'As the guards clustered around Ahmed and me, demanding to know what was going on, I saw you were far enough away to be safe, then pointed at your retreating back and shouted *'Look! You're letting him get away!'*

'Him?' I repeated suspiciously.

'Well, of course! I had to let them think you were Gamal Abdel-Maqsoud, and that I'd caught him skulking around and had him in a headlock until Ahmed disturbed us, and he bolted.'

'But, what about your foot? How did you explain your broken foot?'

'I persuaded them Gamal and I had been fighting, and he'd stamped on it.'

'Are they going to let you go?'

'I think I have persuaded them I am not their man,' he said. 'Even so, Merry, after I've taken a minor detour via the hospital, I don't think it would do us any harm to get away from Luxor for a few days while the dust settles.'

He spent the rest of the night and all of the following morning in the hospital. Ahmed deposited him there, and then returned for duty, eager to play his part in throwing up the smoke screen Adam had created. The police hunt for Gamal Abdel Maqsoud was now on good and proper.

Nobody seemed in the least disinclined to believe he had gone to the bad. I gathered, sadly, that it had been the case before that those employed in the service of preserving the ancient monuments were often the ones who took to looting from them when the chips were down. So it had been in ancient times too, when those who carved the tombs were also more often than not the ones who robbed them.

I suffered some slight pangs of guilt over Gamal's shattered reputation but quickly quashed them. Nobody asked him to corner us with a knife *and* baseball bat at the entrance to the tomb, and to use them Adam had been prepared to treat him quite cordially, giving him some cooling-off time. Our misjudgement had been to leave him locked up inside the tomb, between the entrance and the pit shaft, for this cooling-off period. He'd seen the gleam of gold at the other end of the corridor and it had turned his head. From the point he'd broken free of us, he'd made it his mission to make the tomb his own. We couldn't let him steal a march on us, so we had to take him down, by fair means or foul. Once we had him, we just needed to keep him quiet while we enacted Walid's staged discovery, and then we could decide how best to deal with him. I was rather hoping bribery might prove effective.

Adam was discharged at lunchtime. I collected him by taxi, helping him hobble outside on his crutches. His foot was liberally coated in plaster. The X-ray revealed two broken bones, which had been reset before the bandages were applied.

'I need to keep the weight off it for a while, and then be disciplined about the physiotherapy,' Adam said. 'But they're confident it should heal up nicely. All in all, things could've turned out a whole lot worse.'

But he was still keen to put a bit of distance between Luxor and ourselves for a few days. 'Just in case it should belatedly occur to one of those guards, or worse, Ahmed's Commander Abdul el-Saiyyid, to ask what I was actually doing out there near the temple last night,' he explained. 'I'm not sure I could convince them I was out for a moonlight stroll, and simply happened across Gamal up to no good.'

Walid needed a bit of persuading. 'But, what if Gamal should elude capture, and attempt to break into the tomb again while we are gone? Or, what if the police should find him, and he pleads ignorance about last night? Don't we need to be on hand to manage the situation?'

'Ahmed will stay behind,' Adam reassured him. 'We can rely on him to keep us posted. Besides, if we disappear off the scene for a few days, Gamal might be more inclined to show himself.'

Walid frowned, undecided.

'If we need to get back quickly, it won't take long by train.' Adam added, trying hard to dispel his concern.

'Ted's eager for us to join him in Amarna,' I said. 'The dig house is adequate, but it can't compete with the *Queen Ahmes* for comfort.'

Adam nodded his agreement. 'Besides, it might not be a bad idea to humour Habiba for a bit. She's convinced she's hit upon a link between the suitcase papyri and the Copper Scroll. It might serve us well to allow her a couple of days exploring Akhenaten's ruined city. We don't want her to rumble us, and it might look a bit suspicious if we keep the spotlight on Hatshepsut's temple. She was clever enough to dream up her theory that it might be Amun's temple treasures from Deir el-Bahri that were stolen, buried, and itemised in the Copper Scroll. And she's well enough informed to know about the research linking the Copper Scroll to Amarna. I suggest we give her some time to pursue her hypothesis, and distract attention away from here for a bit. It will make it all the more convincing when that philologist from Cairo completes his translation of the large scroll, and she realises it's actually a royal reburial she's searching for, not just a stash of buried treasure.'

What persuaded Walid in the end was the acknowledgement that it would take the philologist a good few days to complete his translation of the large scroll. There was really no useful purpose we could serve by sticking around while he did so.

'But wouldn't Habiba feel happier if Ahmed could come along too?' Walid asked by way of a final token objection. 'He is, after all, the officer assigned to protect her.'

I permitted myself a small smile. 'She'll have us all there in the unlikely event of needing protection. Dan's a big bloke. We can ask him to keep an eye on her.'

Besides which, I was fairly certain a little bit of absence had never been known to be harmful to the heart. In actual fact, I had a sneaking suspicion it might be just what Ahmed and Habiba needed.

We set sail the following morning. When I say, "set sail", I mean literally. Adam instructed Dan, who proved a willing helper in how to unfurl the two huge sails from their diagonal poles strung above the dahabeeyah; although we invited Khaled along to play Captain and be the one to do the actual steering. Before long, we were making rapid progress down the Nile. Both the wind direction and the Nile current were in our favour, and with the motor set on cruise control, there was really little to do but sit back and enjoy the experience.

Habiba had joined us shortly after breakfast, bright-eyed and flushed with excitement. It was rather a shame Ahmed wasn't here to see for himself how fresh-faced and beautiful she looked, eager to get underway on our adventure to the remains of Akhenaten's holy city. But since I felt pretty sure Ahmed was already fully apprised of Habiba's womanly charms, I didn't let the thought bother me for long. We needed Ahmed to be our eyes and ears in Luxor.

We fed Habiba a watered down version of the same cock and bull story we'd told everyone else about how Adam broke his foot. We let her believe Gamal Abdel-Maqsoud harboured a personal grievance against us for being instrumental in his loss of employment (let's face it; it was true). She seemed as willing as everyone else to accept Gamal was now up to no good, and attempting to remove sections of wall relief from Hatshepsut's temple for sale on the black market. We convinced her Adam had been keeping watch because he felt a sense of responsibility, had ambushed Gamal, challenged him and landed up in a vicious fight for his trouble. Amazing how it's possible to twist and distort the truth when the occasion demands. But I didn't scruple for a moment about the string of mangled half-truths that tumbled from our lips. They were necessary to the wider scheme we were embarked upon. Habiba murmured her concerns and sympathies in all the right places. Gratefully, we were able to proceed without unwelcome questions being asked.

I served mid-morning coffee for us all up on deck, and passed round a plate of my peanut crunch cookies. The view drifting past was of rural Egypt: the inky blue of the Nile, the soft green of the narrow strip of cultivated land on both banks fading away into the tawny gold of the desert and mountains beyond, all soft-focused with dust, and pastel-shaded under the a pale, water-colour-washed sky stretching endlessly above. Here and there the pastoral scene was broken up with tumbledown buildings, scruffy children playing in the dirt, skinny cattle grazing on grassy sandbanks and stoic donkeys pulling carts laden with sugarcane and other crops along the riverside.

Dan; less inclined than the rest of us to appreciate the Egyptian scenery flowing past, decided to make conversation instead. I have to concede his choice of topic came as something of a surprise to me.

'So, what makes you think the treasure itemised in this Copper Scroll you mentioned has never been discovered?' He addressed himself to Habiba.

I rolled my eyes, thinking Ted had already given us a perfectly acceptable response to the self-same question.

Habiba sipped her coffee and brought her gaze from the view across the landscape to focus on Dan's sunburnt face. 'Oh, I'm not saying that at all,' she admitted. 'I think it's perfectly possible that some of the treasure has been discovered; although perhaps it wasn't recognised as such.'

'You mean; it wasn't recognised as being part of what was listed in the Copper Scroll?' I queried, feeling my interest begin to spark.

'Exactly that,' she smiled at me. She really did have the most beautiful smile. It quite took my breath away. 'But I'm certain the majority may still be hidden, awaiting discovery. I am quite keen to test out my own theories before the large scroll is translated, which may perhaps tell us for sure.'

In this hope I knew she was destined to be disappointed. Still, as Adam had pointed out, we were here to humour her, so it couldn't hurt to let her pit her wits against the possibilities. She had no idea we had a prototype copy of the Copper Scroll even now locked away inside our safe. And all the while it stayed that way, her theorising was just fine with me.

'So, tell us about the treasure you say has already been found.' Adam invited, sitting with his plastered foot up on a cushion. 'You think it was some of what was listed in the Scroll, just not identified as such?'

'That's right. As part of the research for my thesis, I studied several translations of the Copper Scroll. Until very recently, scholars considered the locations itemised in the scroll to be in Jerusalem or Canaan. Nobody suggested they might be right here in Egypt until the link to Akhenaten was established.'

'By decoding the strange Greek characters inserted apparently at random into the text.' Adam nodded.

She gave him a sharp look. 'Ah, so I see you *do* know about the Copper Scroll.'

'Only a little,' he qualified quickly. 'I've spent some time reading up about it on the Internet since you hit us with your supposition at Hatshepsut's temple the other day. It's fascinating stuff.'

This time it was him she assaulted with the dazzling affect of her smile. 'Isn't it?' she agreed.

'So, what did you find out by studying the translations?' I asked, surrendering to the need to break into her smile. I'm secure in Adam's affection, but hey, there are limits.

'There is a section that refers to *"the sepulchral monument",* where *"there are one hundred light ingots of gold",'* she said. 'The only other reference to gold ingots talks about *"the carpeted Old House of Tribute".'*

We all stared at her. I daresay it was the mention of gold that captured our attention. For all that we'd seen a lot of it while in Egypt, it still had the power to magnetise the senses.

'In the northern group of the tombs of the nobles in Amarna, is the tomb of Huya, who was Steward to Queen Tiye, Akhenaten's mother,' she went on. 'The wall reliefs inside include a scene dated to year twelve of Akhenaten's reign. It shows Nefertiti being borne on a carrying chair to the Hall of Foreign Tribute. Below and to the side of it are pictures of visiting emissaries paying homage to Pharaoh. I believe the *House of Tribute* referred to in the Copper Scroll was almost certainly this Hall of Tribute at Akhet-Aten,'

'What makes you so sure?' Adam asked. 'I can see the similarity in title, but…'

'The Hall of Tribute was a large altar area within the Great Aten Temple,' she said. 'It's quite likely it was carpeted for the comfort of the foreign dignitaries who were required to prostrate themselves at Pharaoh's feet before handing over their gifts. Don't you agree it is highly suggestive when compared to the translation?'

'Well, yes; I can see where you're coming from,' Dan said, setting aside his scepticism for once. Perhaps he too had succumbed to her smile and hoped she would turn it on him.

'Well then, it's possible this was the location mentioned in the Copper Scroll, which says "*in the cavity... in the third platform sixty-five gold ingots*".'

I felt my eyes grow round.

She observed my reaction and nodded. 'I take this to mean that under the raised platform three levels down, someone hid the gold.'

'And you're saying it's been found?' Walid questioned, sitting forward and nursing his coffee cup between both hands.

She flashed her dizzying smile again. 'Well, listen to this, and then make up your own minds. In 1926 a team led by a Dr Frankfort began excavating the ancient city of Akhet-Aten. When the dig reached the Central Western Quarter of Tell el-Amarna, as it was called back then, the workmen unearthed a large buff-clay, matt-brown painted jug. When they prised off the lid, out popped a gold bar followed by twenty-two more. Dr Frankfort speculated that what they'd found was part of a thief's loot, raided from the Hall of Foreign Tribute less than a mile away. The excavation site is now known as 'Crock of Gold Square'.'

'But I thought you said there were sixty-five gold bars and, earlier, you mentioned a hundred of them,' Dan said. 'That's a bit different from twenty-three.' He wasn't an accountant for nothing. There was certainly nothing wrong with his maths.

Habiba smiled again. 'I said *ingots* not *bars*. What makes me think Dr Frankfort's team unearthed the gold mentioned in the Copper Scroll is the weight. Their treasure trove of gold bars they unearthed in Amarna weighed 3,375 grams in total. The ancient Egyptians used a unit of measurement called a 'Kite' to weigh gold and silver. Assuming the gold ingots referred to in the Copper Scroll were cast in moulds to produce the standard 'Kite' unit of weight, then the weight for 165 of them would be 3,366 grams; almost identical to the weight of the gold found at the Crock of Gold Square in Amarna. Now, don't you think that's a bit more than suggestive? The theory is that the historical thief melted down the 165 light gold ingots to produce the twenty-three gold bars, which he then stashed away, perhaps needing to cover his tracks.'

It occurred to me that if she should ever choose to give up her highfalutin career with the Ministry of State for Antiquities, Habiba would make a fine teacher. She had a natural flair for storytelling. I felt a moment of regret for Ahmed's absence. He would have loved to be here to hear this. I brushed it away. If my inkling about those two proved to be correct, there would be plenty of other opportunities.

'The gold bars are now on display in the Cairo Museum,' she informed us. 'The label says they are from Amarna. I would like to go one further and say they are from Amarna, yes, and also as described in the Copper Scroll. And if they are indicative of the buried treasure itemised in the Scroll, just imagine what else might be still hidden awaiting discovery! Hatshepsut's Amun treasures, for sure! We just have to re-study the translations and think 'Amarna' rather than 'Jerusalem' or 'Canaan' and who knows what we might find?'

'Who would've thought we'd end up with our own onboard Copper Scroll expert in place of Ted?' I asked, helping Adam put down his crutches and climb into bed later that same evening.

'One of those bizarre coincidences that proves life sometimes really is stranger than fiction,' he agreed, easing his foot under the cotton sheets.

'It makes our discovery of the clay tablets seem rather redundant though,' I muttered. 'She seems to know bits of the translations by heart.'

Adam put his head back on the pillow and smiled at me. 'Ah, that's better. A good night's sleep is exactly what the doctor ordered. You know, I was telling the truth today when I said I'd Googled the Copper Scroll. There are translations of the whole damn thing online, if you care to search for them. That said; the scholars who've completed them still don't seem to agree on where the described locations are. Israel and Jordan are still the front runners.'

'The link to Akhenaten isn't widely accepted?'

'Some people seem to think the insertion of those Greek characters is some kind of elaborate hoax.'

'Perpetrated by whom?'

'That's just it; nobody has a viable explanation. But from what I was reading on the Internet, the favoured theory is that the first half of the Copper Scroll describes the hidden locations of the Temple treasure. They still mostly prefer the conjecture that the temple in question is either the First or Second Temple of Jerusalem.'

'And the second half?'

'Get this; there's some suggestion it describes the hiding place of the Ark of the Covenant and the Tabernacle. The caves around Qumran are thought to be the most likely spot.'

I pulled my T-shirt over my head and stared at him. 'Moses again. Wasn't the Ark of the Covenant a kind of portable golden chest in which the Israelites stored the stone tablets Moses brought down from Mount Sinai containing the Ten Commandments?'

'Yes,' he said. 'And the Tabernacle was a sort of tent where the Ark was kept when it wasn't being transported.'

'My God! If archaeologists could unearth them it might even knock the discovery of Akhenaten and Nefertiti's tomb into the shade!'

He grinned at me, putting his hands behind his head on the pillow, elbows sticking out. 'You know what, Merry? I think you've phrased that just about right. That's a find for the archaeologists to make, not us. We need to be generous-spirited enough to leave a few bits and pieces from ancient history for those who are properly qualified in this stuff to dig up.'

I didn't mind him pulling my leg like this, since he always did it with a liquid soft expression in his eyes and a mobile smile tugging at his mouth.

'All I'll say is this,' he went on. 'Those clay tablets are anything but redundant. They prove, beyond any shadow of a doubt, that the Temple treasures originated from Akhenaten's holy city of Akhet-Aten. The Temple in question was the Great Aten Temple.'

'And if Habiba can work out the location of even a tiny part of it, it will be another discovery to rock the world,' I said, running a brush through my hair.

'Treasure to stir up a media frenzy.' Adam predicted. 'Let's face it; Meryre was the High Priest of the Aten, so he had access to all the Temple treasures. And Meryre II was the Overseer of the Treasuries and could lay his hands on what we presume was the wealth of the nation.'

I unclipped my bra and turned to look at him. 'So if the first half of the Copper Scroll as replicated in the clay tablets turns up any treasure at all, it will be all the evidence anyone could ever need of the origins of the Dead Sea Scrolls being right here in Egypt.'

'And if the letters Ted's translating do go so far as to tell the story of the Exodus, then it might bring the second half of the Copper Scroll into sharper focus – perhaps even specify the location where the Ark of the Covenant and the Tabernacle are hidden.'

'All in all, our trip to Amarna is ripe with promise,' Adam grinned. 'Now, come on Merry; it's time for bed. You can't sit there half-naked like that and not expect me to react.'

Chapter 14

Another solid day's sailing brought us to Amarna. Ted was waiting and waving from the quayside as we came into view, shielding his eyes against the fierce glare of the late afternoon sun. Khaled and Dan leapt onto the jetty to secure the docking ropes, while Adam supervised proceedings from the deck, leaning on his crutches.

As soon as we had the gangplank lowered, Ted came on board so we could say hello properly in the air-conditioned cool of the lounge bar. 'Heavens above! What happened to you, my boy?' he asked in concern as Adam levered himself down the spiral staircase and I handed him his crutches at the bottom.

'It's a long story,' Adam said with a meaningful glance, which Ted saw and correctly interpreted. 'I'll tell you all about it later. In the meantime, let me introduce Habiba Garai, on secondment from the Ministry of State for Antiquities. She and Walid have teamed up to carry out security inspections of the historical sites in response to the reports of illegal digging, vandalism and theft.'

'Professor Kincaid,' Habiba stepped forward, eyes shining, to shake his hand. 'I know you by reputation, of course. Yours is an important name in Egyptology. It is an honour to meet you, sir.'

I watched the pleasure sweep across Ted's weathered face. A little nicely phrased flattery from a beautiful girl never failed to hit the spot. He lifted her hand to his lips and kissed it in an age-old gesture of gallantry. Watching him, it occurred to me it was a shame such gentlemanly conduct was dying out. Men of my generation simply didn't go about kissing ladies' hands any more. They'd probably be lynched if they tried it. I thought this a pity. It was a gentle as well as a gentlemanly gesture, and conveyed something rather more gracious than a handshake. Still, I felt sure if Dan or Adam should try it, Habiba wouldn't respond with half so much demure delight as she was exhibiting now. I daresay it would be considered corny, like a dodgy chat-up line. The cynicism of this day and age turned old-fashioned chivalry into something a bit sleazy. In spite of my whole-hearted belief in equality between the sexes, watching Ted and Habiba's little performance, I couldn't help but think we were worse off for it.

'You are not worried about security here in Amarna, I hope?' Ted said: releasing her hand and pushing his glasses back up onto the bridge of his nose. 'The excavation team here runs a tight ship.'

'I would like to do a check while we are here,' Habiba said. 'But no, professor; that is not the primary reason for our visit.' She cast an uncertain glance at Walid. 'Dr Massri, am I permitted to take Professor Kincaid into our confidence?'

While her polite deference was nicely pitched, I thought it was rather late should Walid happen to say no. She really gave him little choice but to consent. Fortunately we'd told her of our friendship with Ted, so I guess she knew she was onto a winner, but perhaps didn't want to appear too presumptuous.

'Naturally,' Walid said with a slight inclination of his head. 'I shall be interested to hear what the professor makes of your theories. I have told him already, of course, of our remarkable discovery.'

'Ah yes,' Ted said, picking up his cue. 'This would be the mysterious suitcase bricked up inside KV20. What an intriguing find. And it contained papyri, you say? Yes; I am eager to hear all about it.'

Uncrossing my fingers from behind my back, I dispensed tall glasses of my homemade chilled lemonade, while Habiba regaled the professor with the whole story. He'd heard it all before, of course, and knew all about the role we'd assigned Habiba as agent-of-the-staged-discovery. But he managed to convey exactly the right degree of astonishment and fascination. We were becoming a rather fine troupe of actors. If we carried on like this, I'd be forced to apply for an Equity Card for each of us.

Luckily, we'd forewarned him too about Habiba's scholarly knowledge of the Copper Scroll, so he managed not to fall off his chair when she got to that part of her narrative.

'And so, you see, I'm wondering if that line of text *"Aten is key"* on the papyrus architect's drawing of Hatshepsut's temple is pointing us here to Amarna,' she finished.

Ted took a long swallow of his lemonade and then put the glass on the cabinet beside his chair. 'You're quite sure the papyri you discovered inside the suitcase relate to buried treasure?'

Habiba nodded. 'While we don't yet have a complete translation, the large scroll speaks of "precious jewels", "sacred shrines", and "golden images". The other two are the architect's drawing I've already mentioned, and a transcription of Akhenaten's Hymn to the Aten. So yes, it all adds up to treasure, and it all points here to Amarna. If I can use my knowledge of the Copper Scroll to identify possible locations here in Amarna where the treasure was hidden, I think we may just have one of the most important discoveries in Egyptology on our hands.'

'Yes; I see.' Ted said sagely.

I didn't dare catch his eye. It was interesting how someone could be at once so completely right and so completely wrong. But that was easy for me to say; sitting here with my insider knowledge of a hidden tomb, a set of clay tablets, and a cellar full of wine-cum-storage jars containing

258

possibly the most explosive correspondence in history. Perhaps if I didn't hold all the pieces I'd also have made a jigsaw with the picture turned upside down.

'So professor, I'm hoping to use this visit, short though it may be, to do a spot of treasure hunting.'

I had to hand it to the girl; she was endearingly candid.

Since Adam was incapacitated, Dan went with Ted to collect his overnight bag so he could settle back into his usual cabin on the *Queen Ahmes*. He would still work at the dig house on his translations during the day. It boasted the facilities for proper conservation of the ancient parchment letters, as well as huge lockers for their secure storage when not being actively worked on.

I prepared a fine meal, and we ate up on deck under the stars. I found myself missing Ahmed. I liked Habiba, but her presence made it impossible to speak openly. Now Habiba's version of the story was told, we found ourselves avoiding any mention of the Copper Scroll or the papyri. The potential for one of us to trip up and say something to give the game away was simply too great.

'So, tell me, Professor Kincaid...' Habiba said when the companionable silence had drawn out too long to be truly companionable anymore and was becoming awkward. '...What brings you here to Amarna? I understood you were retired. Are you here for work or pleasure?'

I glanced nervously at the professor, thinking this was a question we ought to have predicted.

Ted sat back in his chair, folded his napkin neatly, and carefully placed it alongside his empty plate. Ted's movements were often neat and measured like that. They spoke eloquently of his character. He looked up and smiled at her. 'I am fortunate enough to be able to say they are one and the same thing. Egyptology is my life's work and has always been my most profound pleasure. I wonder how many people can say that, hmm? It may not have made me rich, but it has certainly made me happy.'

I looked back at Habiba to see how she would respond to this rather nifty sidestep. She didn't. Respond that is, just sat in an expectant silence, politely waiting for Ted to answer her question.

Left no choice but to say something if he didn't wish to rudely blank her altogether, Ted took a small sip of wine and collected his thoughts. 'I have been asked by the field director here to translate some documents recently come to light. They would appear to date from the period immediately after Akhenaten's demise. We are hoping they may illuminate this rather confused period and tell us something of the legacy he left behind.'

'Are they diplomatic documents, like some of the other discoveries made here?' Habiba asked.

'I think they are more theological in tone,' Ted replied. 'I am hoping they will cast some light on the true nature of what we might call Akhenaten's new "religion". I'm not sure it has ever been fully understood.'

'I would very much like...' Habiba started, but Ted held up one hand and forestalled her.

'It sounds as if your time here in Amarna is likely to be short since I'm sure you'll need to get back to Luxor once the translation on the scroll is complete. Now please, my dear, don't allow me to distract you with boring accounts of doctrinal scriptures. They may fascinate fusty old professors such as myself, but you young people are here to pursue much more exciting ventures. I trust Walid to keep a watchful eye on you so you don't disrupt the work of the archaeology team here, but I wish you well. If I were a few years younger I'd ask for a couple of days off so I could join you. But, for now, I suggest you leave my dreary documents to me, while you go off and search for your buried treasure.'

I'll say that for Ted; when he'd tried and failed to sidestep and then tackle his challenger head on, his ability to turn the tables was both deft and impressive.

He yawned in somewhat exaggerated fashion, and patted his stomach. 'And now, if you will excuse me, I have eaten well and am ready for my bed. I have an early start tomorrow, and so do you. Barry has offered to give you all a tour of the site. It's an honour he doesn't extend to all and sundry, so I'd bite his hand off if I were you. He's been working here for upwards of thirty-five years, and no one knows Amarna better.' He smiled at Habiba. 'If you want to start interviewing someone about possible locations for your hidden treasure, I'd suggest he's your man. Now, I'll bid you all goodnight, and thank you for a most pleasant evening. It's wonderful to be back on board the dahabeeyah again, and to see her looking as good as new.'

He leaned over to kiss my cheek as he passed my chair. Before pulling back, he whispered in my ear. 'That was a delightful meal, Merry; thank you. Oh, and by the way, I know who the Pharaoh of the Exodus was.'

* * *

Barry was a rather grizzled looking British Egyptologist with a full sandy-coloured beard streaked with grey, and a friendly manner. I guessed him to be in his mid-to-late fifties, or possibly early sixties. The bone-dry Egyptian climate had the unfortunate affect of prematurely ageing the skin, so he could really have been any age within maybe a fifteen or twenty-year range. He had the distinction of having worked at Amarna for all the years of my life. It was a track record I stood in awe of, almost as much as I did of the man himself.

He greeted Walid respectfully and with a warm handshake, then said hello to the rest of us as we introduced ourselves. 'Ah yes, some of you were here with Nabil Zaal a few weeks ago. Your discovery of Panehesy's wine cellar brought the media to descend on us.' It was impossible to tell from his tone whether he considered this a good or bad thing; although I thought I discerned a twinkle in his eyes. 'Friends of Professor Kincaid's are welcome here. I had the privilege of attending his lecture series many years ago. There's not much about Egyptology the professor doesn't know. I'm hopeful he may be, even now, unravelling some of the mysteries surrounding the aftermath of Akhenaten's reign. I've worked here in his city for more years than I care to count, but... as Howard Carter once famously said... "*The shadows move but the dark is never quite uplifted*". Perhaps the professor's work here will change all that. I'm waiting with baited breath to find out. Now, since there are five of you, I've brought the old safari vehicle. It's quite good over this rough terrain. Jump in...'

We all piled on board, helping Adam hoist himself up the metal steps. Moments later we accelerated away from the quayside in a cloud of dust. I held onto my hat and squinted through my sunglasses.

Barry shouted out to us above the engine noise while he drove. 'Now, as you can see, Amarna is mostly desert. We have this narrow strip of riverbank lined with palm trees, but as we head inland it's mostly sun-baked sand and rock.'

I could see that for myself. Amarna was a flat expanse of mostly nothing, bordered in the distance by a semi-circle of cliffs rising like fortresses from the desert plain. Here and there reconstructed columns pointed like fingers towards the sky, and boundary walls and enclosures marked out the positions of ancient buildings and temples. But there was nothing to compare with the vast and grandiose temple ruins we were more used to from Karnak and Luxor Temples in what was once ancient Thebes.

Barry drove us to the main excavation site, pulled up in another cloud of dust, and swung round in his seat so he could address us. 'Now, what you need to know is that some thirty-three centuries ago, perhaps 20,000 Egyptians, or maybe twice that number, followed their king to what was then an empty stretch of desert beside the Nile, much like you see it today. Once here, they built a city, and named it Akhet-Aten, The Horizon of the Sun.'

I gazed about me, trying to envisage a newly completed city.

'Within a generation they had all left, never to return. Akhet-Aten became a ghost town. Gangs of workmen systematically dismantled the stone temples and transported the blocks away for re-use elsewhere. The centuries then settled down to reducing the remainder of the habitation to sandy hillocks. But if you ever get the chance to look from above, you'll see it never quite lost the semblance of a city. It remains by far the largest area of readily accessible domestic occupation from ancient Egypt. Put simply, it's the only city you can come and see.'

I glanced at Dan. He was gazing about him as if he wasn't at all sure what he should be looking at. Where we were parked, it was a mishmash of tumbled down stone walls, a few broad steps and sections of flooring covered over with tarpaulin. The excavation work going on around us seemed mostly to be being done with paintbrushes, a few people crouched over indiscernible objects half covered in sand.

'This is the place that's supposed to be so boundlessly fascinating?' Dan muttered. 'I'm not sure why I bothered to bring my camera. Not exactly photogenic, is it?'

Barry heard him, and smiled. 'I'm not sure it's so much the place itself that people are drawn to. I think it's more a case of how archaeology can shine a light into a period of history we thought was lost, and hint at the character of the man who created it.'

'Was Akhenaten a dreamer or a tyrant?' Walid mused. 'An eccentric or a megalomaniac; an enlightened theologian or an intolerant despot?'

Barry smiled again, his lips disappearing into his bushy beard. 'I'm not sure we will ever know. The pharaohs who came later described him variously as the criminal, the enemy and the rebel. Some historians have suggested these titles imply he was not the rightful heir and took the throne by force...'

I wondered vaguely if his Hebrew ancestry might have something to do with this.

'...To me, this is the language of conflict, perhaps even of civil war,' Barry went on. 'And I think we know why. Akhenaten engaged in a theological schism the like of which had never been known before.'

'He displaced something like two thousand gods and goddesses.' Walid commented. 'It was hardly a move designed to secure his popularity.'

Barry nodded. 'Perhaps if he'd lived longer, established a more solid line of succession, he might have laid a firmer foundation for the longevity of his early form of monotheism. As it was, the signs are the common people found it too austere, too unappealing to take hold.'

'Austere in what way?' Adam asked.

'Akhenaten swept aside centuries of imagery and symbolism. The sun moved across the sky on its own; it did not voyage in a solar boat; a divine scarab beetle did not propel it. There was no night-time realm through which the sun journeyed, beset by dangers. There was no kingdom of Osiris. What existed was what you saw, not what blossomed in the imagination. I think this was what sowed the seeds of Akhenaten's destruction, and gave later pharaohs their justification for seeking to obliterate him from history. His theological vision was too dull and lacking in poetic metaphors to be engaging. We've found archaeological evidence all over

Amarna that worship of the Egyptian Pantheon continued among the common people in the privacy of their own homes. Atenism had an uneasy co-existence with what had gone before, and people happily abandoned the pretence once the pharaoh was dead. Perhaps that was Akhenaten's crime: he robbed his people of their old beliefs.'

Habiba listened to all of this in a thoughtful silence. She tilted her head to one side consideringly, and the sun cast a shadow across her face where she'd pulled forward the folds of her headscarf. 'You know, I'm wondering if they called Akhenaten a criminal not so much because he stole what was in their hearts but because he stole something much more tangible: the treasures from the traditional temples.'

Barry looked at her in surprise. 'You have evidence of this?'

'Not yet,' she admitted. 'But it makes a certain sort of sense, don't you think? And, once Akhenaten was dead, his priests and those who did share his unconventional religious beliefs feared reprisals and so buried the evidence.'

'She means it quite literally,' Dan interjected. 'That the Atenist priests hid the temple treasures and then fled in fear of their lives.'

I sat back and let my gaze drift over the vast open spaces of Amarna while she propounded her theories. The ground plan was such, set out in a series of large rectangular boxes; I felt it might almost be possible to reconstruct the ancient buildings on top. This was not a city whose temples and palaces had disappeared beneath the sands and could be excavated out again. This was a city that had been systematically dismantled and carried away.

'Yes, I have heard of the Copper Scroll, of course.' Barry said when she'd finished. 'And I'm aware some historians have cited a link to Akhenaten. But it seems tenuous to me. Really, what are the chances of finding hidden treasures buried 3,500 years ago? Not good, I'd suggest. Assuming you are correct, surely the most likely scenario is that the Theban priests guessed what had happened, searched out the most likely hiding places, and simply dug them up again. If quantities of treasure were buried at sites across Akhet-Aten I'm sure we'd have found at least some of them by now...'

'Then how do you explain Crock of Gold Square?' Habiba challenged.

He looked at her with renewed respect. 'I see you really have made a study of the subject. You researched it for your thesis, you say?'

Habiba nodded. 'And I believe, sir, I could make a suggestion or two about places that might merit deeper excavation.'

'Oh?' It was impossible to tell from his tone if Habiba was pushing her luck, or whether he was willing to run with her on this.

'I have been studying a recent translation,' she said. 'It states the "*tithe vessels and vestments*" are "*in the northern shaft of Matia's funerary structure*". Sir; I have checked the Hebrew for myself. Two Hebrew letters in the name 'Matia' overlap and have been translated as a *tav* – the Hebrew letter for 't'. If you separate them, the letters would translate as *raysh* and *vahv* – the Hebrew letters for 'r' and 'v' respectively. This gives us a rather different translation for the owner of the funerary structure – not 'Matia' but 'Marvyre'.'

My breathing stalled. It nearly stopped altogether as she went on.

'There is one name from the Amarna period that is remarkably close to this sound. He was the High Priest of the Aten and his name has been found on tomb inscriptions among the Northern Tombs here.'

'Meryre,' Barry said.

Habiba nodded, looking excited. 'I think we should be looking for a shaft to the north of Meryre's tomb.'

Barry stared at her for a long moment. Finally, he spoke. 'Directly behind Meryre's tomb, some sixty metres to the north, there is a deep burial shaft on the summit of the ridge.'

We all sucked in a collective breath.

'It has already been plundered,' Barry said flatly. 'We found no body or funerary objects inside.'

But Habiba wasn't to be deterred. 'Perhaps it might pay dividends to dig further down into the shaft, well below where the corpse would have lain?'

Barry allowed the silence to draw out again. We all waited respectfully to see how he would react. Finally he sighed.

'Well, the tombs are next on our itinerary in any event. I will willingly show you the shaft, and you can tell me if it looks a promising location for further excavation.'

Adam and I asked to be excused. We'd made a tour of the Amarnan tombs with Nabil Zaal, Ted and Walid on our last visit here a few weeks ago. Dan and Walid could be relied on to watch Habiba didn't overstep the mark. Even if she should somehow use her feminine guile to persuade Barry some additional digging might be a good idea, it wouldn't happen today. We could look forward to a full report later. In the meantime, I'd told Adam the tantalising words the professor had whispered in my ear last night. We were impatient for some time alone with Ted to hear the next part of the story.

The dig house was en route, so Barry dropped us off before driving off towards the cliffs with the others. I held the door open so Adam could hobble inside on his crutches. Ted saw us arrive and got up from his desk to greet us.

'Your young friend Habiba is a firecracker,' he remarked with a smile, moving across the room to fill the kettle after seeing Adam settled on a chair with another to put his plastered foot up on.

'You don't know the half of it,' I said. 'We're still reeling from her latest revelation.'

'Oh?'

'Yes; she's only gone and identified Meryre from the Hebrew of the Copper Scroll.'

'A clever girl, that one.' Ted smiled, dropping tea bags into three mugs. 'You say she's been running rings round poor Ahmed? I should imagine he'll have his work cut out keeping pace with her.'

'Well, she seems to have backed off him a bit since he rescued her from those knife-wielding thugs who broke into the Luxor Museum.'

'Ah yes! Now you thought our foe Gamal Abdel-Maqsoud might have put them up to it. So, tell me, has that young upstart been causing more problems? I imagine from the look of your foot, Adam, he's stirring up trouble again.'

'To be fair, I'm not sure I can lay the responsibility for my broken foot at Gamal's door,' Adam admitted ruefully. 'He's only to blame insofar as he was our reason for needing to check out the tomb. You see; we thought he might be holed up inside it. '

Between us, we brought Ted fully up to speed on recent happenings in Luxor and our reasons for getting away for a few days. We sipped our tea as we spoke, dunking the digestive biscuits the professor found inside a colourful tin in the cupboard. It looked like a throwback to the colonial days of the British Empire, perhaps brought to Amarna by Flinders Petrie himself as the first archaeologist to excavate here. Thankfully, the biscuits inside were fresh, purchased somewhat more recently.

We finished up with Habiba's attempts this morning to beguile Barry into digging for the Copper Scroll's treasure.

'You never know! If she works her charm on him, he might just give in.' Ted smiled. 'And, who knows? Even if the Theban priests did dig most of it back up again, it's possible something still remains. So, she's been clever enough to work out that Meryre played his part in hiding the Copper Scroll treasures, and she's proposed that he and his followers made a run for it to avoid capture by the old guard. But she hasn't made the next mental leap...? She hasn't gone so far as to identify Meryre as Moses...?'

'Not yet,' Adam said. 'But then she's never met Nabil Zaal. It's possible, if she gets chatting to Barry today and he tells her about that television interview Nabil gave here...'

Ted's pale blue eyes gleamed behind his wire-rimmed glasses. 'Then he'll tell her he thoroughly pooh-poohs the idea that Akhenaten didn't die but somehow stuck around to lead the Israelites out of Egypt. We still have the exclusive on that particular story.'

I grinned at him. 'So – *we* know who Moses was. And *you* know who the Pharaoh of the ~~Exodus~~ Oppression was. Come on Ted; you've kept us in suspense long enough. Time to spill the beans.'

Chapter 15

'Ok, so let me start by testing you both on your knowledge of the Old Testament.' Ted said. 'I'm going to pose you a couple of questions. Firstly, what can you tell me about the burning bush?'

Adam put down his empty cup and leaned back, his bandaged foot still propped on a chair in front of him. Adam liked a challenge almost as much as he liked the opportunity to impress his mentor. Knowing this, I was generous-spirited enough to let him take this one. The fact my religious education was woefully lacking may also have had something to do with it – although you'd never persuade me to admit it to these two. Adam flashed me a quick smile. 'The Bible tells us Moses was tending a flock of sheep on Mount Horeb and saw a burning bush,' he said. 'It is the occasion of God's first appearance to Moses. God tells him to return to Egypt to free the Israelites from bondage and lead them out of Egypt to the Promised Land.'

'Good,' Ted approved. 'The key question is, why now?'

'Why now?' I echoed, confused.

'What I mean to say is why does God choose this moment in time to appear to Moses? Moses has spent years in exile in the Sinai desert. What has changed? Why is God instructing him to return to Egypt?'

Adam glanced at me and then looked back at Ted. 'The Pharaoh of the Oppression is dead.'

Ted smiled at him. 'Exactly! Exodus 1.8 tells us, "*Now there arose up a new king over Egypt, who knew not Joseph.*" The Bible is typically oblique and gives no name by which we can identify this new pharaoh. So, my second question is this... What do you make of this statement "*who knew not Joseph*"?'

Adam scratched his temple. 'Well, I may not be a Biblical scholar, but I'm Egyptologist enough to know which pharaoh succeeded Horemheb to the throne of Egypt.'

'Precisely, so we can perhaps have an educated attempt at working it out.' Ted invited.

I felt the pieces start to slot together in my mind, and sat forward to express them. I was neither Egyptologist nor historian, but I was convinced there was a place for the enthusiastic amateur. 'We know Nabil Zaal had it right when he identified Biblical Joseph as the Vizier Yuya,' I said. 'Yuya served as a young man at the court of Thutmosis IV, and perhaps as a middle-aged man at the court of Amenhotep III, who married his daughter, Tiye. It is not beyond the bounds of imagining that he was an old man during the reign of Akhenaten, his grandson.'

Ted was nodding, approving the logic of my deductions as I elucidated them, so I went on, gaining in confidence as I spoke.

'We know Horemheb achieved prominence as a General of the Army in Akhenaten's reign. So it is entirely plausible that Horemheb knew Yuya/Joseph. And yet, maybe the pharaoh who succeeded him, coming to the throne many years later, did not.'

Ted looked pleased. 'I think you're on the money, my dear. Horemheb seized the throne after the last of the four Amarnan pharaohs, Ay, was dead. He ruled for perhaps fourteen years, subjecting the Hebrews to slavery and harsh labour.'

'Horemheb was the Pharaoh of the Oppression.' I said.

'That's right. But he was not the Pharaoh of the Exodus.'

I thought he was about to name the pharaoh who was. Like Adam, and despite my lack of Egyptological credentials, I was well aware who succeeded Horemheb to the throne. I could feel his name burning on the tip of my tongue. But rather than speaking it aloud, Ted instead returned to the question he'd started with. 'Ok, so we've established why the timing was important. Horemheb was dead and there was a new pharaoh sitting on the throne in Egypt. So, let us reconsider the Biblical story of the burning bush. Now, would it surprise you to learn this was the sign the fleeing Atenist priests agreed on to make contact with each other?'

Adam and I both stared at him.

'You mean...?' Adam started.

'Yes.' Ted nodded. 'The burning bush was not the miracle through which God spoke to Moses. It was the device by which the group who'd split off and spent their years in hiding on the Elephantine Island got back in touch.

'Meryre II.' I breathed.

'That's right,' Ted concurred. 'When Horemheb died, Meryre II brought the news of it to Meryre/Moses and his group living in exile in the Sinai. He set the bush alight to announce his arrival, and make it clear he was a friend coming in peace. It was the agreed sign. The burning bush was meant to signify the divine light of the Aten.'

'So Meryre II travelled the length of Egypt and into Sinai to announce the pharaoh's death.'

'Yes, and of course he brought news of the new pharaoh who had taken his place. And herein lay the problem. As the three of us are well aware, the new pharaoh was not of royal blood.'

'Neither was Horemheb,' Adam pointed out.

'True. But he'd legitimised his claim through marriage to Ay's daughter. The man Horemheb named as his successor served alongside him in the military, and commanded his northern garrison in the Delta; hence the likelihood that he never met the Vizier Yuya. In his own right he had no claim to the throne whatsoever.'

We couldn't put off identifying him any longer. 'The army general Paramessu.' Adam said.

'He became the first ruler of the 19th Dynasty.' Ted nodded. 'But he came to the throne a relatively old man, having spent his career in the army. He already had a grown up son, which is possibly why Horemheb chose him. Horemheb died without children, but he appointed a successor who was loyal to the old ways and came with a ready-made heir. Perhaps Horemheb saw it as his last act as pharaoh to ensure Egypt would not slip back into the religious turmoil of the Amarnan years by strengthening the inheritance of the throne through the next generation.'

I leaned back in my chair and finally named this new pharaoh who would secure a new Dynasty in Egypt, using the appellation by which the world had come to learn of him. 'Ramses I,' I said. 'His son was Seti.'

We looked at each other in silence for a moment, letting the implications sink in. Then Ted spelled them out.

'Ramses I had no royal blood in him at all; neither did his son Seti. But Meryre/Moses did. He was Akhenaten's brother, brought up as a Prince of Egypt within the Court of Amenhotep III.'

'You're saying he didn't go back to Egypt just to free the Hebrew slaves from oppression...' Adam started.

'... He returned to Egypt to stake his own claim to the throne.' Ted confirmed. 'And that of his son.'

'His son?' I gasped

'Yes. Meryre and Setepenre became parents during their years in exile. Now remember, Setepenre was the youngest daughter of Akhenaten and Nefertiti. So she had the blood of Amenhotep III and his forebears in her veins. Sure, it was all mixed up with the Hebrew blood. But if Meryre/Moses' claim was tenuous, his son's was far stronger. His name was Gershomre.'

I gaped. 'But how on earth did Meryre/Moses hope to prove his identity after so many years living in the wilderness?'

Ted smiled at me. 'You'll remember how the Bible tells us God taught Moses to lay down his staff and transform it into a snake...?'

'Yes...?' I nodded, not following.

'It's become known as the magic rod of Moses.' Ted said. 'Well Panehesy reminded Meryre/Moses that one of the treasures he brought with him out of Egypt when fleeing Horemheb's henchmen was the Pharaoh's staff of office. It was one of the treasures he kept when his brother Akhenaten died.'

I felt my eyes widen.

'Meryre/Moses had with him part of the royal regalia?' Adam exclaimed.

'Yes.' Ted said. 'It was a long, gold staff of office topped by the rearing head of the divine cobra goddess, Wadjet.'

'Wadjet protected pharaoh and his right to rule,' Adam remarked. 'It would be a pretty powerful symbol to take back into Egypt and lay before the new King; and an incredibly provocative one – equivalent to laying down a royal gauntlet. Is that what he did? I thought the Bible said that the Lord gave Moses three magical signs that would confirm his identity as the Messenger of God.'

'My word,' Ted smiled. 'You have been beefing up on your Bible studies! You're correct of course. First, he would transform the rod he was carrying into a snake and then restore it to its former state. Second, he would make his hand leprous, as white as snow, and then heal it again. And third, he would pour water onto the ground and it would turn to blood.'

I nodded as the Old Testament story came back to me from the murky recesses of my memory. Unlike Adam, who'd been reading up on this stuff on the Internet since Nabil Zaal whetted his appetite, I had to trawl back as far as primary school scripture classes to dredge it up.

'But magic implies the existence of a realm of power that transcends Nature and the deities.' Ted went on. 'It is an attempt to influence events by the occult and is therefore in complete contrast to Atenism as the early form of monotheistic belief practised by Meryre/Moses. The ancient Egyptians cast magic spells to protect the dead on their journey through the underworld. But Akhenaten swept this all aside when he banished the Pantheon. Meryre/Moses eschewed any form of 'magic'.'

'So how are we supposed to interpret the part in the Bible about these acts Moses is supposed to have performed in front of Pharaoh as proof he was a messenger of God?' Adam asked.

Ted smiled. 'As I think we are coming to learn and, as Nabil Zaal has been suggesting for some time, the writers of the Old Testament were seemingly skilled at taking a grain of truth and weaving a new story that threw a veil over reality, whilst leaving certain clues as to what actually happened.'

'Dan describes it as a tissue of lies from start to finish,' I remarked.

'Hmm, well I'm not sure I'd go that far,' Ted said, then shrugged. 'But it's certainly a clever re-imagining of historical events, with lots of poetic licence and a large dollop of creativity thrown in.'

'So... the three signs from God...?' Adam prompted, bringing us back to the point.

'Panehesy's letter home to his wife Nebt-Het tells us Meryre went before Ramses I in Memphis to stake his superior claim to the throne. He took Panehesy with him. In the Bible, Panehesy has been re-named Aaron, the brother of

Moses. Naturally, Ramses asked him to prove his identity. So Meryre produced Akhenaten's royal staff of office topped with the rearing cobra. He also demonstrated his knowledge of a series of rituals the kings of Egypt performed in their *sed* festivals for the purpose of rejuvenating their power. Now, I've been checking this out, since Panehesy does not describe these in his letter, probably assuming his wife is familiar with the details. The tomb of Kheruef, one of Queen Tiye's stewards, contains scenes showing her husband Amenhotep III performing rituals at his *sed* festival. The scenes include both a 'serpent rod' and 'hand' rituals, although it's not completely clear what they entailed.'

'So Meryre performed these same rituals in front of Ramses I to establish his royal authority,' Adam said.

'That's right,' Ted nodded. 'The wise men of the court were gathered to decide which out of Ramses I and Meryre had the superior claim to the throne of Egypt. According to Panehesy, when they saw the sceptre of royal authority and Meryre's performance of the *sed* festival rituals, they bowed in front of him, confirming he was the rightful ruler.'

I felt my eyes widen. 'I don't imagine Ramses was impressed.'

'He was infuriated. But he had more to worry about than just Meryre turning up to stake a claim to his throne. When Panehesy and Meryre entered Memphis, they found it in chaos. The Nile was flowing red due to some kind of contamination in the water. It killed the fish and drove the frogs onto the land, where they died, causing infestations of flies and lice. The livestock became diseased and people were falling sick and dying due to eating contaminated food and drinking poisoned water.'

Adam was staring. 'Which was likely to affect the first born, since they would be given priority over younger siblings.'

'Pfisteria,.' I said. 'A naturally occurring series of disasters, just as we thought.'

'But you can see how they might have become associated in folklore with the appearance of Meryre back in Egypt to stake his claim to the throne,' Adam remarked.

'Exactly.' Ted nodded. 'Ramses ordered Meryre and his small group of companions to leave Egypt, saying he would let them go if they left quietly. Meryre agreed to leave on condition he could take the Israelites, that is, his extended family of Hebrew relatives with him. He intended to form an army and come back and enforce his claim. Ramses acquiesced, and Meryre sent messages to all his mother's people living in the border city of Zarw. Panehesy sent a desperate message south to his wife, but it seems she didn't receive it in time. Ramses changed his mind, realising the greater threat posed by Meryre plus a potential fighting force, and sent his army to crush the rebels. Meryre and his people were forced, once again, to flee for their lives.'

'And so the Exodus began,' Adam murmured.

'That's right.' Ted said. 'Ramses I was the Pharaoh of the Exodus. And that is as far as I have got in my translations so far. There is one remaining jar I have not yet opened.'

We spent the next couple of hours, while we waited for the others to re-join us at the dig-house, eagerly poring over the texts that revealed the story Ted had told us thus far. Panehesy's letters home to his Mistress of the House Nebt-Het were scratched in faded ink on rolled pieces of parchment, cracked, yellowed and brittle with age.

These particular relics from the past, perhaps more than any of the others we'd had the unbelievable privilege to find and study, had the potential to rewrite history. It was a staggering realisation and an awesome responsibility. The weight of it was just starting to press down on me.

'Who gets to make the decision about how the contents of these letters get published to the world?' I asked.

'Well, I'll share them first with Barry, of course.' Ted said. 'And then he will need to go to both the Government and the Ministry of State for Antiquities to register the find and ask permission to publish. I guess a press conference is the most likely scenario, at which Barry, and perhaps myself, will be invited to speak.'

'But the Ministry will make all the decisions and take the lead?'

'That is my understanding. Any artefacts found in Egypt nowadays automatically become government property. That's as it should be, of course. But I can't help but share Walid's qualms about the timing in view of the political unrest. Ultimately, it will fall to army chief General Abdel Fattah el-Sisi, or perhaps Adly Mansour as the newly appointed interim president, to decide what becomes of these letters and the knowledge they contain.'

Adam was resting on his crutches, leaning forward to study the parchment scrolls. He nodded, and then shrugged. 'We have to hope Walid's change of heart about the timing doesn't prove to be an error of judgement. If it weren't for Gamal Abdel-Maqsoud snapping at our heels I'm not sure he could have been persuaded to stage the discovery of Akhenaten and Nefertiti's tomb with things as they are. But now he's saying he hopes it can be the common interest Egypt might need to unify opposing factions and entice tourists back again. Let's pray he's right and we're not about to blow this fragile peace sky high with what we've got planned.'

'Walid knows the Antiquities Minister, Director Ismail,' I reminded him. 'I'm sure, when the time comes, he'll manage the staged discovery with all due regard to the political sensitivities.'

'Let's hope so,' Adam said. 'Because to drop this bombshell of the Exodus at the same time might just create a fallout Egypt may never recover from. An undiscovered royal tomb is one thing. A re-telling of the Bible is quite another. There's been enough religious strife already, without inviting a whole load more once the identity of Moses is revealed and the world learns he was an Atenist priest.'

The sun was starting its slow descent towards the west by the time the others returned.

'Here they come now,' I said. I'd been standing at the window, scanning the horizon for some time. I saw the cloud of dust thrown up by the old safari jeep before I could make out the shape of the vehicle itself. We'd expected them back long before now.

'Habiba has no doubt proved herself a beguiling visitor,' Ted smiled. 'She's a persuasive young lady, and knowledgeable too. It wouldn't surprise me if Barry has succumbed to her charms and treated her to the tour of a lifetime.'

'Hmm, she's probably been leading the poor man a merry dance inspecting potential dig sites for the Copper Scroll treasure all over Amarna.' Adam muttered. 'She's determined to make a name for herself by proving she was already onto it before that philologist from Cairo completes his translation of Ay's large scroll. She's convinced herself it's going to point to the location of the buried treasure...'

'...And she wants to be able to say she got there first,' I said with a smile. 'Ah well, I don't mind giving her the chance to make her mark. Just think how disappointed she's going to be when she learns it's only a royal burial she's party to discovering, not a whole stash of stolen temple treasures.'

'*Only*?' Adam echoed. 'What you're describing with that little throw-away word just happens to be the most sought-after royal tomb in the entire history of Egyptology.'

It was obvious something was wrong from the moment Barry brought the safari jeep to a standstill in front of the building. The expression on his face, as well as the matching countenances of Walid and Habiba said it all. The absence of the fourth face told its own story.

'Where's Dan?' I asked, rushing forward.

Barry climbed out from behind the steering wheel and slammed the driver's door closed behind him. Walid stood back to allow Habiba to descend the metal steps at the back of the jeep ahead of him. I had the strongest impression they were avoiding making eye contact with me. Adam hobbled out of the dig house behind me, with Ted bringing up the rear.

'I'm sorry to say we lost him,' Barry said gruffly.

'Lost him?' I squeaked. 'What on earth do you mean; you *lost* him?'

'Just that, Merry,' Walid said awkwardly.

'How can you possibly lose someone in a place like this?' I demanded, not letting him finish. 'It's a wide open space for the most part!' Then I remembered Panehesy's cellar. 'Unless he fell down a hole, or something, is that what happened? Did you check to see whether he'd fallen into a burial pit, or a half-excavated shaft, or something like that?'

'No! That's not what happened.' Barry said stroking his beard in a gesture I could only imagine betokened embarrassment. 'And whilst Amarna is largely open space down here on the plain, it's anything but once you get into the gullies and ravines up among the cliffs near the Royal Tomb.'

'The Royal Tomb?' I parroted. Nothing was making any sense.

Habiba stepped forward. She reached out for my hand, pressing it between both of hers. It was such an oddly sympathetic gesture; I felt a real panic take hold of me as I stared wildly into her face.

'You did say, "*lost*"?' I stammered. 'You didn't mean "*de...de...dead*"?'

'Dan's not dead,' Walid said. 'At least, we don't believe so. We just don't know where he is.'

Strangely, I did not find this in the least bit reassuring. Perhaps it was the middle part of what he'd said that caused my knees to buckle.

It was Habiba who stopped me falling, since she still had hold of my hand. Adam was propping himself up on his crutches so was in no fit state to catch me.

'This is my fault,' she said softly, helping me towards a chair as the others crowded into the room behind us. I collapsed thankfully into it, feeling a bit like a rag doll whose stuffing had been pulled out, and stared up at her. 'I was the one who saw the man following us. I shouted out, and Dan gave chase.'

'What man?' Adam asked, levering himself forward on his crutches with a frown.

'That's just it; I don't know who he was,' Habiba said, dropping her head forward and slumping her shoulders. In that attitude she looked like a wilted flower and I felt suddenly sorry for her.

'Why don't you start at the beginning and go from there,' I suggested, feeling a little calmer now I had the chair to prop me up.

Walid sat down opposite me, and Habiba perched on Ted's desk. It was Walid who started to speak.

'We made a slow inspection of both the southern and northern tombs after visiting the main sites of the city,' he said. 'Habiba was reciting what she could remember from the translations of the Copper Scroll, and looking for possible burial sites for the treasure that matched up with the terrain and archaeological evidence we were exploring.'

'I believe the tombs of Meryre and Panehesy are both promising locations since they were both Priests of the Aten who served under Akhenaten,' Habiba explained, a trifle defensively I thought. 'I had a strong sense of being watched while we were looking at these northern tombs,' she went on. 'But every time I glanced over my shoulder there was no one there.'

'Then Barry suggested we should finish our tour with a visit to the Royal Tomb of Akhenaten,' Walid said. 'As you know, it is a drive through the cliffs, and then a bit of a walk to get there.'

'It was as we were coming out of the tomb after our visit that I spotted him,' Habiba said. 'A young Egyptian, although wearing Western clothes. He was crouched behind a rock on the cliff face with a pair of binoculars trained on us. He jumped up and started to run as soon as I shouted. Dan, who was just behind me, saw him too and sprinted after him, scrambling over the rocks and calling out for him to stop.'

'We lost sight of them as they disappeared behind a fissure in the cliff face,' Walid said.

'We shouted and waited, and shouted some more,' Habiba added. 'But Dan didn't come back.'

'Didn't you go after him?' Adam demanded.

'Of course we did,' Barry responded, looking a bit affronted.

Walid ran his palm over the wispy hair covering his bald patch. 'We spent the next two hours climbing all over those cliffs, shouting and calling, and scouring the terrain for any torn clothing or anything else to indicate where they had gone. But there was no sign of Dan or the young man he had run in pursuit of.'

'No sign of a scuffle; no blood, no gunshot?' Adam pressed, rather more graphically than I might have liked, although, let's face it; I was thinking it too.

'Nothing at all,' Barry said. 'I know those cliffs pretty well. If a body were lying there somewhere, whomever it may have belonged to, we'd have found it. Somehow the young man who was spying on us got away. I can only presume your friend somehow went with him. It's possible the young man had a vehicle of some sort hidden off-road up there on top of the escarpment.'

'Oh my God! Dan's been kidnapped!' I cried in horror.

Barry looked at me in confusion. But I could see the realisation dawning on the other faces staring at me.

'Gamal Abdel-Maqsoud has somehow followed us here! Before you know it, we'll be receiving a ransom note. And I don't imagine we'll need three guesses to work out what it will be asking for in return for Dan's skin.'

Chapter 16

Habiba was the only one to look startled. 'You mean, this individual will go to the length of kidnapping your friend in order to get back his job?'

I looked at her in dismay, realising I had once again blurted my mouth off before my brain was in gear.

Adam, quick-thinking as ever, stepped smoothly in to cover my blunder. 'It may just be that he will demand money before he's prepared to hand Dan over to us. I'm sure he knows he'll never be accepted back within the Ministry for the Preservation of Ancient Monuments in Luxor. I daresay he thinks we owe him compensation.'

Habiba looked confused. 'You said you found him somewhere he shouldn't be. What on earth did you catch him doing?'

I'd had time to recover my wits by now and decided the lie should be mine. 'We caught him trying to chip a relief from the wall in Hatshepsut's Temple.' To be fair, it wasn't a complete fabrication, just a stretching of the truth, and with a big distortion of the timing. I decided not to go into more detail. Habiba was no doubt clever enough to work out that if Gamal was somewhere he wasn't supposed to be; then so were we. And our encounter with him could hardly have taken place during normal opening hours. We were as open to suspicion as was he. But I opted not to volunteer further information or attempt to make up any excuses. If she asked, I'd have to get creative. In the meantime, if I could get away with the barest possible explanation I felt it had to be preferable. I knew all about the risks of overdoing the verisimilitude and had no intention of falling into a verbal trap of my own making.

Luckily, wonderful Walid was willing to add some verisimilitude of his own. 'It's what brought me to Luxor from my job at the Cairo Museum,' he said, also preferring an extension of the truth to an outright lie. 'Our ancient monuments do indeed need protection. It is just a shame we must tighten security against those whose job is meant to be to preserve them.'

I considered we'd said quite enough on the subject of Gamal Abdel-Maqsoud, for all that I'd been the one to introduce it, and determined to change it. 'Our priority now needs to be to rescue Dan,' I said. 'I suggest we put a call into Ahmed to tell him what's happened so he can be on heightened alert now we know Gamal followed us here. He needs to be on the lookout for the two of them to return to Luxor. Then, before it gets dark, I'd like to do another sweep of those cliffs, just in case you somehow missed him, and Dan's alone out there among the snakes and the scorpions. Adam; you'd better go back to the *Queen Ahmes*. There's no way you can scramble over the rocks on your crutches. And its possible Gamal will attempt to make contact tonight. The rest of us; let's go.'

We didn't find him of course. The hills were deserted, but for the best-avoided creatures already mentioned. With night falling fast, as it always does in Egypt, we had no choice but to drop Barry back at the dig-house and head back to the dahabeeyah. My first thought once onboard was to check Dan's cabin in the futile hope we might somehow have imagined the whole thing and would discover him lying on his bed with his nose in the latest spy novel. Futile proved sadly accurate. He wasn't there.

'Anything?' I demanded of Adam the moment I clapped eyes on him as I entered the lounge-bar, while the others dispersed to their own cabins.

'Nothing.'

I dropped down onto the divan, feeling sick. 'This is all my fault. If it weren't for me, Dan wouldn't even be here in Egypt. What if Gamal hurts him?'

Adam levered himself down beside me, put his crutches on the floor at his feet and took my hand in both of his. 'Now Merry; you mustn't think that way. If we're right in supposing what Gamal wants are the Aten discs, then it's in his best interests to keep Dan alive and well.'

294

'What the hell am I going to tell Jessica? And my own mother, for God's sake! She sent him here to bring me home and instead I've been instrumental in getting him kidnapped!'

'Hopefully nothing,' Adam said firmly. 'For now, we say nothing. We just have to sit tight and wait for Gamal to make his next move.'

'But sit tight, where?' I demanded. 'Are we supposed to wait here in Amarna for some kind of contact, since we know he was here today? Or should we head back to Luxor? Once we're sailing along the Nile, it's going to be much more difficult for him to reach us. God, Adam; this is terrible. I don't know what to do.'

'Well, there's not much we *can* do until morning. Now, come on, let's knock up something for dinner. Sitting about doing nothing and feeling awful about it isn't going to get things moving any quicker. We'll have to hope Gamal wants this thing over as quickly as we do and makes contact tonight. In the meantime, we have guests who need feeding.'

A small part of me was relieved when the longed-for contact didn't come overnight. We had a pretence to keep up in front of Habiba, and if the demand for the Aten discs came through while she was on board, I wasn't sure how we were going to square it. All things considered, I thought we'd be much better placed to deal with things once we were no longer required to offer her our hospitality and she could return to her hotel. I felt sure she might protest an early departure since we'd only just arrived in Amarna, and she'd had barely any time to search out promising locations for the buried treasure she hoped to find. But Dan's disappearance put a whole new slant on things. She really was in no position to call the shots, no matter what we decided.

Of course, the other person inconvenienced by a precipitate departure was Ted. He'd only just moved his belongings and overnight bag from the dig house back into his cabin on the dahabeeyah. But Ted was a gentleman, and would understand.

In the end it was decided for us. Walid joined us in the kitchen first thing in the morning, where Adam and I were preparing the breakfast things.

'Any news?' he asked.

We both shook our heads.

'I'm sorry to hear it. Merry, you look as if you haven't slept a wink.'

I tried to look a little less careworn as I spooned coffee into the cafetière. But the truth was I was worried sick and had spent the night tossing and turning. It was of no great help to learn that it showed.

'I've just had a call from Ibrahim Mohassib at the Luxor Museum,' Walid said without any further ado.

We both looked at him expectantly.

'The philologist has completed the translation of Ay's scroll,' he announced. 'Mr Mohassib is in a state of great excitement. He refused to divulge to me on the telephone what the papyrus has revealed – not that I need telling, of course. But he has entreated me to return to Luxor with the utmost urgency. Would it…? I mean, do you think we could…?'

'It's alright, Walid.' Adam cut across his agitation. 'Merry and I had already come to the conclusion that we need to head back to Luxor. If Gamal was planning to contact us here, he'd have done so by now. He's probably there already if he travelled with Dan by car. He's used chloroform once, so there's no reason to suppose he won't do so again. Dan's a big chap, and it's a pretty effective way of keeping someone quiet on a long journey.'

I flinched at the image this created in my mind, but did my bit to put Walid's mind at ease. 'Adam's right. And if, for any reason, Gamal should happen to be still here, then he's followed us once, so can no doubt do so again. Of course we should head back. Perhaps you'd be kind enough to let Habiba know so she understands the urgency.'

'I'll let Ted know we need to head off, as well,' Adam said, slipping his arm into a single crutch and hopping towards the door. 'He won't be able to come with us, of course. His job here is not done, and there's no way he'd be allowed to take that last jar away with him. Hopefully, he'll be able to join us back in Luxor in a few days' time.'

'Hang on a sec,' I said, calling him back. 'You know, it occurs to me, we may still have a chance to steal a march on Gamal Abdel-Maqsoud.'

'What do you mean?' Adam asked, turning back into the room.

'He'll be expecting us to sail back to Luxor. If we head back by train instead, there may be still be time to put our original plan for staging the discovery of the tomb into action before he knows we're back. He thinks now he's got Dan that he holds all the aces, but I think we could still outplay him.'

I watched the fire blaze alight in Adam's eyes. 'You're right! We mustn't admit defeat just yet. But we must act quickly. We'll ask Khaled to sail the dahabeeyah back to Luxor. I agree the rest of us need to go by train. I suggest we take the Aten discs with us, just in case.'

We took Habiba with us of course. Speed was of the essence and we may yet still need her to play the part we'd assigned her. Ted waved us off at the ferry port, since we needed to cross the Nile to reach the train station, a short taxi ride away on the east bank. 'Just be careful,' he called after us. 'And promise to keep me posted.'

We arrived in Luxor in the early afternoon, after a three-and-a-half-hour rail trip. It felt horrible to be travelling without

Dan. But since there was nothing we could do about it until Gamal Abdel-Maqsoud made his next move, we had to get on with it. As Adam had pointed out, there was no point moping about feeling sorry. If there was even the smallest chance of getting one step ahead of our nemesis, we had to take it. We all piled into a taxi and gave instructions to the driver to take us directly to the Luxor Museum. Walid had the Aten discs securely locked inside his overnight bag. It was a proper modern one with a combination lock to which only he knew the code. He was adamant about being the one to carry them.

'I'm the idiot who insisted on the ill-advised letters that started all this,' he said. 'The responsibility is mine.'

I'm not sure either Adam or I was in the mood to argue, even if we'd wanted to.

Ibrahim Mohassib came running the minute he heard we were in the building. 'Oh, Dr Massri! I am so pleased you have come quickly! I am quite breathless with excitement!'

'If only his news were my only reason for making haste.' Walid murmured.

We followed the two museum curators along the corridor and into the now familiar laboratory, where the three scrolls were still secured within their glass plates.

'I have such a story to tell you! I am not sure you will believe your ears! But it is true!'

Walid glanced around. 'The philologist; is he here?'

'He worked through until the early hours of this morning.' Mr Mohassib cast a quick look at Adam and me. 'I believe you call it "burning the midnight oil"? This it the correct expression, yes?'

I nodded; glad to have my suspicion confirmed that his English was far from *inadequate*, as he would have had us believe at our first meeting.

'I told him to return to his hotel for some well-deserved sleep. Of course, he is sworn to secrecy and silence until after I have shared with you what we have learned. Then we can decide what to do.' He was almost rubbing his hands together with glee to be involved in something so momentous; as well he might be, I thought.

'His translation of the scroll is complete…?' Adam prompted.

'Ah, yes,' Mr Mohassib nodded delightedly. Then he glanced from Adam to me, and looked uncertainly at Walid. 'Er… These people…?'

'Are my trusted associates,' Walid assured him. 'They were present when we found the suitcase containing the papyri. Director Ismail's representative, Miss Garai here, can vouch for them. It is only right that they should be included in whatever this story is that you have to tell me.'

I was certain Habiba might baulk at being asked to vouch for us in Director Ismail's name. Especially since I was pretty sure her boss had never so much as heard of Adam

300

and me. But I wasn't about to quibble. Time was running out. To my way of looking at things, Walid's equivocation was wholly justifiable in the circumstances.

Thankfully, Habiba seemed willing to let it go since she hadn't been asked a direct question. Glancing at her, I could tell she was impatient to cut to the chase. And Ibrahim Mohassib seemed eager enough to accept Walid's assurances, no doubt due to his own impatience to tell us what he knew.

'So, what has the papyrus revealed?' Walid asked.

'Dr Massri, Miss Garai and – er – associates, I will be as succinct as I can. Now, you will recall, the early part of the document referred to "precious jewels" being undisturbed...?'

'Yes! Buried treasure, golden shrines, sacred images...' Habiba nodded, then added as an aside, 'No doubt statuary stolen from temples the length and breadth of the land.'

Ibrahim Mohassib looked as if he might explode with the importance of what he was about to impart. 'That, my friends, is where we had it wrong. The "precious jewels" are people.'

'*People*?' Habiba parroted, beating Walid to it by a second. He was acting of course, but was convincing enough.

'Specifically, a pharaoh and his great royal wife,' the curator said, eyes like bright chips in his walnut face. 'The term "precious jewels" was a kind of code. But you will never guess...'

'Akhenaten and Nefertiti!' Habiba cried out.

We all stared at her in genuine astonishment.

'It has to be!' she exclaimed. 'Don't you see? The Hymn to the Aten... the line of script reading *"Aten is key"*... It's all pointing to Akhenaten!

Ibrahim Mohassib looked devastated that she'd stolen his thunder. He opened and closed his mouth a few times, his eyebrows snapping up and down. I felt quite sorry for him.

'It was a very long scroll,' I interjected. 'We noticed it had the cartouches of both Tutankhamun and Ay. Did it fill in any of the gaps from history?' It seemed important not to jump too far ahead of ourselves, as well as to give poor Ibrahim Mohassib his moment in the sun.

He sent me a grateful smile. 'Ah; such a story as you will never believe...'

'Try us...' Adam invited sweetly.

'The papyrus, it must have come from Tutankhamun's tomb,' Mr Mohassib started. 'It is a mystery indeed how it came to be bricked up in KV20. Some opportunistic workman perhaps...? We will never know. Anyway, the scroll is a sort of pledge written to Tutankhamun by Ay.'

'But Tutankhamun was already dead when Ay succeeded him to the throne,' I frowned, trying to make the same comments as the first time around.

'That is true,' Mr Mohassib nodded. 'Ay wrote the scroll after tomb robbers broke into Tutankhamun's tomb. He dealt with them, and then must have had his papyrus placed inside the tomb when it was resealed.'

'What sort of pledge?' Walid asked.

'The scroll is a promise to keep the "precious jewels" safely hidden where none will ever find them.'

'Are you telling us this papyrus,' – Habiba pointed to it as she spoke – 'gives details of the secret burial place of Akhenaten and Nefertiti?'

'It does indeed,' the curator confirmed.

'Then it must still be there,' she said. 'Akhenaten and Nefertiti have never been found!'

I heard a thump, and looked round to find Walid had slumped forward onto his knees. He started wheezing.

'Get him some water,' I yelled. 'It's shock.'

We helped Walid – giving the performance of his life – to a chair and put a glass of water into his shaking hands. Habiba sat down too, also looking as if her legs might give way at any moment.

'I think you'd better start at the beginning and tell us the whole story.' Adam suggested, settling himself and propping up his foot on a stool.

Mr Mohassib gabbled his way through it, his words running together and falling over themselves in his eagerness to get them out. Half way through, I reached for a chair too. It was an incredible story, even hearing it the second time around.

When he was done, I summarised the essential point. 'So basically Tutankhamun and Ay outfoxed Horemheb by using the removal of Smenkhkare's remains from Akhet-Aten to a hastily built tomb in the Valley of the Kings – KV55 we presume, since Horemheb immediately desecrated it – as a cover for the secret reburial of Akhenaten and Nefertiti.'

'You have it exactly right,' Ibrahim Mohassib said, clapping his hands together.

'But you haven't told us where!' Habiba said, jumping up. 'You said the papyrus gives details of their secret burial place! So where is it?'

Ibrahim Mohassib looked suddenly as if he might burst into tears. 'Miss Garai, I am sorry; I have misled you,' he babbled. 'The papyrus does not reveal the location. It only says the "precious jewels" will remain undisturbed for all eternity, "no one seeing, no one hearing".' He looked quite dejected; his shoulders slumped forward. His bubble of excitement of a few minutes ago had well and truly burst. Perhaps it was the impact of a beautiful girl glaring at him as if he'd offered her a priceless gift only to snatch it away again.

'But I think Ay has left us some clues about where to look.'

It was Walid who had spoken, pushing himself up from his chair and walking towards the glass plates on legs that looked as if they were made of elastic. We all moved across to join him in staring down at the three papyri secured under their glass plates.

'I feel as if we have the pieces of a puzzle,' Walid said. 'We just have to work out how they fit together.'

'*Aten is key... Aten is key...*' Adam repeated over and over. 'You know, when we were inside the Hathor Chapel inside Hatshepsut's temple a few days ago, we were all struck by the sheer number of sun discs carved into the walls...'

'But they are all associated with Hathor, not the Aten,' Habiba frowned.

Adam shrugged. 'Nevertheless, if you were planning on secretly burying your precious jewels somewhere their enemies would never think of looking for them, don't you think you might choose somewhere dedicated to the rival gods, but with enough of a nod to the new religion to be acceptable?'

I could see enlightenment dawning on her face. 'You think that architect's drawing is actually a map of the burial site?'

Adam looked at her intently. 'That line of script has surely got to mean something.'

He was willing her to make the mental leap, but she just continued to stare back at him. Adam is a handsome man, so perhaps it was just his mesmeric gaze that held her transfixed. Whatever, I felt a little gentle nudge in the right direction wouldn't go amiss.

'What if it's a literal key we're supposed to be looking for. You know; of the turn-in-the-lock variety.' I had a feeling these may have been the very words I'd used the first time around, when we were trying to figure out what it all meant for ourselves.

'You're suggesting there might be some kind of keyhole in the Hathor Chapel; and something Aten-related is the key to unlock it?' Walid asked a bit breathlessly.

I shrugged, shaking my head. 'It's just a thought.'

'No, no; I think you might be onto something.' Habiba cried, as I appeared to dismiss the idea. 'There are deep gashes in the wall all over the chapel. What if one of them should prove to be a keyhole?'

We all gaped at her; I think perhaps in genuine amazement that she had finally cottoned on.

'We have photographs, don't we?' Habiba rushed on excitedly. 'You took loads of them the other day, Adam.'

Adam pulled his iPhone from his pocket, tapped on it until the photographs opened onto the screen and then handed it across to her.

'Look, here!' Habiba exclaimed. 'See this gash beneath the Hathor relief... Doesn't that look worthy of investigation?'

She'd struck the bulls-eye at her first attempt.

'But we don't have anything to use as a 'key',' I protested, trying to ignore Walid's overnight bag, which seemed to be emitting some kind of electromagnetic signal.

'Surely we need to work out what the original 'key' might have been,' Walid said, struggling to keep us within the bounds of reason and reality.

I remembered the scribbled note Ahmed had found stitched into the lining of Howard Carter's suitcase. We still desperately wanted to keep Howard Carter out of this, and his reputation intact. But at the same time we needed to fast-track our reasoning so we stood the best chance of getting ahead of Gamal Abdel-Maqsoud, to protect the tomb from his avaricious clutches and get Dan back.

'If Aten is key, then we must need a physical Aten disc,' Habiba suggested, thoroughly immersed now in puzzling it out. I recalled Adam and I had got that far in our own deductions first time around, and silently congratulated her. She was a bright cookie, this one, unknowingly playing her part to perfection.

'Where on earth are we going to get one of those?' Adam asked. 'Or, are you suggesting we go and take some measurements and try to manufacture one?'

'I'm just wondering…' Walid started, and we all turned to look at him. '…Whether there might be any chance of there being something among the Tutankhamun treasure to help us out.'

I realised we were all playing our parts as if acting were a skill we'd been born to. 'Well, you know the artefacts from his tomb better than anyone…' I prompted.

Walid was gazing at the photograph on Adam's phone. Habiba followed his glance.

'The Aten disc is between the upraised cow-horns of the goddess Hathor,' she said thoughtfully. 'Dr Massri, can you think of anything in the Tutankhamun collection that resembles this…?'

She was actually a step ahead of where Adam and I had been in our logic on that first occasion. We'd known we were looking for something Aten-shaped, but didn't make the connection to the cow-goddess. Walid had used subtlety and suggestion and she'd holed it in one.

'I wonder if we should investigate the Mehet-Weret ritual couch,' he mused. 'She was a cow-goddess associated with the cult of Hathor. But, of course the couch is on display at the Museum in Cairo…'

We all traded glances.

Finally, Walid turned to Ibrahim Mohassib, who'd been strangely quiet throughout. 'You are sworn to secrecy and silence,' he said in that authoritative tone I'd heard him use before. 'We will naturally need to make our report to Director Ismail at the Ministry of Antiquities. If you breathe a word *to anyone* before we have done so, I will personally ensure you are stripped of your office here. Do I make myself understood?'

'Yes, Dr Massri; I understand you perfectly.'

'Good. Then I suggest we look into flights so Miss Garai and I can travel to Cairo tomorrow.'

Chapter 17

It felt very odd not to have the dahabeeyah to return to. But Khaled wouldn't have her back in Luxor until tomorrow. We took a taxi to Habiba's hotel, the Nile Palace. Adam and I had a coffee on the terrace overlooking the clover-shaped pool and the Nile, while Habiba and Walid made their travel arrangements for tomorrow. Successfully staging the discovery of the tomb was now within sniffing distance. Walid and Habiba would lay the whole thing before Director Ismail at the Ministry of State for Antiquities. He could decide whether to risk bringing the genuine Aten discs from between the horns of the Mehet-Weret ritual couch to see if they would indeed unlock the entrance to a hidden tomb behind the Hathor Chapel in Hatshepsut's Temple. I felt sure Walid would persuade him, and urge him to be quick about it.

Walid joined us on the terrace after a little while. 'Habiba has gone to her room. I think she is feeling somewhat overwhelmed.'

'Hard to blame her,' I sympathised. 'It's just taken about an hour to arrive at a point we took several days to get to.'

'It's a lot to take in,' Adam agreed.

'She hasn't mentioned the Copper Scroll,' I remarked. 'Perhaps her tour of Amarna convinced her there's unlikely to be anything left to be found. It's possible the Theban priests dug most of it up again, after all.'

'Speaking of which...' Adam started. '...It reminds me we left the clay tablets in the safe on board the *Queen Ahmes*. If we really are going ahead with our plan to get back inside the tomb tonight, it strikes me we really ought to collect them so we can return them. If a contingent from Cairo is going to arrive at some point over the next few days, I want to be able to look them in the eye; not feel guilty that we've got something stored in our safe which ought by rights to be hidden inside Akhenaten's sarcophagus. Habiba's proved quite effectively that she doesn't need our prototype of the Copper Scroll when the real thing is sitting in a museum in Jordan and is available to look at on the Internet. We don't need the clay tablets. She can carry on with her treasure hunting to her heart's content once the whole business of the tomb is done and dusted.'

'So, how do you propose we get them back?' I asked. 'The *Queen Ahmes* is sailing the Nile something like a hundred kilometres north of here.'

'Sounds like a job for Ahmed,' Adam said. 'He can take the police speedboat as well as my key to the safe.' He fingered the small key on the bootlace at his throat, alongside the crocodile tooth.

'So, we really are going to go back inside the tomb tonight?' Walid asked, looking anxious.

'I don't see that we have any choice,' Adam said.

'As well as putting the clay tablets back, we need to remove the pulley system you rigged up inside the burial chamber, and dismantle the bridge you secured across the pit shaft,' I reminded him. 'If a delegation from the Ministry of State for Antiquities is going to "discover" the tomb…' I made speech marks around the word with my fingers, '…there can be no evidence left inside of our earlier visits.'

'The quantities of dust and stones can be explained as the natural result of a rockfall,' Adam said. 'They're a frequent enough phenomena around here. No one need ever know Mustafa Mushhawrar set off an explosion that caused half the mountainside to implode into the tomb. We'll just have to be careful not to leave any footprints.'

'Then we will have to tell Ahmed to be quick in getting the clay tablets back.' Walid said. 'With you injured, Adam; and Dan currently – er – indisposed, we will need Ahmed's strength to get everything dismantled and brought out of the tomb.'

'We'll also need him to think up some way of distracting the guards,' I muttered. 'I don't see how we're going to pull this thing off if they're still patrolling the place every few minutes.'

'And once he's dreamed up a distraction for them to get us inside and out again tonight...' Adam said. '...he then needs to find a way to ensure security is tighter than ever for the next few nights so it's impossible for Gamal Abdel-Maqsoud to act before the Ministry gets here.'

I nodded. 'Basically, we have a small window of opportunity to put our plan into action tonight, while Gamal thinks we're sailing back from Amarna. No doubt we'll hear from him to name his terms for Dan's release as soon as the *Queen Ahmes* is back dockside tomorrow.'

Adam smiled. 'It's all a question now of good luck and good timing. And once we're out of there, you can travel to Cairo tomorrow, Walid, with a clear conscience that we've done everything in our power to protect the tomb and prepare it for discovery.'

Walid decided to check in at the Nile Palace. He and Habiba were booked on the first flight out of Luxor in the morning, and he needed somewhere secure to keep his suitcase out of harm's way.

'I won't get much sleep tonight if everything goes according to plan,' he said. 'So I'm going to try for a few hours shut-eye now. I'll see you both later.'

Adam and I met Ahmed in one of the coffee shops in town. He sat there in his police uniform smoking a hubble-bubble pipe while we filled him in on everything that had happened in Amarna and at the Luxor Museum.

'So, Gamal Abdel-Maqsoud has taken Dan,' he growled. 'This is bad news that he followed you. It explains why everything here, it has been as silent as…' He cocked his big head to one side, concentrating on dredging up what he wanted to say from his inner mine of colloquialisms. 'Now what is your English expression…?'

'As silent as the tomb.' Adam supplied.

'Hmm, perhaps not the most apposite given the circumstances.' I remarked. 'If Gamal hurts Dan, I'll personally make it my business to ensure he ends up in one, and it won't be Akhenaten's, that I promise you.'

Ahmed bared his even white teeth. 'A prison cell in Egypt can be much like a tomb,' he said. 'Kidnap of a British national is a very serious business. When we catch him, I can perhaps give him the choice between prison and his own tomb. It will be interesting to see which he prefers.'

Ahmed's supreme confidence that we would win out in the end was just what I needed, and reassured me immensely. It was hard having an enemy who could wreak such havoc without showing his face. It felt uncomfortably like a war of attrition. I wondered how Gamal Abdel-Maqsoud would set about making contact and issuing his ransom demands: whether he'd find some oblique way of naming his terms or be assured enough in his superior negotiating position finally to come out in the open and confront us head-on.

Adam stirred a brown sugar lump into his coffee. 'We just have to hope that we can bring everything to a happy resolution before the Ministry officials arrive, so that all Habiba's hard work in sleuthing her way through the papyri pays off.'

Our police pal seemed intrigued to hear about Habiba's involvement in figuring out the location of the tomb. 'She worked most of it out herself,' I said. 'With only one or two gentle nudges in the right direction.'

'She is a very clever young woman,' Ahmed said, with a strange glint in his eye. It sparked and went out. 'Perhaps too clever,' he added.

'You like her, don't you?' I fished, deciding this was too good a lead to let go.

Ahmed drew on the water pipe, and breathed out a stream of fragrant-smelling smoke on a long sigh. 'Yes,' he said simply.

This was unusual for Ahmed, who never used one word when tens of dozens would do. He didn't need to say more. His single statement spoke volumes.

'Then you should ask her out,' I encouraged him. 'You'd make a fine couple. Head-turning at any rate.'

Ahmed sighed again. 'I would like a lady in my life; somebody my mother and my sisters would approve of. But I look at the young women of Luxor and I don't see anyone special, lovely though many of them are.' He glanced from my face to Adam's and back, and a strange expression softened his features. Ahmed wasn't usually given to speaking about his personal life, about which I knew next to nothing, so I decided to keep quiet and not interrupt him. Adam, sitting alongside me, sipped his coffee and also remained sensitively silent. 'I watch the way the two of you are together,' Ahmed admitted. 'And I wonder if it might ever be possible for me to find the same: a woman who could be my equal partner, who is intelligent, quick-witted and fearless…'

'Merry is already taken,' Adam murmured drily. 'I have a feeling they broke the mould when they made her.'

I overlooked this since I was really rather overcome. Not knowing quite what to say, I reached across the table and squeezed Ahmed's hand.

'Habiba is the first woman I have met, who I think is a little like you,' Ahmed said. 'But of course she is very beautiful…'

I wasn't sure quite how to take this, thinking this perhaps was where the comparison between Habiba and me stopped. I'm self-aware enough to know I'm passably attractive. But beautiful…? No; beautiful was definitely a word for Habiba, not for me.

Ahmed had only paused for breath. 'Somebody like Habiba would never be interested in someone like me.'

316

'Why ever not?' I demanded. 'You're a good catch for any young woman, Ahmed. You're kind-hearted, loyal, good looking, and you have a good job.'

'But she has her degree and her career in the Ministry... She is very focused on her work and wishes to make a name for herself.'

Adam put down his coffee cup and looked Ahmed squarely in the eyes. 'Mate, we have an expression back at home that all work and no play makes Jack a dull boy. Your Habiba would do well to heed it.'

'Jack?' Ahmed frowned, looking confused.

'It's just a figure of speech,' I explained. 'Basically the saying means that too much work, without any light relief makes someone both bored and boring.'

'If you ask me, you could be the making of that young lady,' Adam said. 'And she should count herself damn lucky that you're interested.'

Ahmed, much bolstered by our support for his suit, agreed to his mission to retrieve the clay tablets from the *Queen Ahmes* by commandeering the police speedboat for the afternoon. River patrols were part of his regular duties, so he didn't need to ask special permission. He'd just be going a little further along the Nile than usual, that's all. Ok, a lot further. But the extra miles didn't seem worth mentioning. I think we'd convinced him that once the tomb was cleared and we knew the lay of the land where Gamal Abdel-Maqsoud was concerned, there was really nothing to stop him making a play for Habiba.

Left at a bit of a loose end, Adam and I debated checking in to a hotel, but decided there was little point. We could live without a night's sleep without suffering too many ill effects, and it was money we didn't need to spend given the parlous state of our income. Instead we found a quiet spot in the newly finished garden along the Corniche overlooking the Nile and put in the promised call to Ted. Adam pressed the speakerphone button so we could both participate in the conversation. It was time to bring him up to speed on everything that had happened since we left Amarna first thing this morning.

'No word on Dan…?' he asked as soon as we'd said hello.

'Radio silence this end,' Adam said. 'And you?'

'Nothing to report here either I'm afraid. Which is a pity, since you told me Dan was especially interested in finding out what Panehesy's letters might have to say about the parting of the Red Sea…'

'You've translated another scroll?'

'I've been hard at it since you left here early this morning. It helps to focus on something other than worrying about Dan and the rest of you. I'm dreading speaking to Jessica. If we can't get this thing sorted and assure ourselves of Dan's safety in the next couple of days, I think I'll have to avoid taking her calls.'

It was good to be reminded that Dan was family to more than just me, rhetorically-speaking of course. There were lots of people who cared about him. But, as Ted was suggesting, perhaps it was best not to dwell too much on that right now. I hated to think of him in the clutches of the malicious Gamal Abdel-Maqsoud.

'So, what's the latest tale home from the Exodus?' Adam asked. 'If I remember rightly, we'd just reached the point where Ramses I ordered Meryre and the descendants of the tribes of Israel to leave Egypt peaceably; and then changed his mind and set off in pursuit of them. Does Panehesy shed any light on the parting of the waves? Was it a tsunami that sucked all the water out so the Israelites could cross before sending it crashing back in a huge tidal wave to drown pharaoh's infantries, in the way some scientists suggest?'

'Well, the first thing to clear up is that it wasn't the Red Sea at all that the Israelites crossed while fleeing from Pharaoh and his armies,' Ted said. 'That is a mistranslation of the term "Yam Suph" that has perpetuated down the centuries. It was actually the "Sea of Reeds", one of the many salt water lakes fed by tributaries and canals in the Nile Delta region, near the Mediterranean coast.'

'And the pillars of fire and smoke mentioned in the Bible...?' Adam enquired. 'Some geologists have suggested a volcanic eruption in Santorini, some five hundred kilometres away, might have been visible in Egypt...?'

'The truth, I fear, is much more prosaic, and closes the historical gap of some two hundred years between the Santorini eruption and the actual expulsion of the Israelites from Egypt,' Ted said. 'The Hebrews' fire pots were placed in front of the column of fleeing men, women and children, in the nature of a military guide-on. However, as Meryre and his retreating people pretended to be boxed in against the water of the Sea of Reeds, they moved their fire pots to the back of the column. This was a ruse to give the pursuing Egyptian Force the impression the Hebrews were facing them, preparing for a daylight confrontation. It also meant the glare of the fire pots caused night blindness, permitting the Hebrews to leave at night from the far, or new back, side of the column without detection.'

'So you're saying that under cover of darkness, and with the aid of the fire-pot ruse, the Hebrews retreated across the water barrier?' Adam interjected.

I found the image forming in my mind's eye of the parting of the waters, as depicted in Cecil B. DeMille's film *The Ten Commandments.*

'Yes,' Ted confirmed. 'Now, you need to forget all the movies you may have watched,' he advised, apparently reading my mind. 'Remember, Akhenaten's religion rejected magic. Panehesy's account most certainly does not recognise the hand of God at play in the escape of the Israelites. There was no miracle. What secured the ultimate release of the Israelites from Pharaoh's pursuing army was the knowledge Meryre and Panehesy had of a series of man-made canals dating back to Joseph's time.'

Neither one of us interrupted him this time, so Ted went on.

'This canal system was called the "*Bahr Youssef*" and was built as an irrigation system to mitigate the seven years of drought foretold by Joseph, or Vizier Yuya, as he became. There was a north-south canal, which defined the eastern border of Egypt, called the Samana Canal. It was approximately forty miles long. It extended from Lake Timsah on the south to the Pelusiac arm of the Nile. As well as providing irrigation, it served as a defensive wall against invaders. There was also an east-west canal on the southern side of Goshen, extending from Lake Timsah on the east to the Nile on the west. It was called the Wadi Tumilat Canal and extended some one hundred kilometres. Both canals had waterways of some two hundred feet in width. The Isrealites gave the appearance of being hemmed in at the junction of these two great canals, unable to cross Lake Timsah, the Sea of Reeds.'

Adam raised his eyebrows. 'If that's true, there must be some geological evidence still remaining to back it up...?'

I could almost hear Ted's smile coming through the receiver. 'Funnily enough, I have looked it up online this afternoon. Geological research has indeed identified soil markings to confirm the existence of these two dried-up waterways. The writers of the article I read say the scale of the undertaking was a remarkable bronze age canal system, predating the Suez Canal by more than 3,000 years.'

'Wow!' Adam said. 'And we thought the pyramids were impressive!'

'There's even evidence the ancient Egyptians used a system of locks to cut off areas of water for moving ships, and built dams to manoeuvre the monoliths they used in their building programmes on and off of watercraft,' Ted enthused.

'I'm starting to get an inkling of how a working knowledge of canals, and locks, and dammed water might have aided the Israelites in making good their escape from Egypt,' Adam commented.

'But we'd still like to hear the story,' I added quickly.

'Ok then,' Ted said. 'Meryre and his retreating people bled the waters through sluices to reduce the water level of Lake Timsah on either side of the cofferdams. This allowed the Hebrews to move forward on a dry surface and minimised the possibility they might inadvertently march into the body of water on either side of the roadway. Once on the other side they obstructed the end of the channel. As dawn approached, Ramses I, and his army in pursuit were required to break rank and follow the Hebrews onto the narrow causeway in their chariots in almost single-file. There was no way for them to regroup in any kind of formal military phalanx.'

'And then the Hebrews breached the canal walls...' Adam deduced, '... emptying dammed water from both sides of the roadway, sending it crashing in on both sides like a double tidal wave.'

'Ramses I, and his charioteers drowned,' Ted said. 'It was a quite brilliant military ambush.'

'We know from the historical record that Ramses I ruled for only a year, two at most,' Adam nodded. 'So it fits with what is known.'

'Quite,' Ted agreed.

'So, what happened next?'

'Well, the Bible goes a bit quiet at this point, as you may recall,' Ted said. 'Moses leads the tribes into the Sinai desert, where they wander in the wilderness for forty years. The next major event for Moses is receiving the Ten Commandments from the Lord on the holy mountain.'

'Why do I have a feeling you're going to tell us it wasn't quite like that?' I murmured.

'Ramses I had a son who was already a grown man, as I'm sure you both know.'

'Seti,' Adam nodded. 'He became Pharaoh Seti I on his father's death.'

'That's right. On hearing about the ambush in the Sea of Reeds, Seti set out to recover his father's body so it could be prepared for the rites of mummification. Seti's troops also collected up the bodies of all the dead charioteers, and recovered the chariots, shields and spears to prevent the Hebrews further arming themselves. Now, if Seti had simply retreated back into Egypt at that point and let the Hebrews go, things might have followed a more peaceful path. But he didn't...'

'He followed them?' I asked.

'Not only that,' Ted said cryptically. 'I think Seti harboured a secret, one that has been preserved through the centuries.'

'A secret?'

'I can't be completely sure as I haven't quite finished my translation of the last scroll,' he qualified. 'I'll tell you what; why don't you both head over to Karnak and call me back from there?'

'Karnak?'

'I think you'll see the relevance if the next part of Panehesy's narrative says what I think it does... I just need to double-check a few of the passages.'

I was pleased to have something to fill in the time before tonight and also distract me from worrying about both

Dan and our ability to pull off our plan for preparing the tomb for discovery.

Karnak Temple was a walk of about a mile from the Corniche gardens. It was a distance not to be sneezed at in the summertime temperatures. But both Adam and I were pretty well acclimatised by now, and we managed it with only some depletion in the quantity of bottled water we were carrying. Adam's crutches slowed us down a little, but he'd mastered them now and swung himself along at my side quite easily.

There were the usual armed guards on duty in the sentry post, but otherwise the great temple complex was virtually deserted. Despite the lack of visitors, we were able to buy entrance tickets from a sleepy-eyed individual in the ticket hut. He looked at us a bit askance, but couldn't rouse himself sufficiently from his torpor to question our visit, and waved us through.

'I still can't get used to seeing the archaeological sites like this,' Adam remarked as we descended the wide steps between raised ram-headed sphinxes on stone plinths and approached the gigantic entrance pylon. 'I'm so used to dodging the tour groups, it seems strange to be here completely alone.'

'What a privilege though,' I said. 'I wonder how many people on the planet can say they've had Karnak Temple entirely to themselves. You see, there are a few upsides to the dire political situation.'

He dropped one of his crutches and reached for my hand. 'I love your ability to see only the positives, Merry; but unless the tourist ban gets lifted soon this will become the norm rather than the exception. I don't know how long the economy can survive.'

'D'you know what? I'd rather not be reminded that our days in Egypt are probably numbered,' I said. 'Let's just live in the moment and enjoy it while we can, huh? We've got enough to worry about without adding our uncertain future into the mix.'

He pulled me against him and hugged me one armed and then leaned back to look at me. 'And d'*you* know what, lovely Merry? You're right. I don't know why I'm being so damned defeatist. Look at me! Come what may; right now I'm in one of my favourite places on earth, with my very favourite person. I'm going to take your advice and enjoy every second.'

'Good. You know, I feel quite nostalgic being here again with you,' I admitted.

He smiled at me. 'It was kind of our first date, wasn't it, coming here?'

'You told me your life had burst into Technicolor since meeting me,' I reminded him a bit shyly.

He leaned forward and kissed me. 'And it's stayed that way ever since. Meredith Pink, you have been the time of my life! I adore you!'

'Amen to that!' I grinned.

'Amen, did you say? Or Amun? We're here in a temple dedicated to the latter.'

'Which only goes to show how much influence Egyptian theology has had on modern religion,' I smiled. 'Now, let's get into the shade before we call Ted back and get on with hearing the inside track on the "Greatest Story Ever Told".' I made quotation marks with my fingers around the words. 'I think I'm about to expire with the heat.'

Adam picked up his abandoned crutch, and crossing the open court we entered the jaw-dropping hypostyle hall, with its towering sandstone columns rising all around us.

'You know, Seti I is credited with starting the building of this part of the temple,' Adam said. 'It was completed by his son, Ramses the Great.'

I stared around me at the forest of immense columns, trying to imagine them fully painted, as they were originally. There was still some faded pigment clinging to the stone in places.

Adam added, 'It was Seti I and Ramses II who restored the might of the Egyptian Empire at the start of the 19th Dynasty, after the years of chaos that characterised the ending of the once glorious 18th.'

I nodded, remembering our visit to Seti's fabulous tomb; the deepest and most richly decorated in the Valley of the Kings. 'Seti had a reputation as a great warrior, didn't he?'

'Yes; probably the best since Thutmosis III.'

'I wonder what his mysterious secret was.'

'Only one way to find out.'

We perched in the shade on the plinth surrounding one of the enormous columns, and called Ted.

'My dears, where are you?' he greeted us.

'Hypostyle hall.' Adam said.

'Good. Ok, now I know it's hot, but I want you to head outside to the exterior northern wall and tell me what you see.'

We got down from the plinth and did as he'd asked, emerging into the blinding sunshine on the temple's northern side. Navigation in Egypt is a straightforward business since the Nile divides the country in half north to south. So long as you know where you are relative to the river, and which bank you are on, it's simple enough to work out your bearings. We shielded our eyes and gazed up at the immense carved walls.

'They look like war reliefs,' Adam said into his iPhone. 'They stretch across the entire northern wall of the temple.'

'Exactly correct, my boy.' Ted approved. 'Specifically they are Seti I's war reliefs, giving a full military account of his campaign against the Shasu.'

'The Shasu?' I repeated.

'The name 'Shasu' was used by the Egyptians to designate the Bedouin tribes of Sinai, nomadic people who spoke a Semitic language. There can be little doubt, however, it is also a derivative of the word 'Hebrew'.'

'Seti campaigned against them?' Adam asked.

'He did. The temple wall reliefs you are looking at right now prove it. Only the link has never been made explicitly to the Biblical Exodus. But I now have the proof in Panehesy's correspondence that the term 'Shasu' also denotes the Israelite group Moses led out of Egypt. Ok now, the king's first war is shown on the bottom row of the eastern side of the wall. See it? It is dated to Seti's first year on the throne.'

We made our way to the eastern corner of the temple and Adam pointed out the scenes to me, waving one crutch at the relevant reliefs.

'There is evidence this campaign took place immediately after the death of Ramses I,' Ted said. 'Before the process of mummification, which took seventy days, had been completed and before Seti I had been crowned as the new Pharaoh.'

'So, he followed the escaping Israelites into the Sinai,' Adam said. 'I imagine his objective was to capture or kill Meryre to obliterate his claim to the throne.'

'Correct,' Ted confirmed. 'But on his first attempt, he did not succeed. Shortly after his coronation, he set out again and, once more, his campaign is recorded in front of you. The second and middle rows of relief show the relevant military manoeuvres.'

Adam pointed with his crutch again, and I squinted through my sunglasses, looking at the carvings of chariotry and infantry set deeply into the stone.

'Ok, my dears; I have shown you where the historical evidence is to be found. I suggest you head back into the shade, and I'll tell you the rest.'

We returned to the hypostyle hall, and perched back on the same plinth as before. Adam propped his crutches against the column, and levered himself up beside me.

'Now, just to fill in a couple of Biblical gaps,' Ted started. 'The whole story of Moses receiving the Ten Commandments from God on the Holy Mountain gets only a passing mention from Panehesy. As I recall our friend Nabil Zaal citing, the Ten Commandments are in actual fact a re-phrasing of Spell 125 of *The Book of the Dead*, the assurances a dead person had to give before Osiris and his forty-two judges in the Hall of Judgement. Since Meryre, as an Atenist, no longer believed in Osiris or the rest of the ancient Egyptian Pantheon, he took it upon himself to re-transcribe the spell as a set of Laws, teachings, or commandments, if you prefer, for his people to follow.'

'Makes sense,' Adam nodded.

'And the worshipping of the golden calf story is also an incident blown out of all proportion in the Old Testament,' Ted continued. 'The truth is that Meryre caught Meryre II with a gold statue of Hathor. It was one of the treasures stolen when Akhenaten's henchmen closed the traditional temples, and the treasurer had brought it out of Egypt with him.'

'Could it have been stolen from Hatshepsut's Temple?' I broke in excitedly.

'Specifically from the Hathor Shrine,' Adam added, catching my drift.

'The letters don't say where it originated from,' Ted remarked. 'But I'd say it's a distinct possibility.'

'So Habiba really is onto something,' I breathed.

'Yes, for sure.' Ted confirmed. 'It's clear they weren't worshipping the golden calf as the Bible suggests. Remember, these were Atenist priests. Meryre accused his namesake of keeping the statue for his own personal enrichment, and confiscated it. It's fair to say it caused a rift in the camp. I guess the later Biblical authors needed to find an explanation for the squabbles that broke out between the Hebrews, which are quite well documented in the Old Testament. I imagine the row over the golden calf had become folklore by then, and they found a way of re-telling it, and linking it to the Ten Commandments, without revealing Meryre's identity.'

I tilted my head on one side, gazing at the columns surrounding us. 'It's interesting how the thread of what actually happened runs through the embellished Bible stories.'

'But there are bits the Old Testament leaves out altogether,' Ted said. 'And Seti's secret is one of them.'

'His secret being that he killed Meryre/Moses, I presume?' Adam said.

Ted was silent for a moment. 'Well, yes; that of course.'

'That's not all?'

'Let me ask you a question,' Ted said. 'From what you know of the historical record, how many children did Seti have?'

Adam scratched the side of his head. 'Two for definite: a daughter, Tia; his son, Ramses, obviously; and possibly a second daughter, making three.'

'Interesting you should use the word *"obviously".*' Ted remarked.

'We know Ramses was Seti's son,' Adam said in confusion. 'He's recorded on various monuments as the Crown Prince, and we know he followed Seti to the throne as Pharaoh Ramses II.'

'Most of what you say is true,' Ted agreed. 'But he was not Seti's natural son. At the time of his father's death, Seti had sired only daughters.'

'But...' Adam started and trailed off.

Ted allowed his pause to draw out by a beat or two. 'Seti did not have a son, but Meryre did: Gershomre. He was a small boy at the time of the Exodus. Seti pursued the fleeing Hebrews into the Sinai and, yes, he killed Meryre. But he spared Gershomre. Instead of slaying him, he took him back with him to Egypt to be brought up at the royal court, changing his name to Ramses. That was Seti's secret.'

Chapter 18

Walid's eyes nearly fell out of his head when we told him, later that same evening, eating a quick meal in the Nile Palace restaurant before setting out for our planned night-time excursion to get the tomb ready for discovery.

'You're telling me Ramses the Great, possibly the best known of all the pharaohs after Tutankhamun, was in actual fact the son of Moses?'

'Well, perhaps we should just stick with calling him Meryre's son,' Adam advised. 'But yes, that's right.'

'But... that means... I can scarcely believe it... he was related to Akhenaten by blood!''

'Akhenaten, and all the previous pharaohs of the 18th Dynasty,' I said. 'He was Akhenaten's nephew; or half-nephew if we're going to be precise.'

'Which means, he also had the blood of the Hebrews flowing in his veins.' Adam added.

'Did he know it?' Walid gaped. 'Was he brought up knowing his "father" the pharaoh kidnapped him from the fleeing Israelites?'

'I don't think we can ever know that for sure,' Adam said. 'And, of course Panehesy's correspondence is silent on that particular point. He only tells us Gershomre was a small boy when Seti took him, but doesn't give us his age. But if you look at Ramses II's throne names, you'll notice something rather suggestive.'

Walid was Egyptologist enough to be able to reel them off. 'His prenomen was "*Usermaatre Setepenre*" and his nomen was "*Ramses Meryamun*",' he said. Then he let out a strangled kind of exclamation and went very still, staring across the table at Adam with bulging eyes.

'*Setepenre* was his natural mother's name,' Adam nodded. 'She was Akhenaten's youngest daughter as you'll recall. And it seems to me that *Meryamun* is simply a swapping of the deity whose protection is sought. If we replace Amun with Re, we're back to Meryre.'

'Of course, this could be simple coincidence,' I remarked. 'But, as Adam says, it's incredibly suggestive, don't you think?'

'But Ramses worshipped the traditional gods,' Walid protested. 'There's no sign of Aten worship in his reign. In fact, he did more to eradicate the Amarnan period from the historical record than any of his predecessors.'

'Political expediency?' Adam suggested. 'Ramses II became possibly the most powerful Pharaoh in history, especially considering the length of his reign: upwards of sixty years. Perhaps he was determined to assert his own authority, and didn't want to raise any doubts in the minds of his people by in any way associating himself with the social and religious upheaval that might still have been just about within the living memory of a few elderly folk.'

Walid looked thoughtful. 'What I think it's possible to say for sure about Ramses the Great is that he worshipped himself above all others. You only have to look at the sheer quantity and scale of the statuary that's survived from his reign. Ramses II saw himself as a God. Perhaps, in his own mind, that was his way of unifying the disparate beliefs of his ancestors, whether consciously or not. By elevating himself to the status of a divine being, he obviated the need to nail his colours to the mast, beyond maintaining the traditional status quo for his people.'

Adam nodded. 'What we can be definite about,' he said, 'is that Ramses II was not the Pharaoh of the Exodus, despite his candidacy in popular culture. Sure, he built a new capital city, Pi-Ramses in the Delta region. But, although he used the foundations of the earlier city, he didn't use Hebrew slaves to complete it.'

'What I don't understand, is how the Old Testament and the Qu'ran and the Torah could go on to describe the life and influence of Moses in leading his people to the Promised Land if he was already dead at the hands of Seti I.' Walid frowned. He pushed the food around on his plate with his fork without once raising it to his lips.

Adam put down his own knife and fork. 'Ah, yes, it's the final piece of the story. The Book of Exodus in the Old

Testament makes reference to a "veil" of Moses. The Bible states that when he comes down from the mountain after collecting the second set of tablets containing the Ten Commandments his people are afraid to come near him, and from then on he wears a veil of some description whenever he speaks to the tribesfolk. Biblical scholars have never known quite what to make of this.'

I could resist no longer, and leaned forward. 'But it falls into place when you realise that Meryre is dead, Gershomre has been kidnapped, Setepenre has died of a fever, and that it is in fact Panehesy who returns to the Hebrew camp from the skirmish with Seti, but wearing Meryre's robes, and with headcloths wound around his face so they won't recognise him.'

'Panehesy?' Walid gaped. 'You're saying it was Panehesy who led the Israelites through the wilderness towards the Promised Land?'

'Yes. His last letter home is to say goodbye. With Meryre dead, Panehesy knew he had to be the one to see that Akhenaten's beliefs were passed down through the generations. He and Meryre had made a pledge, and he was determined to keep the new faith alive.'

'So Panehesy became Moses.'

'He did. And I think it's safe to say we have Panehesy to thank for ensuring enough of the original teachings survived for the Qumranites to set down in the Dead Sea Scrolls several hundred years later. He also made sure the record of the treasure they'd buried when leaving Amarna so many years earlier was passed down; and set Meryre II to work on recording the hiding place of the golden casket in which they kept the tablets with the Ten Commandments inscribed on them. Today we refer to it as the Ark of the Covenant. Eventually, of course, the whole thing was translated from its original hieratic into Hebrew, and then copied onto the Copper Scroll.'

'Speaking of which...' Adam started.

'Ah yes,' I nodded, catching his eye. 'We have one last thing to tell you.'

Adam leaned forward. 'Ted signed off by telling us that the Barry is quite excited about that shaft near Meryre's tomb in the northern cliffs. He's had a metal detector of some sort down there, and it seems there might be something buried below the surface after all.'

'P'raps we should hold off telling Habiba, huh?' I suggested. 'Just until he's sure.'

Ahmed arrived just as we were finishing our after-dinner coffee. The carefully wrapped package under his arm proved he'd been successful in his mission to recover the tablets from the *Queen Ahmes*. He handed the key to the safe back to Adam.

'Khaled is going to sail through the night. He will be here in the morning.' Then he looked at me. 'I have asked the Receptionist to allow me to put a call through to Habiba, but he refuses to disclose the room number.'

I smiled at him sympathetically. 'It's because you're not in uniform tonight. Habiba is a single woman travelling alone and hotels – rightly – have strict policies on things like that.'

'I knocked to ask if she'd like to join us for dinner,' Walid said. 'But she'd already ordered from room service. She said she wishes to rest before our trip to Cairo tomorrow. It has been a busy and eventful few days.'

I nodded. 'That sounds sensible. And, fingers crossed, it's about to get busier and more eventful over the next few. At least it means we don't have to make up any excuses for leaving the hotel en masse and without her.'

'So, should we get going?' Adam asked, calling for the bill.

The night was still, with no breeze to speak of, the warm air somewhat suffocating in its dryness, as if every last drop of moisture had been sucked from the atmosphere. Put it this way; there was nothing fresh about it. While it was dark, it most certainly was not pitch-black. The stars were bright pinpricks spangling the heavens, and a perfect half-moon hanging in the sky bathed the landscape in a pale milky opalescence. It didn't bode well for evading the guards but it made for a beautifully scenic night-time walk.

We approached the temple from the south. Adam's rucksack contained the Aten disc;, mine the clay tablets, while Ahmed was lugging a heavy zipped-up canvas bag containing the tools we'd need to dismantle the pulley system and bridge the boys had rigged up inside the tomb. It left Walid to carry the backpack with our flashlights and bottles of water. All in all, we looked as if we were setting out on a camping expedition. If we were stopped, it seemed to me this might be our best explanation for why we were laden with so much baggage. I could only hope nobody would think to search us for tents.

Adam had dispensed with the crutches. His plastered foot meant he hobbled, but he was determined to play his part tonight.

With Hatshepsut's temple in sight, breathtaking in the moonlight, we hunkered down behind the rocky outcrop near Mentuhotep's crumbling ruins, where Ahmed had so nearly stumbled across Adam and me the other night. Silent and trying to keep our breathing shallow, we kept watch. Fifteen minutes passed, then twenty. There was no movement from the guard post. We stuck it out for another twenty minutes, and then I turned to Ahmed.

'Why aren't they patrolling tonight?' I whispered suspiciously. 'What did you tell them?'

'I telled to them only that Commander El-Saiyyid, he has posted a police unit to monitor the west bank sites and reinforce their efforts.'

'And is that true?'

He shifted uncomfortably. 'It is very nearly true. I am the police unit in question.'

'But you're off duty.'

Ahmed shrugged. 'I was posted here for several nights. They do not know my shift pattern, or that of my colleagues.'

Adam peered towards the guard hut. 'Even so, you'd think they'd still put up a token effort at least. Surely they don't think the police will take over their duties from them and assume all the responsibility for keeping a lookout.'

Ahmed shrugged. 'They can be lazy, these men.'

Walid looked at him sharply. 'Then you'd better make sure the police patrols become a reality from tomorrow. Their idleness may work in our favour tonight. But if Gamal Abdel-Maqsoud decides to make his move, assuming he thinks he can trade Dan for the Aten discs, I want to know he'll be caught.'

His voice was so stern I thought for a moment Ahmed was going to salute. He contented himself instead with pulling straighter. 'I will catch the villain,' he vowed. 'Have no fear.'

'Do you think we ought to check on the guards, just to be sure?' I asked as a horrible thought struck me. 'What if

Gamal has somehow been keeping watch on us, knows we're here, and that we must have the Aten discs with us, and has decided on an ambush? He might somehow have incapacitated the guards. He's used chloroform before, remember!'

'One man against four guards?' Adam said dubiously. 'One man against four of us?'

But I could see I'd put a sliver of doubt in his mind.

'I'll go,' I volunteered. 'I'm light on my feet. Besides, they'd recognise you from the other night, Adam; and they know you, Ahmed. Walid, you stay put, and look after the Aten discs for me. You're too important to risk getting caught.'

I slipped the rucksack off my back, passed it to Walid, and crept out from the shelter of the rock. I felt as exposed as if a spotlight were trained on me in the pearly glow of the moonlight. Ducking low, I moved forward, watching the ground in front of my feet for stray rocks that might trip me up.

I made it to the guard post without mishap. Stretching up on tiptoes I peeped in through the window, half expecting to see the guards sprawled unconscious on the floor.

They were clustered around a television set, smoking and watching a movie. It was obviously a comedy of some sort if the frequent bursts of laughter were anything to judge by.

I eased myself away from the window and turned to make my way back to the others. I'd swear I didn't make a sound, but as I moved, the door behind me opened. A rectangle of artificial yellow light spilled across the desert floor, and me with it.

Caught like a startled rabbit in headlights, there was only one thing I could think of to do.

I spun to face him and smiled brightly. 'Er – hello – do you speak English?'

The guard stared at me, looking perhaps more surprised than I did. I don't suppose it's a common occurrence to have a young Englishwoman turn up in the middle of the night. His string of incomprehensible Arabic answered my question. The television set went silent. Suddenly I had all four of them clustered around me.

'Officer Ahmed Abd el-Rassul,' I said loudly. 'Is he here?'

They evidently recognised the name and exchanged a few rapid-fire sentences. Ahmed's name was repeated, but other than that I didn't understand a word.

I decided my best bet was to keep talking. 'It's just, he helped my – er – my boyfriend a few nights ago.' I pointed to my foot and made a wincing face to indicate pain, then made fists of my hands and threw a few punching motions, pretending to be in a fight. 'Adam? Adam Tennyson? Officer Abd el-Rassul took him to hospital. I wanted to say thank you!'

One of the guards glanced at his watch and raised his eyebrows at me in a way that eloquently expressed his view that I'd chosen a damned strange time to pay a visit. It was almost midnight. But at least it proved I was making myself understood, at least to one of them. As the caleche and taxi drivers in Luxor are master linguists, it's easy to make the mistake of thinking all Egyptians speak English. But outside of the tourist trade, where their living depends on it, it isn't so.

'I know it's late,' I babbled. 'I have been out of town for a few days. I called at the police station, and the officer on duty told me Officer Abd el-Rassul was posted here again tonight. I imagine he sleeps during the daytime. I just wanted to express my gratitude, that's all.'

I shoved my hand into the pocket of my cropped cotton trousers and drew out a fistful of notes. Money in Egypt speaks a language all of its own. Tipping for any service, large or small, is a way of life. All at once their bright avaricious glances were on my hand, not my face.

'He comes,' the English-speaking guard informed me. 'Officer Abd el-Rassul, tonight he comes, yes. But not here yet. You leave?' He indicated the notes clutched in my hand. It was the money he was suggesting I should hand over; it was not an invitation for me to depart.

I made a great play of reluctance. 'I would much prefer to wait, if it's all the same to you. I would like to say thank you personally.'

I was gambling on this being not what they would want at all. I crossed the room and sat down in front of the television set, looking as if I was perfectly happy to hang around for as long as it might take for Ahmed to show up. I saw the perplexed glances they exchanged.

'No, no.' The guard pointed to the money I was still holding tightly. 'You leave. I give.'

I smiled sweetly. 'That's very kind of you. But I really think it would be better if I could give this token of my thanks to Officer Abd el-Rassul myself.'

He looked affronted. 'You no trust?'

'It's not that,' I assured him. 'I'm quite sure you're all fine, upstanding pillars of the community. It's just, the officer was very kind to my boyfriend.'

He stared at me, possibly understanding very little of this, possibly trying to work out how best to eject me. I made a play of looking at my watch, appearing undecided. 'That said, it's much later than I realised... Perhaps it might be better after all...'

'I have something...' He pulled out a drawer from the desk in the corner and rummaged about inside it for a moment, then held up an envelope. I didn't blame him for not knowing the word. He handed it across to me. 'You write name. I give,' he said.

This seemed like a perfectly reasonable compromise so I decided not to argue further. I accepted the pen he held out to me, slipped a few notes inside the envelope, sealed it, and wrote Ahmed's full name on the front. Getting up, I dug back into my pocket and handed them each an Egyptian twenty-pound note. This was worth approximately two-pounds in sterling, so hardly likely to break the bank. But its value was immeasurably higher to them in these tough times. It seemed a gesture worth making. Whether I was bribing them not to break into the envelope or to let me go without further issue, I wouldn't have liked to say. But with smiles all round, it seemed to do the trick. One of the guards even bowed as he held the door open for me.

I saw Ahmed duck back down behind the rock as I stepped back out into the moonlight, and deduced he'd been just about to come in after me.

'Goodnight,' I called back loudly, making it clear I was leaving without any great disaster befalling me. I turned towards the road, rather than heading straight back towards the others. The charade needed to be completed to be convincing. 'My scooter is just over here. Thank you for your help.' I waved, even though the door had already closed behind me. Only then did I let out a shuddering sigh of relief and allow myself to notice how much my limbs were shaking.

I waited at the roadside for a while, just to be sure they didn't follow me out and that the coast was clear, and then doubled back to join the others.

Adam pulled me into his arms the moment I was within reaching distance. 'My God, Merry; that was a close shave. We were just about to send Ahmed in to get you.'

'That would have taken some explaining, since he's not in uniform.'

'Exactly. That's why we waited. I knew if anyone could talk herself in and back out of there, it was you. Thank God you're ok.'

I smiled at the compliment. 'Well, it's proved the guards are as right as rain,' I whispered. 'Although I'm sorry to say I interrupted their television viewing. But hopefully it means I was wrong about Gamal Abdel-Maqsoud. Let's pray we'll be as lucky getting into and back out of the tomb.'

We didn't dare stir from our spot until we were absolutely sure the guards were staying put.

'I still don't understand why they're not patrolling,' Adam said with a frown.

'Maybe with everything so quiet for the last few nights, they've decided the danger has gone away,' I shrugged. 'I think that guard only opened the door for some air earlier. He certainly didn't look as if he expected to find me standing outside on the doorstep.'

'They are probably debating whether to open my envelope.' Ahmed growled. His aggrieved tone was that of a man who really did think it was *his* money the guards might be considering swiping, perhaps in the belief he'd never be any the wiser.

'If it keeps them off our backs, they can have it with my blessing,' I said. 'It's a small price to pay if we can get into the temple undisturbed. Come on, unless we're going to sit here tense and anxious all night, I think we should make a move.'

Walid handed me back my rucksack and I shrugged into it. Keeping low, we skirted the ruins of the Montuhotep temple, following the same route Adam and I had used the other night.

Ahmed helped Adam across the shallow incline of the lower cliff face bordering Hatshepsut's Temple and then to negotiate the southern boundary wall. But all in all Adam was doing a pretty good job of keeping up despite his plastered foot.

Once safely inside the Hathor shrine, we leaned against a couple of the pillars to wipe the sweat from our brows and get our breath back.

'I will be glad, once the tomb is safely discovered, not to have to do this anymore,' Walid murmured vehemently. 'Each time I come here, it takes years from my life.'

I knew exactly what he meant. It was hard to think of a more stressful pastime. Even so, I was determined to relish every moment. Whatever the outcome after tonight, be it the carefully staged discovery of the tomb by the Ministry of State for Antiquities or the sacrilege of it by that blasted Gamal

Abdel-Maqsoud, this would be our last time here. It made me strangely sad.

I hoped Akhenaten and Nefertiti, if they could see us from wherever they might happen to be, would understand and forgive us for not letting them forever rest in peace. Tutankhamun and Ay pledged that their "precious jewels" would remain undisturbed for all eternity, no one seeing, no one hearing. It was an awesome responsibility we were taking on, planning to wrest them from the silence of their shared grave and shove them unceremoniously into the media circus of the twenty-first century.

I wondered whether Howard Carter found himself troubled by such thoughts when he dug up the boy king almost a century ago. Maybe the press frenzy his discovery unleashed back then explained why, knowing of this tomb, he decided not to bring it to the attention of the world. Instead, he'd bricked up the papyri that revealed its existence inside a wall in an unprepossessing tomb in the Valley of the Kings. Perhaps if he'd left things there, the story might have turned out differently. As it was, he'd devised his ingenious trail of cryptic clues, and I was the one who'd happened across them. It could have been anyone. But it had been me.

Even then, if I'd heeded Dan's advice to leave well alone, it might all have come to nothing. But I'd been hell bent on having my Big Adventure.

Well, I'd had it, and then some. I let out a long sigh.

'Are you ok, Merry?' Adam reached for my hand in sudden concern.

'Are we doing the right thing?' I asked doubtfully.

'You're having cold feet?'

'I just feel this overwhelming sense of responsibility.'

He squeezed my hand. 'Walid's the one who's calling the shots on this. It's not down to you. We both know it's not a decision he's made lightly.'

'That's true. It's just I can't help but think if I hadn't been so determined to step off my hamster wheel last year, then Dan wouldn't now be kidnapped by a baseball bat-wielding opportunist, and the tomb would be still safely hidden away and undisturbed.'

'You mustn't think like that,' he admonished me softly. 'You didn't plan any of this. It's just the way it's turned out. All you've done is played the hand life has dealt you. Besides, if it hadn't been you, it might well have been someone else; someone not half so bothered about the outcome for Akhenaten and Nefertiti.' He leaned forward and kissed me lightly on the lips. 'We'll get Dan back from Gamal, don't you worry about that. Just look into my eyes and tell me honestly you'd want to have missed out on living this last year of your life…despite some of the scrapes we've had…'

I gazed into his eyes as asked. '…You know I can't say that.'

He smiled, his whole face softening as he looked back at me through the shadows. 'Well then, my suggestion is to just go with the flow tonight. We're here for all the right reasons, Merry. Come what may, this will be our last time here. Let's make the most of it, huh?'

This time it was me who leaned forward for a kiss. 'Come what may,' I murmured.

Ahmed collected up the heavy bag of tools while Adam hooked the key out of his pocket and unlocked the door to the interior Hathor Chapel. Once inside with the door safely closed behind us, we retrieved a couple of flashlights from Walid's backpack and switched them on. I was used to the way the wall reliefs seemed to leap to life by now. It was no longer quite so unnerving.

'Ok, now the Aten discs...' Adam said, holding out his hand.

I shrugged my rucksack off my back, unbuckled the straps and pulled them out one by one.

'Right; ready to get this thing done, have a last private viewing, and then get the hell out of here?' he asked.

We moved across the room to the familiar gash in the stonework. Adam slotted one of the Aten discs into it. With it sitting proud of the wall, he pressed down with all his strength.

I remembered the breath-catching sense of anticipation and wonder with which I'd first observed him do this. The awful sense of anti-climax when, for long seconds, nothing happened. But now I was cognisant of the long pause. I knew exactly how many seconds to count. It was nevertheless a wondrous and heart-stopping moment when the hidden panel started to shift aside, letting out a long groan of exertion as the ancient mechanism caused rock to move against ages-old rock.

We all stared at the square dark hole for a moment. I decided I could watch this spectacle every day for the rest of my life and it would never lose its sense of awe-inspiring magnitude.

'Ok, let's make a start on dismantling that pulley system,' Adam said prosaically, bringing us all back down to earth.

We dropped down onto all fours to crawl through the hole. Adam shone his flashlight through to light the way.

We all froze.

The black interior of the entrance corridor was not the only thing Adam's torch illuminated. There, standing inside the passageway, were three sets of legs.

One set was encased in suit trousers and smart shoes. The second wore chinos and trainer; while the third happened to be a nicely shaped pair of calves encased in nylon, with slim ankles, and feet shod in a pair of kitten-heeled court shoes.

We stared in shock.

The legs encased in the suit trousers moved as their wearer knelt down to look at us, squinting and raising one hand against the beam of Adam's torch.

'Good evening. And thank you for joining us at last. We have been waiting for some time for your arrival.'

Chapter 19

'Director Ismail!' Walid gasped.

'Dan!' I cried.

'Habiba! I mean, Miss Garai!' Ahmed exclaimed.

'This explains why the guards were so happy to look the other way,' Adam murmured.

'And why Habiba opted for room service rather than join us for dinner,' I muttered.

'Indeed,' Director Ismail said smoothly, switching on his flashlight. 'Miss Garai has been keeping me closely apprised of your activities. We felt sure you would attempt a visit here tonight; although I don't think we'd appreciated quite how much work you had to do to return the tomb to its original state. It was important the guards should allow you to pass unchallenged. Please... Do come and join us...'

We had little choice but to crawl through the hole. I noticed we all kept our mouths firmly shut as we did so. The biggest bigwig from the Ministry of State for Antiquities had caught us in the act of entering the tomb. Until he made it clear what he intended to do with us as a result, silence seemed our best bet.

Director Ismail was a tall, well-built man with closely cropped black hair, greying at the temples, and a courteous manner to match his smart suit. He spoke softly, but I sensed a leashed in quality about him. My instincts suggested he was a man not to be crossed. I couldn't help but wonder a bit bleakly if we had done so already.

I noticed the quick glance Ahmed and Habiba exchanged. He looked shocked, horrified and perhaps a little devastated. It was impossible to read Habiba's expression. I think I expected to see a look of smug superiority on her face. Let's face it; it was clear she'd been stringing us along the whole time. Instead, I thought I read discomfort, perhaps even a hint of apology in the way her gaze dropped away before his.

Dan looked... well, Dan just looked like Dan, big, gangly-limbed and a bit shaggy-looking, standing there in his crumpled shirt and with a couple of day's worth of stubble darkening his jawline and his hair sticking out at improbable angles all over his head. My bone-softening relief at seeing him fit and well was marred somewhat by the truly condemnatory look he sent me. It was almost as if I could hear the words *another fine mess* ringing on the airwaves.

'The bridge over the pit shaft and the pulley system are quite ingenious in design,' Director Ismail said conversationally. 'I imagine you wanted to take a look inside the sarcophagus? But it is a shame about the thick coating of rock dust covering everything. It appears there has been an explosion of some sort; since there was no mention of a rockfall when first you entered in here. Perhaps you'd be kind enough to explain…?'

I was starting to have my suspicions as to what might have happened to bring him here. Perhaps Gamal Abdel-Maqsoud had perceived some greater advantage in shopping us to the authorities than in attempting to break into the tomb himself. Although that didn't explain how Dan…

Walid stiffened his back and met the Director's gaze without flinching. 'I carry sole responsibility for everything you see here. If you wish to hold somebody accountable, that person is me.'

Director Ismail smiled at him. It was really rather an attractive smile, revealing a set of large, evenly-spaced teeth in the torchlight. One of the molars was gold, I noticed irrelevantly. 'I understand perfectly the role you have played, my friend. We can have a nice long chat about it later.' While his tone remained pleasant, it was hard not to read an implied threat into his words. 'But you forget your manners. You have not introduced me to your friends…'

Walid cleared his throat and started to speak but the director silenced him with a gesture. It was the merest flick of his wrist as he held up one finger, but it had the desired effect.

'Don't worry, my friend; I think I can manage.' His gaze came to rest on my face. 'My dear, you must be Meredith Pink. Now, I feel I must apologise to you that the housekeeping of one of my employees was so lapse that you found yourself trapped inside the Howard Carter Museum after closing time.'

I stared up at him and opened my mouth to speak. He didn't give me the opportunity, carrying on in that same smoothly polite tone,

'But I do wonder whether by rights you ought to have handed over the scrap of paper you found inside the picture frame you accidentally broke.'

Feeling the full weight of Dan's gaze on me, I shut my mouth again realising it was hanging inelegantly open and that I really had no idea what to say in any event.

The Director smiled. My discomfort seemed satisfaction enough. His eyes snapped sideways away from my face. 'Young man, I take it you are Adam Tennyson.'

'Sir,' Adam acknowledged.

'Yes; it was a singularly clever notion of yours to hit on the idea of weighing and measuring the original Mehet-Weret discs from among the Tutankhamun treasure so you could make replicas. This is one of them, I take it?' He picked up the Aten disc where it had dropped through the slot to the floor, and held it up so he could study it in the torchlight. 'Hmm, most creative.'

Without giving Adam a chance to respond, his gaze snapped sideways once again. 'Officer Ahmed Abd el-Rassul,' he said.

Ahmed pulled himself straight. Aside from Dan, he was the only one of us as tall as the Antiquities Director. He managed to meet the Director's gaze levelly but couldn't prevent himself biting his lip.

'You come from an illustrious family of tomb robbers, I understand. It is a pity, given your current profession, that you have not been able to shake free of your ancestry. It is my sad duty to inform you that breaking and entering into closed-to-the-public historical sites do not feature on your job description.'

Perhaps following the lead Adam and I had established, Ahmed remained silent, but I saw his head drop forward. If guilt and shame were the emotions the Director planned on eliciting, he'd achieved his objective with no difficulty whatsoever.

I opened my mouth to defend our police buddy and claim all the liability for leading him astray, but a gentle nudge from Adam stopped me. We were in this together and we'd each played our part, as the Director had just pointed out with cool efficiency. Trying to dissemble was pointless.

It was left to Walid to broach the lengthening silence. He took a breath and stated aloud the simple fact that was glaringly obvious to every one of us. 'Either Dan has proved himself surprisingly loquacious, or, more likely, you have a copy of the letter we all signed.'

The Director's appraising glance shifted back to his face. 'I have the letter; although Mr Fletcher has been most helpful in fleshing out the bones of its contents. It was quite an undertaking, Walid, to require such a large group of people to put their names to it – most impressive. And right now we are missing only... Now, let me see...' He started to count on his fingers. '...Professor Edward Kincaid and his daughter Jessica. I understand from Mr Fletcher here that she is at home in England preparing for their nuptials. Next, your colleague from the Museum, Walid: Mrs Shukura al-Busir. And, finally, a young gentleman employed by the Ministry for the Preservation of Ancient Monuments here in Luxor, a Mr Mustafa Mushhawrar. Now that is quite a list. How on earth did you hope to secure their silence...?'

'If you've read the letter, then you'll know that in itself it was supposed to be a surety, or guarantee if you prefer, that we would each wait until I felt able to make a decision about what to do. Given the political turmoil...'

'I believe I understand your reasons. But do you think it is within your jurisdiction, Walid, to play at being God?'

For the first time our friend's calm self-assurance slipped. 'As things have turned out, it was clearly a huge error of judgement to delay. Perhaps, if Mustafa Mushhawrar had toed the line...'

'But he did not, did he?' Director Ismail rapped out sharply. 'Mr Fletcher informs me he lost his life when you caught him robbing this place. He brought a rock fall down on himself and sadly sent half the mountainside crashing into the tomb.'

'I'm afraid that is true,' Walid admitted, perhaps wondering, as I was, why Director Ismail had asked for an explanation earlier if he knew the answer the whole time. 'I'm ashamed to say that since then I have lost control of the situation rather badly.'

'To the extent that Mr Mushhawrar's copy of the letter fell into the hands of an individual who saw the opportunity to blackmail you.'

We all stared.

'Ah yes, you will no doubt be wondering how the letter has come into my possession. So allow me to enlighten you. A couple of weeks ago, I received a package from the landlady of an apartment block in the Heliopolis district of Cairo. Your letter was in a sealed envelope inside. The covering note from the lady in question explained that one of her tenants, a young man by the name of Abdul Shehata, had given her the envelope and asked her to post it to me at the Ministry in the event that anything should happen to him. I imagine the young man was in fear for his life...?'

'He was killed in the rioting outside the presidential palace,' I said flatly, roused from my silence by what I imagined he was implying. 'He chose to go there to join in the demonstrations.'

'I see; so you were not hunting him down to retrieve the letter...?'

'We won't deny we wanted to retrieve the letter,' Adam admitted, similarly provoked to offer an explanation. 'But he got himself killed before we were able to get to him.'

'Ah; so perhaps he suffered a pang of conscience in leaving the matter of the letter to be cleared up after his death,' Director Ismail shrugged. 'I guess we will never know whether he feared it would be at your hands or in the unhappy incident that did in fact rob him of his life...'

'We're many things,' Adam said tightly. 'But we're not murderers.'

'I don't believe I have accused you of being any such thing,' Director Ismail countered mildly.

My brain was whirring at a million miles per hour. I suddenly realised the unseen enemy we'd supposed to be stalking us wasn't Gamal Abdel-Maqsoud.

I shook my head again as suddenly it all slotted together in my mind, the pieces falling neatly into place. Then I fixed my gaze on Habiba. 'It was *you*; wasn't it? You've been spying on us!'

She met my accusatory stare for a moment and then, once again, dropped her gaze away. The others were staring with bulging eyes. I'm not sure they'd cottoned on as yet, but it was all becoming increasingly clear to me.

'Miss Garai has been following my orders.' Director Ismail informed me matter-of-factly. 'The letter was testimony enough to your misadventures. But it was dated over a year ago. There are some distinguished names among the signatories, individuals acclaimed in the field of Egyptology, as you are well aware. Dr Massri here is prominent among them. And of course Professor Kincaid has a stalwart reputation internationally. I needed to know what you were doing now, and to what extent the tomb might be at risk, before I started throwing my weight around wielding my big stick'

'So you sent Habiba to check us out,' I deduced. 'I imagine she used chloroform on Adam so she could conduct a search of our dahabeeyah for the Aten discs? Ahmed mentioned something about her giving him the slip...'

Habiba gave the slightest inclination of her head, having the grace to look a bit shamefaced.

'And set out to see what information she could wheedle out of Ahmed...?' I pressed on, not letting her evident discomfiture sidetrack me.

Ahmed gaped, looking hurt. 'But I did not give anything away.'

'You didn't need to,' I said grimly. 'She already knew the whole story; didn't you, Habiba? I imagine you were just testing to see if we had any leaks in our otherwise watertight defences.'

'I didn't find any,' she mumbled. 'Your security onboard the dahabeeyah was unassailable, and Officer Abd el-Rassul proved himself equally guarded. Charming, but guarded,' she amended with a quick glance at him from under her lashes. His response was to proudly puff out his chest. Typical Ahmed.

'Then you invited Ahmed and me to join you on your inspection of the Valley of the Kings,' Habiba went on. 'When we entered KV20, I discerned your plan at once. I realised you wanted me to play a role in helping you to stage the discovery of the tomb.'

Clever! Just as I always believed! Even now, I felt a sneaking admiration for her. She was flirting with Ahmed even at a time like this. And he was lapping it up. There might be hope for these two yet, I thought.

'And the break-in at Luxor Museum?' I frowned. 'What was that all about?'

Habiba shrugged. 'I think it was exactly what it seemed. Just some desperate locals willing to risk everything to feed their families.'

'Oh.'

'But it made me realise you were worried somebody else might know about the papyri, and perhaps therefore, the tomb.'

Not for the first time I cursed my stupid blabbermouth. 'Is that why you attempted to force your way in here that night? I assume it was you who broke into the Hathor Chapel and tried to work the mechanism without an Aten disc?'

'I thought anything pressed into the gash might release the hidden panel. I needed to know how badly at risk the tomb might be.'

'Shame about the scuffs and scratches you left on the reliefs,' I said critically.

She managed to look embarrassed. 'I'm sorry about that, but checking to see if it was truly impossible to get in without an Aten disc was critical so I knew if it was safe to leave Luxor for a few days. Director Ismail had instructed me to find a reason to go to Amarna.'

'We knew Professor Kincaid had gone there, but not why.' the Director nodded. 'I needed to find a way to keep tabs on him, too, since as a group you had decided inconveniently to separate.'

'So all that stuff about the Copper Scroll...?' I queried, confused.

'Oh, that was all true enough,' Habiba declared. 'I did make a study of it for my thesis. It's just, it suddenly struck me when we were in the Chapel out there...' she indicated the room on the other side of the hole in the wall, '...and you were making such a song and dance of pointing out the Aten discs between Hathor's horns... that this might be my way of carrying out Director Ismail's orders whilst also keeping you from getting suspicious that I might be getting to grips with the clues in the papyri rather too quickly.'

'But why kidnap Dan?' Adam asked, finding his voice at last.

'Mr Fletcher seemed our best bet for hearing the whole story,' Director Ismail said unapologetically. 'We wanted to know what Professor Kincaid was working on. We wanted to understand everything that had occurred since the letter was signed a year ago. Let's just say he didn't seem quite as *invested* as the rest of you, and we felt he might be our best bet for learning everything we wanted to know. I have to say he has proved a most illuminating interviewee.'

'There's nothing like having a top brass identity badge waved in your face, not to mention a pistol, to loosen a man's tongue.' Dan said drily.

'So you know all about...?' I trailed off, deciding it was time to stop giving things away.

'I understand Professor Kincaid is exploring some quite fascinating links between Pharaoh Akhenaten and the Old Testament of the Bible... and even our very own Qu'ran.' Director Ismail said. 'There has been speculation before, of course. But now you have the proof, eh?'

None of us spoke. Dan, it seemed, had filled in the gaps in the Director's knowledge quite nicely. But then, he'd been banging on about coming clean with the authorities right from the start. In some strange way I supposed I should be pleased for him that he'd had his chance. I'm sure it was a weight off his mind.

'And of course by having your friend in my custody I knew it would force you to act. I was keen to talk with you. I felt the tomb itself was the best location for this conversation. And I was right. You are here.'

'Director Ismail… Feisal,' Walid began, appealing to the part of their relationship that went beyond the purely professional. 'I can understand that you wanted to test us; to see for yourself what manner of people we were in the wake of this immense find and what our motivation might be going forward. But surely our plan to stage the discovery of the tomb … our being here tonight to put it back to rights … Surely these are proof enough that all we have sought to do is protect it…?'

'Walid, my esteemed friend, your integrity has never been in question. Just, perhaps, your wisdom…'

'Dr Massri has acted with the very best of intentions every step of the way,' I piped up staunchly. 'None of what has happened has been his fault.'

'Count me in to second that,' Adam said at my side. 'It's down to us that he's standing here needing to give an account of himself.'

'The same is true for Officer Abd el-Rassul,' I added, deciding it was now or never to have our say. 'In fact, the same goes for every single name on that list, except for

Adam's and my own. The only reason they got dragged into this whole affair is because Adam and I were trapped in here and they came to rescue us!' Adam and I are the ones who broke in!'

Director Ismail met my gaze for a long moment. Hoping I'd said enough, I held my breath.

'The participation of Ms Kincaid and Mr Fletcher here – and perhaps that of Mrs Al-Busir – I can possibly overlook,' he said. 'It seems to me their involvement was peripheral – although, of course, Mrs Al-Busir is employed in the service of the Ministry and should know better than to sign her name to...'

'But...' I started to argue.

He held up his hand in an abrupt gesture for silence. 'Mr Abd el-Rassul, however, is an officer of the law, employed in the Antiquities division. He should never have allowed his questionable instincts to cloud his professional judgement.'

This time it was Habiba who spoke up. 'I have found Officer Abd el-Rassul to take his duties incredibly seriously.'

The Director arched one eyebrow. 'As I have already pointed out, if one can consider those duties to include unlocking off-limits tombs and "borrowing" keys from the officials in charge of our archaeological sites in order to grant his friends unauthorised access, I might be inclined to agree with you. As it is, I am fast forming the opinion there may be some element of bias creeping into your view, my dear.'

I saw the flashing glance Habiba sent Ahmed and the steady gaze he met it with. They needed to talk, those two; although I suspected most of what needed to be said had already been communicated in that shared look. Habiba turned to face her boss directly. 'Then, please allow me to dilute it by saying I have come to like and respect all of these people. It is my conclusion that they are exactly what they seem: ordinary individuals caught up in extra-ordinary events.'

With that stalwart statement of support she won me over for good. Given a chance I would have hugged her. As it was, Director Ismail's forbidding expression kept me rooted to the spot.

He narrowed his eyes on Habiba's beautiful face. 'Nicely put, my dear. And in the case of Miss Pink and Mr Tennyson, you may well be right. They are, after all, guests in our country; although Mr Fletcher here informs me they harbour hopes of setting up in business. But how am I to excuse Dr Massri's involvement; and Professor Kincaid's?'

'Now, hang on a moment,' Walid said quickly. 'The only thing Professor Kincaid is guilty of is a bit of illicit translation. As soon as we knew about the tomb, he handed the papyri over to me for safekeeping. My sole reason for removing them from the Museum vault was so that I could bring about the proper discovery of this place. The work Ted is undertaking at the moment is at the explicit invitation of the field director in Amarna. It's properly authorised and completely above board. The fact the content of those jars is proving so explosive is pure luck. We couldn't possibly have guessed at what they would reveal. We thought they were wine jars.'

Director Ismail met his gaze. They stared at each other for a long moment, almost as if waiting to see who would back down first. In the end, Director Ismail sighed heavily. 'So, in the final analysis, Walid, my friend, it all boils down to you. You have played fast and loose with the rules and regulations laid down by those who first set up the Antiquities Service here in Egypt.'

'Yes,' Walid admitted levelly.

'You brought solid gold discs from among the Tutankhamun treasures in the Museum...'

'...So, I imagine, did you.' Walid murmured softly. 'How else did you get inside here tonight?'

The Director appeared a little taken aback by this counter-attack, however lacking in heat it was. 'Er, yes... It was my only option. I knew, once I had detained Mr Fletcher here; that you would want to move quickly. But the point is, Walid, you have played reckless games with the authority vested in you...'

'You also know, thanks to Habiba – er, Miss Garai – that everything was in readiness for you to make the discovery of the century,' Walid shot back. It was clear he wasn't prepared to go down without a fight. 'If you'd left us alone tonight then within a few hours from now, Miss Garai and I would have presented ourselves at your office and laid the whole matter officially before you.'

Director Ismail held his gaze for the longest time. When I was just starting to wonder if he'd somehow turned to stone, he let out his heaviest sigh yet. 'And that, my friend, was exactly what I came here tonight to prevent.'

I felt my jaw drop. We all stared at him with blank incomprehension. With that sigh his whole demeanour changed. It was as if he dropped his façade, and all pretence with it. In a completely different tone, almost of a man in a confessional, he went on,

'If you'd informed me of the possibility of an undiscovered royal tomb – particularly an Amarnan royal burial – in my official capacity as the Minister for Antiquities, I'd have had no choice but to notify the new puppet president Adly Mansour. He, in turn, would have been duty-bound to advise the Military Chief Abdel Fattah el-Sisi. And then the whole thing would have been taken out of our hands.'

'What are you saying?' Walid asked hesitantly.

'That I needed to come and see for myself what we were dealing with.'

'And?'

'And ... As Allah is my witness ... Words fail me. It really is the most magnificent discovery ever made, isn't it?'

'In Egypt, certainly.' Walid agreed.

'And now, from what this young man informs me...' He indicated Dan on his right. '...Professor Kincaid is perhaps on the verge of eclipsing it with the new insights he is bringing to light about Moses...'

'Well, it depends on your liking for religion which discovery you find most appealing,' Dan muttered, perhaps feeling he'd been invited in on the conversation. 'Personally speaking, I could have happily lived my life without knowing of either one of them.'

Everyone ignored him.

'So I find myself caught on the horns of the same dilemma you faced a year ago, my friend.' The director admitted, looking Walid in the eyes. 'And I am equally torn.'

'I had thought, well, that a discovery such as this might be exactly what our country needs to set her once more on her feet...?' Walid offered.

'Perhaps.' Director Ismail conceded. But he didn't look convinced. 'And if we misjudge it; what then? If this marvellous tomb becomes a pawn in a political power struggle, or becomes a reason for Western governments to intervene in the running of our state affairs; how will we live with ourselves then?'

What could Walid say? These were the self-same arguments he'd wrestled with himself. After a moment he reached up and placed his hand on the other man's shoulder.

'Do you think it is within your jurisdiction, Feisal, to play at being God?' he said quietly.

'I don't know,' the director was candid. He looked at each of us in turn. 'I don't propose we should all sign our names to a letter,' he said with a wry smile. 'But I am wondering if I can ask you all to give a pledge of silence...? Of course, I will need to speak with Professor Kincaid, and with the field director in Amarna. I will also have to find an explanation to satisfy Ibrahim Mohassib and the philologist who translated the papyrus. But with such a lot at stake...'

'What are you suggesting...?' Walid frowned.

Director Ismail met his gaze. 'I believe I am saying that your original strategy was the right one, Walid. For now, for the sake of this tomb, and for the sake of Egypt, we wait. We wait and see how the political landscape unfolds.'

'But...'

'No, please do not attempt to dissuade me. I am pulling rank on you, my friend, as it is within my authority to do. I relieve you as of now of any responsibility for this tomb. And I swear each and every one of you to secrecy and to silence about this and also the contents of those Amarnan jars, and anything else you may suppose you know that is not officially recognised. These are now matters for the Ministry of State for Antiquities, as should have been the case from the start. I will be the one to determine if, when and how the world will come to learn of these things.'

'But what does that mean for each of us?' Walid asked.

'You, my friend, will return to your post at the Museum in Cairo, and I will rely on you to have a quiet word with Mrs Al-Busir. Similarly, Miss Garai and Officer Abd el-Rassul may resume their usual duties; although I imagine Miss Garai may prefer a posting here in Luxor...? Perhaps Ibrahim Mohassib can find something suitable for her at the Luxor Museum.'

I rather enjoyed spotting the twinkle in his eye as he said this.

'And the rest of us...?' I ventured.

'Well, it strikes me that Mr Fletcher here is most eager to head home to see his fiancée. And I imagine, after the conversation I plan to have with Professor Kincaid, that he also will wish to spend time with his daughter in the run up to her big day.'

'And Adam and me?' I stammered.

He cast me a look of some benevolence. 'You have both been caught up in a thrilling adventure, I perceive.'

For some inexplicable reason I felt my chin starting to wobble and pinpricks stabbing by eyes. 'It's been the time of my life,' I whispered.

'Nevertheless, my dear; it is my very strong advice to you that you and your young man should leave our country for a while. Let the dust settle a bit, hmm?'

Sensing me about to crumble, Adam reached for my hand and squeezed it tightly. 'Look on the bright side, Merry,' he said. 'It means we can go home and get properly married!'

Out of the corner of my eye I saw perplexity sweep across Dan's face, his brows drawing sharply together in a scowl. 'What do you mean *properly*?' he demanded.

Epilogue

It was as we were preparing the Queen Ahmes for dry dock, entrusting her to Khaled's safe-keeping, that we discovered the swollen and distended body caught up in some netting underneath the hull.

'Ugh,' I shuddered. 'Do you mean to tell me we've been dragging him around with us the whole damn time?'

'So it would seem,' Adam muttered grimly. 'Gamal Abdel-Maqsoud R.I.P.'

The End

Author's Note

As I write this footnote to my story, Ridley Scott has just released his film Exodus: Gods and Kings. In popular culture Ramses II (the Great) is most often first choice as the Pharaoh of the Exodus. Possibly, excepting only Tutankhamun, this is because he is one of the few pharaohs people have heard of. To what extent this is the result of the legacy he left behind him in Egypt (his immense statuary if nothing else), and how much it is down to his prominence in popular culture is hard to say. It's one of those never-ending circular arguments.

In reality, there is very little evidence for Ramses II's candidacy as the Pharaoh of the Exodus; if indeed historically such a person ever actually existed.

The primary argument in favour of him seems to be that the Bible states the Pharaoh of the Oppression subjected the Hebrew slaves to harsh labour building his store cities of Pithom and Ram'ses. The only pharaoh known to have built a new capital city (besides Akhenaten) was Ramses II. Called Pi-Ramses (or Piramesse), its remains have been discovered under the modern town on Qantir in the Eastern Delta, close to a branch of the Nile that silted up approximately 1,000 BCE. Some historians believe it was also the site of the Hyksos city of Avaris, as well as the border town of Zarw, identified by some as Biblical Goshen.

This possible link to Zarw is interesting. As historian Ahmed Osman has pointed out, the army-general-turned-pharaoh Horemheb appointed his fellow army-man Paramessu as Vizier, Commander of Troops, Overseer of Foreign Countries, *Overseer of the Fortress of Zarw* (my italics), and Master of the Horse, before naming him as is successor. So Paramessu (Ramses I as he became later) was the most powerful man in Egypt after Horemheb. In the Bible, which never names the ruling pharaoh but gives the name of the Eastern Delta city built by the harsh labour of the Israelites as 'Ram'ses', the name may conceivably derive, not from the pharaoh, but from the Vizier Paramessu, who personally forced them to work.

The truth is, there is no evidence whatsoever to allow us to say with any confidence in whose reign the Exodus took place – if indeed it took place at all.

Geologists point to the Santorini volcanic eruption to explain the ten plagues as occurring as a result of natural phenomena. This would place the Exodus some two hundred years earlier than my story. The reign of Ramses II of course came shortly afterwards, perhaps some fifty or so years after Akhenaten ruled Egypt. The other natural explanations for the plagues are as described in the story, and could have occurred at just about any time in Egypt's long history. My sense is there is likely to be some kernel of truth in the account that found its way into the Old Testament, plus a lot of embellishment. I think it entirely plausible that the Biblical authors took these naturally occurring events and decided to turn them into ten plagues to add drama to the story they were telling.

To my way of looking at it, the circumstantial evidence pointing to the Exodus taking place during the reign of a pharaoh who ruled shortly after the Amarna period is overwhelming. It is a fact that Akhenaten's priests and nobles disappear from the historical record at the time of his death – with perhaps only one or two exceptions. It is certainly the case that they were never buried in the tombs they'd no doubt paid huge sums to have carved and decorated in the hills surrounding Amarna. So where did they go? I think it unlikely they were unceremoniously put to the sword by the new regime intent on returning the country to the old ways.

The High Priest Meryre's titles were exactly as quoted. Perhaps the titles "hereditary prince" and "sometime prince" were purely ceremonial. Who knows...? But I can't help finding them highly suggestive. Moses was described as a Prince of Egypt after all.

Everything I have included about the Copper Scroll is as set out in publications by historians and scholars far more qualified than me. The strange Greek characters inserted, apparently at random, into the end sections of text do indeed appear to spell out the Pharaoh's name when positioned sequentially. There is no way of knowing whether Akhenaten swelled his coffers with treasure confiscated from the traditional temples when he ordered them closed. The quantities of buried treasure the Copper Scroll describes are staggering, so it had to have all come from somewhere.

The ancient Egyptian influences in some of the greatest religious iconography extant today seem to me blindingly obvious. Forget the Aten for a moment and its possible roots feeding the great monotheistic religions of the world; just look at the Christian Holy Family and compare it to the Egyptian myth of Isis, Osiris and Horus.

DNA testing on Tutankhamun's mummy and those of his immediate family has not ruled out the possibility of what we might call 'Jewish' genes. Was Queen Tiye Biblical Joseph's daughter? I daresay we will never know for sure; but the circumstantial case is compelling.

Finally, who was Moses? Of course, I don't know. I've sought simply to weave a story that fits the historical and archaeological evidence as I understand it.

And so, finally, I have been left with little choice but to bring Merry and Adam home. The political situation in Egypt through the last half of 2013 and all of 2014 has been such that their business stood no chance of success. As a writer setting stories in the present-day I have to stay true to events as they unfold, even though I failed to foresee them when I started writing my Egyptian series.

Somehow I have a feeling Merry and Adam's adventures will continue. There are many more ancient Egyptian mysteries I wish to explore. I'll choose to see this as a creative challenge, and go from there.

I hope you've enjoyed this sixth book following Meredith Pink's Adventures in Egypt. If so, I would very much appreciate a review on Amazon. As ever, I welcome your comments and feedback on my website: www.fionadeal.com

Fiona Deal
December 2014

If you enjoyed Seti's Secret, you may also enjoy Belzoni's Bequest – Book 7 of Meredith Pink's Egyptian adventures, available on Amazon.

About the Author

Fiona Deal fell in love with Egypt as a teenager, and has travelled extensively up and down the Nile, spending time in both Cairo and Luxor in particular. She lives in Kent, England with her two Burmese cats. Her professional life has been spent in human resources and organisational development for various companies. Writing his her passion and an absorbing hobby. Other books in the series following Meredith Pink's adventures in Egypt are available, with more planned. You can find out more about Fiona, the books and her love of Egypt by checking out her website and following her blog at www.fionadeal.com

Other books by this author

Please visit your favourite ebook retailer to discover other books by Fiona Deal.

Meredith Pink's Adventures in Egypt

Carter's Conundrums – Book 1
Tutankhamun's Triumph – Book 2
Hatshepsut's Hideaway – Book 3
Farouk's Fancies – Book 4
Akhenaten's Alibi – Book 5
Seti's Secret – Book 6
Belzoni's Bequest – Book 7
Nefertari's Narrative – Book 8

Also available: Shades of Gray, a romantic family saga, written under the name Fiona Wilson.

Connect with me

Thank you for reading my book. Here are my social media coordinates:

Friend me on Facebook: http://facebook.com/fjdeal
Follow me on Twitter: http://twitter.com/dealfiona
Subscribe to my blog: http://www.fionadeal.com
Visit my website: http://www.fionadeal.com

Printed in Great Britain
by Amazon